THE

TRUCKER'S

CAT

CHRISTINA THOMPSON

ISBN-13: 978-1542565233

ISBN-10: 1542565235

The Trucker's Cat

Second Edition

Cover art by Deidre Hof

"Some men think there's a choice
between right and wrong.
Great men know there is none."
~ General Steven Randall

CHAPTER 1

FRIDAY

SAMANTHA RANDALL FLIPPED OFF THE light in her bedroom and stepped onto the second-story stone balcony overlooking the embassy grounds in Washington D.C. Lilacs and classical Russian music permeated throughout the patio garden where a group of diplomats visited during the evening gathering.

Sam spotted her mother on the arm of her husband, Ambassador Dmitri Demas, near the trimmed hedge. With perfectly coiffed sandy brown hair and pristine makeup, her mother had the stature of a queen. Like royalty, Martha ruled her daughter and the staff. She expected excellence and saved her affection for rare occasions.

Bald and pudgy, Dmitri had a round face with rosy

cheeks from either alcohol or happiness. Although he was extremely intelligent in political matters, he still reminded Sam of Humpty Dumpty. Always happy and never uttering a cross word, he loved Martha and relied on her opinions in the social setting.

Looking past the people, Samantha scanned the embassy grounds. The bright green leaves of the closest trees within the patio lighting and the dark foliage behind it would give her enough coverage for her escape plan. Glancing below, she blew out a breath. She pushed her fear aside as her father, General Randall, had taught his soldiers to do when confronted by life-threatening events, such as patrolling hostile regions, evacuating from hot landing zones, or falling thirty feet onto Martha's prize-winning rose bushes.

In her black leggings, turtleneck, and leather dance slippers, Sam stuffed a strand of her long blond hair back under her black Scottish cap. She set her backpack in the corner and climbed onto the wide stone railing. Inhaling the cool air of the Memorial Day weekend, she looked into the starry sky.

"Daddy, I hope you have my back," she whispered.

Sam leapt with the agility of a cat to the next dark balcony four feet away. A light came from the third upper semicircle. Slinking along the edge of the second one, she heard Colonel Seth Williams mumble to Karl Petrov, the ambassador's assistant, through the open doors of the third balcony.

She sprang again to the railing of Karl's office. She had tried to stay away from creepy Karl, especially after their recent encounter. Although it was a necessity, she winced at the thought of his rough manner. With her back against the gray stone building, she balanced on the edge to hear their conversation.

"She doesn't understand," Colonel Williams said.

Karl laughed. "This says different, and it's your fault."

Sam peeked through the open French doors on the balcony. With his black hair slicked into a short ponytail, Karl held a flash drive in his hand. She shivered at his seventies' style tan suit and pointed collar. Tuffs of chest hair peeked out. His gaudy gold Rolex matched the thick chain around his neck. He was the bad guy from every Charlie's Angels rerun, one of her dad's favorite shows.

Sergei, Karl's shorter clone lackey, had his back to the French doors, and her. Tall and in uniform, Colonel Williams would have stood at attention if not for the slight lean against his spiral mahogany cane.

"You will remain on the grounds," Karl said.

"You can't keep me hostage here."

Karl pointed the flash drive at him. "This says I can."

The Colonel scowled and limped from the room. Sam leaned in farther straining to see Karl type in the code to the wall safe. After putting the flash drive inside, he shut the safe door then turned off the light.

"He's under our control now," Karl said to Sergei as they left the room.

After waiting a full minute, Sam dropped to the balcony floor and scanned the party below. Karl escorted Jillian Williams, the Colonel's daughter, to the corner of the patio by the shrubbery. With her ample breasts, thin waist, and thick blond hair, Jillian modeled in sexy swimwear for Maxim and Sports Illustrated. Karl whispered in her ear. Jillian feigned surprise then nodded with a sly smile. Her long manicured fingers touched his forearm, and he drew her closer. Is that what flirting was all about? Sam cringed. Jillian can have him.

Dismissing Jillian and Karl, Sam slipped into the room that smelled of stale cigars. Bruno, Karl's Doberman, growled from his cage next to the carved oak desk. She shivered as he stared.

After taking a beef stick from the box on the shelf, she slowly pushed the treat between the bars. Grateful that Bruno munched on the beef and not her, she quickly found Karl's keys in his cigar box and unlocked the center drawer behind his desk.

Pulling out the top file, she feverishly scribbled down the information of the truck route on the nearby pad. She'd detail it later when she had more time. Hearing footsteps down the corridor, she shoved the file back and ducked behind the brown leather couch. Telling herself that this was bigger than her pride, she stripped off her clothes and tucked the paper into the bottom of her dance shoe. As the door opened, she pulled off the cap and smoothed down her hair.

"Who's in here?" Karl demanded.

"I am," Sam replied, popping up naked from behind the couch. "I was waiting for you."

He laughed. "I'm too busy right now, my странный кошка. I have bigger game to hunt."

"You mean Jillian?"

He laughed again. "Yes, a model's body. I'm curious to see what's under that icy exterior."

"I'm guessing more ice," she replied.

"You sound jealous, my pet," he said, taking his keys—the ones she had just returned—from the cigar box. He twirled the key ring on his index finger. "You can't compete with Jillian. It's a fact."

He lifted her chin and tweaked her plum-size breast. She tried not to flinch at his touch.

"I'll come to your room in the morning. You can amuse me more then. Now, scat before Dmitri or your mother sees you in here," he said as he closed the door behind him.

Relieved that he didn't stay, she quickly dressed. With her cap in hand, she left through the door and glided to her bedroom two doors down. She had no time to dwell on the past.

Feeling the paper in her shoe, she tucked her hair back under her cap and strode to her balcony. The music and laughter continued as she grabbed her backpack. She shimmied down the ivy latticework along the shadowed edge of the patio lights.

Hidden among the trees and bushes, she crept beside the tall stonewall that surrounded the compound. Holding her breath, she abruptly froze behind a fat maple. A security guard walked beside the tree. She waited and eyed the camera on a higher branch. From scouting their security earlier, she knew where every camera was located. Planning is essential, her father had said.

With the guard moving on, she climbed the tree staying away from the video camera. Sitting sideways on a branch, she scooted to the end that hung over the wall. Her petite frame bent the branch slightly. Like a father, the tree gently lowered its child safely to the ground. She whispered a *thank you* and hurried toward the bus stop.

On the last run of the night, the metro bus dropped her off at the Greyhound terminal. While standing in line, she casually slipped her cell phone into the handbag of the elderly lady in front of her. The woman and her friend were heading to Las Vegas. Sam's one-way ticket would take her to Topeka, Kansas.

Since the bus didn't leave until morning, Sam walked to the dilapidated motel across the street. Standing straighter, she opened the office door. An old hippy with a long white mustache like Yosemite Sam checked her out through the bulletproof glass on top of the counter.

"I'd like a room for the night," she said.

He grinned and scooted his stool closer to the counter. "You alone?"

Averting her eyes, she shook her head. "My boyfriend's outside smoking," she replied, sliding two twenties in the gap between the glass and counter.

"He's making you pay?" he asked, stroking one of his mustache handles.

"He's worth it."

He shrugged and pushed a key on a lime green triangular fob to Room Twelve toward her. "The ice machine's broke and make sure you keep the noise down."

Without a word, Sam hurried to the last door of the one-story moss-covered building. Once inside, she locked it, set the chain, and pushed the desk chair under the knob. She shivered and hoped she wasn't starring in some new slasher movie.

After calming her breathing, she set her backpack on the lumpy bed that appeared as if the maid simply threw the bedspread over the top without laundering the sheets. The worn out La-Z-Boy was more inviting. She didn't want to think about that now. Instead, she took out a box of hair color and a pair of scissors from her backpack.

After setting the items on the edge of the bathroom sink, she stared in the mirror. "There's no going back, Sam. You need to finish this. You have no choice."

She started cutting. One and a half foot strands of blond hair fell into the sink. More and more empowered, she chopped it off, trimmed it, and then smiled at her new soft curls that had replaced her straight hair.

"Who would have guessed I'd have some body to my hair?" It shouldn't have surprised her though. Her father had thick wavy gray hair.

After reading the instructions, Sam colored the blond into a reddish brown. Using gel, she spiked it into wafts of curls. She admired her new look with her one blue eye and one green eye.

"I am a freakish cat, а странный кошка."

After triple checking the locked door, she curled up in the chair and unfolded the piece of paper from her shoe. The truck would start in Maryland and head west with specific stops toward its destination.

Her bus would follow the same route. If she played her cards right, she would find it before the end of the route since the bus and truck started at the same time. Her biggest concern now was how to recognize the truck and the driver.

CHAPTER 2

SATURDAY

AT EIGHT IN THE MORNING, Karl knocked lightly on Samantha's bedroom door. In the empty hallway, he tried the knob. With a low growl, he used his master key. He expected to see a Cinderella comforter and matching curtains, but he found a woman's room in tasteful shades of green.

Karl reminded himself that Samantha was twenty-one and not a child. He liked his women young though. After a disappointing night with Jillian, he wanted Samantha. Her naivety was appealing. Jillian had her fair share of men over the years, and he had to work too hard for a taste of the Ice Queen. He'd much rather enjoy Samantha again. He checked her bathroom and found it empty.

After a quick tour of her practice room, the kitchen, and the library, he met Ivan in the second-floor hallway. "Where's Samantha?" Karl asked.

"I don't know," Ivan replied. "Her mother's looking for her, too."

In a foul mood, Karl stalked to his office. Sitting at his desk, he retrieved his key and opened his center desk drawer. The file lay askew. He quickly checked the contents. Everything remained intact and in order. He reached for the pad of paper on the desk and tilted it to see the impressions. As he grabbed a pencil, his desk phone rang.

"Petrov," he said.

"Have you tracked down the truck?" Russian General Yzemikov asked.

"Not yet, General, but everything's in place."

"The only link is that second box and its memory card."

"Yes, General, my men will leave within the hour," Karl replied.

"Have your men meet the truck at its third stop east of the Kansas border. Don't disappoint me with incompetence," he replied, before hanging up.

Karl wrote the information on the pad to be sure. Not that he'd forget, but General Yzemikov demanded perfection. Karl swore as he looked closely at the pad. He

16

couldn't tell if the pad had the file's information on it. He'd assume Samantha had snooped.

"Sergei," he yelled. The door immediately opened, and his aide stepped inside. "Take Bruno for a walk and tell Colonel Williams that I'd like to speak with him."

Sergei nodded and opened the cage. Ten minutes later, Seth Williams limped in with his shiny mahogany cane. Refusing a chair, the Colonel stood behind it.

"We need her here. It'll be easier setting up Samantha than Dmitri," Karl said.

"She left?" the Colonel asked.

"Yes, and we need to find her."

"She's just a kid. She doesn't need to be involved," Williams said.

"Rather it's your kid involved?" Karl asked with a grin.

The Colonel sighed. "I'll send a team to track her down."

"We're worried about her disappearance and want to keep her safe. An underage Amber Alert should help. She looks young enough."

"I understand. We'll need to know every place she's been to pull this off."

"That's your problem," Karl replied, waving his hand as a dismissal.

"I'll check with Martha first," Williams mumbled as he limped out the door.

Karl focused back on the notepad. He ripped off the top piece and used a pencil on the next. The shading uncovered his writing. He hated not knowing why Samantha disappeared.

CHAPTER 3

IN THE LEFT FRONT SEAT of the Greyhound bus, Samantha watched the young driver. Bob had his seat all the way to the steering wheel. Earlier, she peeked around to see if he had blocks on his shoes to reach the pedals. No blocks, just heeled cowboy boots.

While Bob kept a steady speed of fifty-five miles per hour, Sam continued to calculate the miles and hours to her destination. She was never good at algebra.

If the mystery truck kept to the same speed, she thought the bus would need to gas up at the same truck plazas listed in Karl's folder. If meeting the truck during the stops didn't work as Plan A, she'd try Plan B and track it down once it reached its objective.

The bus route on Highway 70 would take her all the way to Kansas. The folder didn't mention much about the driver except that he was military, so identifying the man and his truck caused her the most anxiety.

Hiding a sigh, Sam faked a nap. Next to her, the white-haired grandmother knitted some kind of sleeved thing with red yarn. Lila Speaker headed for Columbus, Ohio, to visit her daughter and grandkids. Thank God, they were almost to Columbus. For the last eight hours of their trip, she knew everything about Laurie, her deadbeat husband, and their kids, Cassidy and Gina. Sam tuned her out after the first four hours.

While Sam pondered her predicament of finding the truck and driver, the bus slowed. She abruptly sat up. Thick black smoke poured from the front engine. It seeped through the vents into the bus. The twenty-five passengers coughed at once.

"Hang on, folks. There's a truck plaza a mile up the road," Bob said.

"What's happening?" Lila asked, hugging the knitting to her bosom.

"Just a little engine trouble," Bob replied casually.

"Just a little?" Sam asked under her breath.

From his rearview mirror, Bob glared at her.

Passengers in the back slid their windows open, which sucked more smoke into the bus making it worse.

"I can't take it! Let me out!" Lila shouted, stuffing her yarn into her canvas bag.

"We're almost there," Bob replied, turning on the windshield wipers as if that would help.

Impressed with his calm attitude, Sam wondered if this happened often. With her backpack on her lap, she breathed through her flannel shirtsleeve. The bus continued to slow as the driver shifted gears. Suddenly the engine caught fire in the middle of the entrance to the truck plaza.

"Everybody out the back!" Bob yelled.

Lila and the rest of the passengers scrambled for the back exit while Bob opened the front side door. He jumped out with his phone. With her bag on her back, Sam followed him with the fire extinguisher. While everyone watched, she sprayed the front engine until white foam covered it.

Bob slid his phone into the front pocket of his jeans. "I would have let it burn."

She set the empty canister next to him and frowned. "People have luggage on board. What are we supposed to do now?" she asked as the group surrounded them.

Bob shrugged. "The replacement bus will be available in six hours."

"But I'm on a set schedule," she replied with her hands on her hips. While the passengers trekked toward the diner connected to the gas station, she grabbed Bob's arm. "That's all you can do?"

Unaffected by their new circumstance, he shrugged again. "Find another ride, wait, or walk. I get paid no matter what."

"You're a big help," she replied, but he had already turned away.

She sighed and thought about her options. Waiting and walking were out. She'd have to find a ride. The last one by the bus, she followed the rest toward the building. She paused at the edge of the driveway as trucks passed her to park for the night.

While she waited, she spotted a big man walking out of the side door of the gas station. He looked like her father's best friend, Bear. Why would he be here? Dismissing the notion that her grizzly Bear had come to help her, she skipped between the trucks.

Maybe that was a sign to call him. She trusted him, but she hadn't seen him in over a year. Since she ditched her cell, she found the pay phone by the car section of the parking lot. She dialed, and his baritone voicemail answered.

"Bear, it's me, Sam." How much should she tell him over the phone? "I'm in a bit of a pickle and could use some advice. I don't have my cell, so I guess I'll try again later." Tears filled her eyes. "I, um, I miss you."

She quickly hung up and blew out a breath. This wasn't a problem; this was an inconvenience. She knew this wouldn't be easy. She could adapt.

Walking toward the diner, she paused as the plaza attendant lowered the American flag for the evening. With a hand over her heart, she respectfully waited. After looking closer at the flag, she glowered and stalked toward him.

CHAPTER 4

FRESHLY SHAVED AND SHOWERED, LOGAN McCormick sipped his black coffee from a window booth in the truck stop diner. While his partner ranted through the hidden communication piece in his ear, Logan watched a smoking Greyhound bus catch fire at the edge of the parking lot.

The passengers scrambled in every direction except for a young woman in a flannel shirt and jeans. She sprayed the engine with the fire extinguisher. It surprised him that she could hold it up; it was almost as big as she was.

"Mick, are you even listening to me?" Barrett asked in his ear.

"I wish I wasn't. You're whining again," he mumbled.

"Well, it pisses me off I can't get a decent cell signal anywhere at this damn truck stop."

"Who are you calling? I'm your only friend." Logan smirked at the non-reply.

The group from the bus raced across the parking lot knowing they'd have a long wait. Glad he already ordered his meal; he continued to watch the young woman by the pay phone. As she walked gracefully toward the diner, her heels never touched the ground. He smiled when she stopped at the lowering of the flag.

When his cell vibrated on the table, he checked the caller ID, winced, and then covered it with his Texas Ranger's baseball cap. Fascinated with the young woman, he pushed his hat aside and leaned forward to see her argue with the attendant. The man nodded apologetically while she shook her finger at him.

Logan sipped his coffee. As he wondered about the wildcat under the cap, the waitress stopped briefly to deliver his steak and scrambled eggs. He wolfed down his meal, and the young woman disappeared into the gas station's convenience store.

The bus passengers overwhelmed the only two waitresses while the manager corralled the busboy to carry around a pot of coffee and hand out menus. Logan chewed his last bite as an elderly woman with a bag of red yarn trolled the diner and eyed his spot.

"How long does it take you to eat?" Barrett asked in his ear.

He set his knife across his plate. "Can I finish my coffee, please?"

Logan held out his mug for the busboy and spotted the young woman scanning the room from the doorway. His wildcat assessment fit. Her body was sleek not awkwardly skinny. The loose curls of reddish brown hair danced around her Scottish cap as she turned her head. He couldn't see her face but knew by her confident stance that she was a spitfire. She caught him staring and moved toward him. Damn it. He didn't need the attention.

Pulling her cap to her brow to shadow her face, she stood beside the table with her backpack in her hand. "Hello, Major."

Barrett thundered in Logan's ear, "What the hell? Who is that?"

"Excuse me?" he asked tensely.

"I'm guessing you were a major in the Army," she said.

He relaxed slightly. "What makes you think that?"

"Your hair is Army short, your watch is military time, your combat boots are Army issue, and your posture is rigid," she said, setting her bag on the seat across from him. She slid in next to it.

"Military maybe, but an officer?" Logan asked.

She shrugged. "You have a superior air about you. I guessed. Was I right?"

Barrett laughed. "She's got you pegged."

Resisting the urge to turn off his com, Logan frowned and crossed his arms stretching his denim over-shirt.

When he didn't answer, she continued, "I'm looking for a ride."

"How do you know I'm not done for the night?" Logan asked.

"I think you prefer to drive at night. You're clean and you just ate breakfast," she said.

Barrett snickered in his ear. "Let her. She's amusing, and you're such a grouch."

"No," he replied to her and Barrett. Two could play her game. "What are you running from?"

She stiffened slightly. "What makes you think that?"

"You have leftover hair dye on your earlobe." She gasped and rubbed her ear. He pointed at her other. "Busted," he said with a chuckle.

"Are you joking with a woman?" Barrett asked. Logan clenched his jaw at Barrett's statement.

Turning her head, she tugged her cap down farther. He thought she'd completely cover her eyes.

The waitress walked by and put his bill next to him. "Honey, you want anything?"

"No, thank you," she replied.

When the waitress hurried away, the wildcat stuck her foot between his legs and pressed her canvas shoe into his crotch. God, it felt good.

"If you give me a ride, I can make it worth your while," she whispered.

Barrett chuckled. "Take her up on it. How long's it been? Two years since your divorce? Mick, don't even think about turning me off. You know the protocol."

Calling her bluff, Logan leaned back, which pressed his cock firmly against her foot. "How old are you?"

"Twenty-one," she replied, wiggling her toes through her shoe.

He was getting hard—so much for bluffing. "Let's see your ID."

"Nice try, Major," she said, glancing around the room. "I'm also guessing you have a nickname like Mac."

Enjoying the banter, Barrett laughed. "Mick, Mac, same thing."

"It's not," Logan replied.

Her mouth opened with some witty reply, but she snapped it shut just as quick. Before he could follow her eyes to the TV above the counter, she applied a little more pressure with her foot. God, and it wasn't his own pressure. Needing to focus on something else, he sipped his coffee.

"How about that ride?" Her foot continued to stroke him. "I'm not a virgin if that's what you're wondering."

He choked on his coffee. "Jesus," he said, looking around.

Thankfully, nobody paid any attention to them. Before Barrett said a word, Logan casually tapped off his com. She looked up at him, and he finally saw her eyes. He stared at her freckled face with a mesmerizing green eye and cobalt blue eye.

She quickly looked away. "I know. I'm Sam the Freak."

When she started to pull her foot away, Logan held it firm with his hand. "They're exotic," he replied, before letting her go.

She smiled. "Thank you, Major."

Stunned, he watched her leave the diner and wondered why he'd said it. He would have liked to take her up on her offer especially after seeing her smile. It curved at the ends like the Cheshire Cat. It seemed genuine and knocked him on his ass. God, he was hard with only a foot and a smile. It had been too damn long.

CHRISTINA THOMPSON

With a sigh, Logan turned on his com. As if he never turned it off, he listened to Barrett continue to swear about protocol and grumble about the reception on his phone. Sam had guessed right although Logan was still an Army Major.

Close to retirement, Sergeant Major James Barrett has known him since basic training and has been his partner on these special assignments for the last three years. Orphaned at a young age, Logan thought of Barrett and the military as his family and home.

Logan looked at the military face of his watch. Was he that obvious? She must have been an Army brat. He shook off his attraction to the wildcat. Although she made an impression, he swore he wouldn't fall for any woman's manipulation ever again. He had jumped through hoops with his ex, and she chewed him up and spit him out like all her meals. He clenched his jaw as he pulled out his wallet.

Their mission came first. He and Barrett had to deliver their high priority cargo to Fort Riley's secret installation in Kansas. Taking twelve-hour shifts, they'd be there in no time. Their protocol required constant communication even while the other slept on the cot next to the cargo in the trailer of the truck.

31

After handing the bills to the waitress, he waited in the long line to pay for another large coffee in the convenience store. The passengers from the bus wandered and crowded the area. He didn't see Sam anywhere, so he hoped she found a ride with a vacationing family in a minivan. On the Saturday of the Memorial Day weekend, they were swarming the place.

"What happened?" Barrett demanded in Logan's ear.

"Sam left," Logan muttered, so the people around him couldn't hear.

"Damn, it would have made the trip less mind-numbing."

With a snort of agreement, Logan paid for his drink and headed toward his semi among the others in the acres of parking. He thought another trucker would quickly snatch his spot for the night's stay.

"You've become a stick in the mud," Barrett said.

"Keep hitting me with those grandpa quotes, old man."

"I can still kick your ass."

Barrett probably could. At six-four and built like a defensive lineman, Barrett had decided to grow a scraggily gray beard as a trucker. Logan's partner was a grizzly mountain man with a Chicago White Sox baseball cap.

"Was she my type?" Barrett asked.

32

"As your daughter," he mumbled. "She had exotic eyes—one blue and one green. You know, I think I should find her. I got a bad feeling."

Barrett swore under his breath. "Yeah, and I'm feeling fatherly. She's no lot lizard."

Logan agreed. At the truck, he set his coffee in the holder and tossed his cell and hat in the center console between the seats. Standing on the step, he scanned the darkness. Only a few halogen lights lit the back of the gas station and larger parking lot.

His eyes stopped at a red, white, and blue cab with an American eagle on the hood. From the cab's overhead bulb, Sam stood hunched on the seat. With her bag on her back, she pressed tightly against the passenger side window. She shook her head and stared at the hunting knife in the man's hand.

"Shit!" Logan reached behind the seat and pulled out a loaded shotgun.

"What? What's going on?" Barrett demanded.

"She's in some perv's truck, and he's pointing a knife at her," he replied as he raced across the aisles.

"Well, hurry the hell up!" Barrett yelled in his ear com.

Logan jumped on the step of the passenger side door and saw a bloated slob with his pants down. "Sam, get out," he yelled behind her.

The sleazy trucker glared at him. "She's mine. You didn't want her."

With Sam frozen in her spot, Logan yanked open the door. The smell of horrid body odor and shitty crotch almost knocked him backward. The guy's belly rolls only partially covered his hairy balls and hard bent cock. Logan re-swallowed his scrambled eggs.

"She ain't leaving," the blob said, stabbing his knife in the air.

While holding onto the outside bar handle, Logan pumped his shotgun with his other hand. "This says different. Sam, come here."

Like a frightened cat, she leapt at him. With a grunt, he swung backward and hit his back against the corner of the cab. Her arms squeezed his neck and her legs wrapped around his waist. He dropped to the ground and ran for his truck. He actually learned a few new curse words from the creep behind them.

"You are a great man," Sam whispered.

Between her breath steaming up his neck and her braless breasts torturing his chest, he disagreed. He inhaled the subtle rose scent of her cheek. He didn't want to think about the parts of her that pressed against his belt buckle.

"What? Damn it! What's happened?" Barrett yelled again in his ear.

"Are they all as ugly?" Sam asked, tightening her grip around his neck.

Logan snorted. "Pretty much."

"What's as ugly?" Barrett asked. "God damn it. Tell me something."

"I don't think yours would be," she replied.

Logan groaned as they approached the truck. He pulled at the door and tossed her up and in. She crawled across his seat. He suddenly felt cold and empty without her in his arms. Dismissing his reaction to her soft warm body, he jumped in after her and shoved the shotgun back in its holder. He shifted toward the highway.

That outcome could have been far worse. What if he hadn't found her in time? He narrowed his eyes as she pulled her knees to her chin. Her backpack set on the floor in front of her.

"What possessed you to leave with that guy?" he demanded.

"He had a patriotic truck," she replied with her forehead against her knees.

"Have you ever heard the saying *Don't judge a book by its cover*?"

Ignoring his rhetorical question, she stared out the front window. A few minutes later, she whispered, "Thank you, Major."

"It's Logan," he bit out. He wasn't ready to calm down yet. A different scenario continued to cross his mind. She should know better. "God, you've never seen one before? I thought you said you weren't a virgin."

"I'm not. I just didn't see it."

Barrett shouted in his ear, "What the hell is going on? Mick, I swear to God you better tell me something or I'm coming up there."

Knowing Barrett couldn't get out until they stopped; Logan glanced at Sam. He didn't want to know, but—hell— he wanted to know. "So? What? A dark back seat with your prom date?"

"No, last week with my stepfather's assistant."

"What?" Barrett roared.

Logan subtly adjusted the volume on his earwig com in his left ear before he went deaf. "Did he take advantage of you?"

She sighed. "Not really."

"What's that mean?" he asked.

"I didn't actually see it."

Barrett swore. "Oh, for God's sake, this is making me mental."

36

Ignoring the rant in his ear, Logan asked, "So he did take advantage?"

"I tried flirting and got in over my head. What's done is done." She looked his way. "Are you married?"

"Was." His body tensed at the mention of his ex-wife.

"She wasn't your best friend?"

"Hardly," he said, turning on his CB radio. He adjusted it to the police channel.

With the dash providing the only light, Sam looked around the cab. An empty bottle of water and a coffee set in the cup holders between the seats. The butt of the shotgun stuck out behind his seat.

His modified truck was a regular semi at a casual glance. If she started probing, she'd notice the high tech security. He'd have to be careful. She seemed to have an eye for detail.

She glanced in the sleeping compartment. "Where are you going?"

"West."

"What are you carrying?"

"Cargo."

Turning her body toward him, she bit her bottom lip and watched him closely. "Where were you stationed? My father was at Fort Riley."

"He was?" Barrett asked in his ear.

"We don't have to talk," Logan said, tensing at the fort's name. That was their destination. Was she a plant? An agent? Who was she working for?

Barrett piped up. "Yes, she does. I want to know her story and why she's on the run."

Logan sighed. "Where are you headed?"

"West," she replied with a grin.

"Who are you running from?" Logan continued.

She tensed this time and turned toward her side window. "I'm looking for someone."

"Who?"

"I'm not sure yet," she said.

"Are you in college somewhere?" Logan asked.

"Does Miss Martin's School for the Proper Lady count? It was my mother's idea."

He chuckled. "Etiquette and manners are a rarity these days. You came from money?"

She shook her head. "I teach dance to grade schoolers. I'd like to own my own studio someday."

"Where?"

She smiled at him but remained quiet. Boy, that playful grin did him in every time. He found himself compelled to smile back. Was that her way of getting answers?

Pissed at himself, he clammed up. He focused on the road and his CB for any upcoming problems. At least, the weather wouldn't slow them down. The forecast called for cool nights and clear skies for the next few days.

While he quietly racked up the miles, Sam did a head bob as she nodded off a few times. He wondered about the wildcat and her dilemma. He felt a need to help her.

Was that her plan for him to save her and make him care before she struck? God, he sounded paranoid, but his ego couldn't take another personal slam. It didn't matter though. She wanted Intel on his cargo. He'd bet on it. What's that quote? *Keep your friends close and your enemies closer.*

In the middle of Illinois, Logan turned on his blinker to enter the rest area. Before he dealt with the St. Louis traffic, he would stretch and clear his head. He could keep his distance from her.

CHAPTER 5

SUNDAY

AT ONE IN THE MORNING, Sam jumped awake as Logan pulled into a truck plaza. After parking in the front lot for easier access back to the highway, he stretched his back and rubbed his neck.

"What's the matter?" she asked.

"My neck's been sore ever since you launched yourself at me."

Remembering, she winced as he leaned forward against the steering wheel. Without asking, she pounced into the spot behind him and started kneading the tight muscles of his shoulders. She moved her fingers to his neck; he groaned. Her first choice had been the right one. She shivered at the thought of her second.

She'd like to think she and Logan had some kind of Army connection. Did her father have her back? While she wondered if she could trust Logan to help her, his body warmed her fingers.

Her flannel shirt wasn't as protective at night as she had hoped, and she had no phone, one change of clothes, and thirty dollars. Her father had lectured her to be prepared but to adapt when necessary.

She smiled at how good Logan felt. He certainly wasn't soft and squishy like Ugly Penis Man. Logan had solid muscles. She liked being pressed against him.

Leaning onto his back, she moved her fingers to his short brown hair and caressed his temples. He moaned and relaxed his shoulders.

"Does that feel better?" she whispered near his ear.

He stiffened. "I won't be used," he replied, pulling away.

"What? I was just—"

He abruptly opened his door and slid out. Turning his head away, he growled, "Shut up."

With her hands still in the air from where she had rubbed him, she stared at his reaction. She didn't understand why he was so angry. She had only tried to help; he had helped her. Why shouldn't she reciprocate?

Running his hand over his head, he looked up at her. "Come on. I heard your stomach growling, almost as loud as your snoring."

She smiled at his jest. He reached out for her. With his hands around her waist, he gently set her on the ground. She trembled. Was it the cold air or his touch?

As they walked toward the building, she boldly slipped her hand into his and moved closer. She shivered again.

"Are you cold?" Logan asked.

"A little," she replied.

He let go of her hand and took off his denim shirt. It engulfed her.

"Thank you, Logan," she whispered as they paused for a conversion van to drive by.

Sam hugged herself and inhaled the Irish Spring Body Wash that lingered on his denim shirt. With a wide gap between them, they continued to the large convenience store. She hesitated at the restroom door and bit her lip.

He snorted. "Sam, I'm not going to leave you here at one in the morning. Your taxi stops at dawn. Besides, you're wearing my favorite shirt."

She nodded and rushed to the stall. After washing her hands and face, she looked at her reflection. Her hair stuck out every which way under her cap. She thought her freckles stood out more with her darker hair. She liked this adventurous Sam better.

At the rate Logan was driving, she'd beat the mystery truck to Fort Riley. She had tried to test him by bringing up the destination of the cargo. He didn't even blink. Well, that would have been too easy.

Debating whether to trust Logan, she left the restroom. The store's attendant put the *Closed* sign on the men's door, so he could clean it.

"Is there anyone still in there?" she asked.

The attendant shook his head and slapped the dirty wet mop on the floor. With a knot in her stomach, she quickly checked the store and the diner. Nauseated by her Amber Alert with five other girls on the TV, she hurried outside. She couldn't see Logan's truck. Too many others hid it. Before she ran toward the space, she heard a commotion along the side of the building.

She peeked around the corner. Next to two large dumpsters inside a wooden privacy fence, Logan held up his hands. Blocking the open gate, Ugly Penis Man pointed his knife at him. He moved closer forcing Logan into the back corner.

"Where is she?" the blubbery man asked with his back to her. He swiped the knife at Logan.

"Who?" Logan asked, calmly stepping back.

44

"That girl."

"I dropped her off a few miles back," Logan replied.

Sam tiptoed toward them and carefully picked up an abandoned hubcap. The man slashed the knife again. Logan rammed his back into the fence. Seeing her, he shook his head.

"I should gut you and leave you to rot. She was mine," the fat man said, jabbing the knife closer.

She snuck up behind him. "I'm nobody's."

Sam swung the hubcap and knocked him in the head. He fell sideways into a stack of cardboard boxes, which broke some of the wood slats in the fence. The rattle and bang brought the attention to a few truckers on their way into the building.

Logan picked her up and cradled her in his arms. He sauntered toward his truck as if he didn't have a care in the world.

"I can't afford to have the cops called," Logan said. When the fat man screamed bloody murder, Logan flipped her around to face him. "Hang on."

Once again, she hugged him around the neck as he lengthened his stride. With her ear against his cheek, she looked over his shoulder. "He's pointing at us," she said.

"I'm hurrying," he mumbled.

"You know I can walk," Sam said.

"You'll only slow me down," Logan replied with an arm around her.

Wrapping her legs around his waist, she should have been scared. She gripped him tighter while he maneuvered between the other parked trucks. She shivered every time his warm breath hit her ear. He panted as he ran, and she squirmed with arousal. She was tempted to kiss him. Loosening her grip, she looked at his profile. This Army man had the traditional strong rugged features. Who could resist him? She bet not many.

He glanced at her and groaned. "I think taking the long way around will give us a chance to leave before they identify my truck."

Nodding, she let her hands linger along his smooth jaw line. While he scanned the area, she looked at his long lashes. She couldn't see what color eyes he had.

"Stop it. We're here," Logan said with a scowl. He yanked open the door and tossed her in.

She sprang across his seat and immediately chilled from the separation. While he pulled in line with other nondescript semi-trucks, she looked out his side mirror to see if anyone followed them. She couldn't tell in the darkness.

"You didn't have to make a scene," Logan said, accelerating onto the interstate.

"He was going to hurt you," she replied.

"I didn't need any help."

"Sheesh, I bet you don't ask for directions either," she said, looking at him.

"I had it under control," he replied. "I was waiting for the right time to overtake him."

"It didn't look like it." She gasped. "Logan, you're bleeding."

"Where?"

Sam grabbed a tissue from the center console and crouched beside him. Her knees touched his thigh. He had an inch-long slice across his upper arm.

"He stabbed you," she said, pressing the tissue against the cut. "Do you have a first aid kit?"

"Behind your seat. I thought he missed."

"Does it hurt?" she asked, scrambling for the kit.

"Just slap a Band-Aid on it."

With his right hand on the wheel, he pulled up his t-shirt sleeve with the other. She peeled open one of the larger Band-Aids. His arms were hard as steel yet they had gently held her twice. Under the guise of making sure the Band-Aid stuck, she caressed his warm skin. She leaned closer and saw the tattoo of an open parachute with skull and sword on his deltoid.

"You were an Army Ranger?" she asked.

47

He quickly pushed down the sleeve. "Once upon a time." He sat up straight and checked his mirrors as if to dismiss her.

She slid back to her seat and wiped her face before he saw the wetness. He was injured because of her. After finding her iPod in her bag, she stuck in the right ear bud. She pulled her knees to her chin and absently counted the reflective green mile markers.

CHAPTER 6

SAM'S LINGERING COLD FINGERS SEARED his skin. Logan probably could have let her run back to the truck, but she felt too damn good. Her moan in his ear and her breasts against his chest again drove him nuts. Her seductive gaze made him dizzy.

His jeans were still tight at her closeness and concern. As he accelerated west on the interstate, Barrett berated him about the incident, which brought him back to reality. Sam was using him for the ride. That was all.

With a clenched jaw, he turned up the police frequency on the CB and entered the City of St. Louis. On the holiday weekend, the night traffic slowed his pace. Blowing out a breath, he finally left the city and continued west on

Highway 70. Out of the corner of his eye, he saw her wipe her eyes on his denim sleeve. Damn it. He softened. She sniffed her nose as she listened to her iPod. He wanted to know what song made her so sad.

"Don't get snot on my shirt," Logan said instead.

"I'm sorry about your arm. It's my fault," she replied, dropping her iPod back into her bag.

"Sam, I'm fine. It's a scratch."

"I should have done what the guy wanted. It shouldn't have mattered. It was just sex."

Waking up, Barrett growled. "Just sex? Jesus, what the hell?"

"It matters," Logan replied.

"Why?" she asked.

"What do you mean *why*? I'd like to think there's more to sex than just sex," Logan said.

"Like what?" she asked.

Barrett piped in. "Yeah, like what?"

"I don't know," Logan replied.

She flashed that sexy smile. "Are you the virgin?"

Logan groaned as Barrett roared with laughter. "Are you harassing me on purpose?" Logan asked.

As a reply, Sam chuckled.

"Go to sleep," Logan demanded to Barrett, who continued to laugh.

50

"Not on your life," Barrett replied.

Sam glanced back into the sleeping compartment. "That's too enclosed."

"I'm not going to climb in after you," Logan replied.

"I wouldn't mind if you did, but I don't like small spaces. It makes me queasy."

He moaned. Sharing the compartment? Too damn late to get those images out of his head. He'd drive into a ditch if he didn't refocus on his mission.

She took a deep breath. "My uncle was an Army Ranger at Fort Riley," she blurted out.

"What?" Barrett asked.

Why bring that up again? Army Rangers weren't stationed at Fort Riley; they trained at Fort Benning in Georgia. For as much as she knows stuff about the Army, she should have known that. What's her angle? He needed to change the subject until he could question her properly.

"Is he someone you should call for help?" Logan asked.

She sighed. "I got his voicemail."

Barrett mumbled in the back.

"You want to try again?" Logan asked. "My phone is somewhere in the center console."

She eyed him for a full minute then searched for the cell phone. It rang. She jumped back.

Logan grabbed it and growled. "What?"

"How are you, Mick?" the sultry voice asked.

Damn it! Why didn't he check his caller ID? He's been avoiding her calls for the last month. Sam distracted him. He couldn't think straight.

"Why are you calling this late?" he demanded. "I'm working."

"I know you prefer to drive at night. When are you coming home? I miss you," she said.

"I don't have a home. You took it." He bit his tongue before he lashed out more. At his tone, Sam shrank into the seat. He sighed and tried to calm his irritation. "What do you want?"

"Mick, I miss you. I've changed. Let me prove it to you. Where are you? I'll meet you somewhere," his ex said.

Barrett fumed in his other ear. "She has not changed! She's still a selfish brat!"

"I know that," Logan growled back.

She chuckled. "I'm so glad you agree that I've changed. Mick, I still love you. Will you give me another chance?"

Logan paused from replying. She had said *I love you* only once before, and he proposed the same night. The first couple of weeks of their marriage had been wonderful, but it went downhill quickly. She didn't understand that he couldn't talk about his assignments. She accused him of cheating and not trusting her. She had cheated and had blamed him for it. Had she changed? He didn't know what to believe anymore. He hated being alone, but he had become more and more resigned to the fact.

Barrett warned, "She's sucking you into her vortex again."

"Logan," Sam whispered.

Snapping back to the present, Logan glanced at Sam. She pointed to an accident a half mile ahead of them. Taillights lit the highway in a red chain reaction as cars slammed on their brakes.

"I'll call you later," Logan said.

He tossed his cell aside and hit his brake. Sam flew forward and fell to the floor. He stopped a foot from a Camry. From the side mirror, the driver's eyes bugged out. Tires screeched around them.

"What's going on?" Barrett demanded. "Me and the cot slid the length of the trailer."

Logan blew out a breath. "An accident ahead. We may have to wait a while."

"Yeah, I got that," Sam said, climbing slowly onto the seat. "I guess that'll teach me to wear my seatbelt."

"You okay?" Logan asked, turning up the police band on the CB. She nodded and fastened her seatbelt.

"That was your ex-wife?"

He nodded and gripped the steering wheel.

"You still care about her?"

"Yeah, I guess, but I don't trust her," he said.

"You can love her without trusting her?" Sam asked.

"No, she's a liar."

"Are you trying to convince me or you?" she asked.

Clenching his jaw again, Logan put the truck in park and checked his mirrors for unusual activity.

Three cars had crashed into one another. A state police cruiser, two tow trucks, and an EMS bus were finally on the scene and were slowly moving the damaged vehicles aside.

He rubbed the bridge of his nose and glanced at Sam. She had her knees to her chest with her chin resting on top.

"I'm sorry she hurt you. You don't deserve it," she said, watching the commotion.

He frowned. "How would you know?"

"I can tell you're a good guy. You saved me," she replied with a smile.

She was actually trying to cheer him up; it was working. He forgot about what's her name.

"Twice," he replied.

"No way," she said, turning her head so her cheek pressed against her knees. "Only once. I saved you twice— once from that man using that rusted hubcap and just now from crashing your truck. You owe me."

He laughed. "I hit the brake in time, and it's your fault anyway. You're distracting me."

"How?" she asked.

"Your feminine wiles," Logan replied.

Barrett laughed. "Thank God, you've finally admitted it. I like Sam a lot better than the She-Devil."

From the dashboard lights, Logan watched her lips curve into a smile highlighting the gleam in her eyes.

"I have feminine wiles?" she asked.

"Yeah, so knock it off." He chuckled as she proudly sat up straighter.

After another hour, the state trooper motioned the traffic around the broken glass on the left side of the road. The trucks and cars merged into one lane, and they eventually drove past the mess. The police band squawked about the hit and run. A silver Lexus with diplomatic plates had cut off the other drivers causing the crash.

Sam tensed. "Did they say *diplomatic plates*?"

Barrett asked the same thing, "Diplomatic plates?"

Logan eyed her. "Yeah, what do you know about it?"

"Just curious." She checked her watch. Barrett remained quiet, too. Using her finger, she wrote on her jeans as if calculating in her head. After a while, she looked at him. "Are you behind schedule?"

"Why would you think that?" What did she know?

She shook her head. "I'm doing a little math in my head."

"Are you late for something?" Logan asked.

"No, but I'm cutting it close."

"Who are you meeting?" he asked as he listened to Barrett grumble in his other ear.

"I'm not sure."

"What does that even mean, Sam?" Logan asked. "Is it someone you met on the internet? Where are you meeting this person?"

She shook her head and hugged her legs to her chest again. An invisible force field surrounded her. She didn't trust him. Well, he didn't trust her either. What was she hiding?

Logan sighed. "We're stopping at a truck plaza east of the Kansas border. We part ways there."

She nodded and reached for her iPod. He silently drove and wondered about the wildcat beside him.

At five in the morning, Logan pulled into the rest area. Sam looked out the window as he passed the cars by the gas pumps. A quiet mew rose from her throat. She crouched down slightly in her seat.

With the area full of parked semis, he followed the long drive to the back of the twenty-acre lot. The edge dropped off into a ravine. A two-foot high rusted guardrail protected the trucks from the edge—not much security for eighteen-wheelers. Apparently, someone thought having a landfill next to the truck plaza was a good idea. He would bet during the summer months the place reeked.

Knowing in thirty minutes dawn would lighten the back lot, he found an empty spot along the edge. Barrett yawned. Logan would stay with the truck giving his partner a chance to use the restroom and grab a bite to eat before they made the switch.

"Keep her with you for fifteen minutes while I check on a couple of things," Barrett said.

With a panicked look, Sam bit her lower lip. "Please, don't leave me here."

"You can call your friend. You're safe in the daylight," Logan replied.

"But I'm not."

"Sam, I can't take you with me," he said.

She blew out a breath. "You're right. A deal's a deal."

She took off his denim shirt and then stripped off her flannel and t-shirt. Before he knew it, she climbed onto his lap. He groaned at her pale breasts jutting at him. She slid her hands up his chest to his neck. He grabbed her forearms to stop her from moving closer. Touching her silky skin provoked him to act. He weakened again. She was so damn close and he was so damn horny.

She looked into his eyes and smiled. "Yours are a vibrant green."

Anger overrode his lust. "Stop it. I won't be manipulated."

She dropped her hands. Her shoulders sagged. "I'm sorry," she whispered.

With tears in her eyes, she scrambled from his lap and slipped on her t-shirt. Without another word, she opened the door and slid down. With her flannel shirt in her hand, she disappeared into the darkness.

Once again, she had enticed him; and like an idiot, he had stopped her. His lonely nights just got lonelier. Of course, he wanted to get lost in her exotic eyes, lick the sweetness from her lips, and make love to her sexy dancer body. Then what? He had an assignment. He couldn't let her continue to ride with him. Barrett would take over in a few minutes. For as much as he wanted to lock them in the trailer with the cot for the next twelve hours, he couldn't. As it was, he was going to catch shit from his boss. Colonel Williams would not be happy that he picked up a hitchhiker.

Glancing at her backpack on the floor, Logan punched the steering wheel. Did she think he'd chase after her to give it back? Hell no, but he was tempted. He already missed her. How pathetic!

CHAPTER 7

SLIPPING ON HER FLANNEL SHIRT, Samantha hiked toward the plaza. Should she have trusted Logan and told him the truth? Was he of the same mindset to help her? She still wasn't sure.

His anger at her pitiful display of seduction kept her from turning back. At least, the embarrassment kept her warm. She had used him. It was a mean thing to do, especially after hearing his conversation with his ex-wife.

Back in Logan's truck, she had seen Sergei and Ivan by their silver Lexus at the gas station pump. How did they find her already? Why did they cause the accident?

While she looked for a pay phone, she saw the Russians by the restrooms. She probably could have walked by without them noticing. Her hair was different, but she couldn't take the chance. She moved closer and hid behind a rack of paperback books. What were they up to?

"The other team is searching for her. What if we see her first?" Sergei asked.

"We'll grab her for an added bonus. The Army guy and the truck are our main concern," Ivan replied.

"How do we recognize him?" Sergei asked.

"He's tall with short dark hair, and he has an Army Ranger tattoo on his right arm," Ivan said.

Sam gasped and steadied herself with the rack. Logan was the one? He was in trouble, and he didn't even know it. She turned away from the Russians and came face to face with Ugly Penis Man, who had a puffy purple eye.

He gripped her upper arm and grinned. "Where's your boyfriend?"

"In the bathroom. Do you want another swollen eye?" she asked, making a fist.

He yanked her toward the door. "You first."

Not knowing which would be the lesser of two evils, she yelled, "Sergei! Ivan!"

The fat man let her go as Ivan and Sergei turned toward them. She darted for the side door. With the Russians chasing her, she leapt onto the hood of the closest semi-truck and ran the length of its trailer. She sprang onto the top of the next one and thanked God the trucks were parked close together. Leaping from island to island, she raced for Logan in the back. He had a shotgun.

Emptiness filled the space where his truck had been while sadness filled her heart. She'd never see him again, but he was safe and away from the Russians. If Logan went through her things, he'd find her drawings and know about the danger. He'd be extra cautious then.

With the regret of hurting Logan and losing her iPod, she stopped at the edge of the last truck before the ravine. At the front of the trailer, Sergei and Ivan stopped to catch their breath. She balanced on the corner edge in the back.

"Stay away from me or I'll jump," she said.

"No, you won't," Ivan replied with a laugh.

"Samantha, your mother's worried. Come home with us," Sergei added.

She shook her head, took a deep breath, and stepped backward dropping into the ravine.

CHAPTER 8

IN THE CAB OF THE truck, Logan grabbed her backpack and unzipped it. Before he could look inside, Barrett yanked open his door and scanned the cab.

"Where's Sam?"

"Somewhere in there," Logan replied, gesturing to the building. "What's going on?"

"Find her. She left me a message for help and so has her mother," Barrett said.

"You know her?" he asked, shoving her bag onto the passenger seat.

"She's General Randall's daughter."

"Shit," Logan said, scrambling past Barrett. "Why didn't you say something?"

"She was safe with us. Now, move your ass."

Logan scanned the area as he jogged toward the buildings. "You should have told me sooner," he said into his com.

"And wreck my fun?" Barrett asked in Logan's ear. "I'm parking closer to the ramp. Something's going on with her, and it may involve our cargo."

"So she was testing me by bringing up Fort Reilly? Does this have to do with that Lexus with diplomatic plates?"

"I think so, and I'll explain later."

"Damn right, you will, Sergeant Major Barrett. As your superior on this assignment, you should have informed me of the danger to our cover."

"Major McCormick," Barrett thundered, "I would have if I thought we were in danger. I had no idea what she was doing and I still don't. Can we discuss this after you find my goddaughter?"

"You're a son of a bitch," he raged as he yanked open the door to the convenience store.

Logan stuck his head inside the woman's head and yelled for her. Hearing a woman—who wasn't Sam—scream, he moved toward the diner. Only a few truckers sat at the counter. They watched the mounted flat-screen TV on the wall. Logan glanced at it and froze.

An Amber Alert on the screen showed five girls and Sam with long blond hair. He read the description.

"She's not really sixteen, is she?" he asked Barrett.

"No, and I don't know why it would say she was. Did you find her yet?"

"I'm working on it," he said, spotting that sleazy trucker leaving through the side door.

Logan followed the slob and shoved him behind the building. Before the loser said a word, Logan punched him in the gut. His fist bounced back from the blubber. Waiting exactly two seconds for him to catch his breath, Logan got in his face.

"Where is she?" Logan demanded with his hand around the jerk's throat.

The bastard shook his head. Logan pushed him against the back of the building and squeezed his fingers. The ass's eyes widened.

"If you don't have the answer I want to hear, you will die in a puddle of your own urine. Where? Is? She?" Logan demanded.

The pig gurgled an answer. Logan loosened his grip slightly.

The bastard gasped for a breath. "Two guys named Ivan and Sergei chased after her."

"When?"

"A minute ago."

Logan squeezed fatty's neck. "If I ever see you again, I will kill you."

Logan punched him once more in the gut for good measure. He could have defended himself at the last truck stop without Sam's help. Of course, she wasn't with him to see it this time.

Logan raced for the parking lot. In the darkness with just a hint of light, he scanned the aisles. He spotted her silhouette leaping across the top of the trucks with two men chasing her. He swore and ran at an angle toward the back of the lot. On the last truck next to the ravine, she stopped and faced the men. His heart sank when she moved to the edge.

"Don't do it, Sam," Logan muttered, sprinting toward her.

"Do what? What's going on?" Barrett asked.

As she stepped off the truck and into the darkness below, Logan grabbed her arm. The force of his momentum yanked her body to the right. He heard a pop from her right shoulder as he pulled her toward him. She let out a short scream and passed out. With her limp body in his arms, he ducked under the semi just before the men appeared above them.

66

"Shit, she really did it," one of the men said with a Russian accent.

"Karl won't be happy," the other Russian replied.

The men dropped to the pavement and looked over the guardrail. Logan carefully laid Sam down. Full of fury, he stalked toward them. The men turned and saw Sam on the ground behind him. The short one with a paisley shirt and pointed collar drew his gun.

The other man in a tan leisure suit smiled. "We're definitely getting a bonus."

The idiot with the gun stepped closer to Logan. "Where's your truck?" the Russian asked. The gun almost touched his chest.

Within a blink, Logan reached out and twisted the gun out of his hand. He punched him in the face. The Russian staggered backward and over the side of the ravine. The other kicked the gun flipping it over the edge.

Logan blocked a second kick and slammed him to the ground. He jumped on top of him and quickly snapped his neck. After tossing him into the ravine, he gently picked up his unconscious wildcat.

"I've got her. Where are you?" he said to Barrett.

"By the ramp leading to the highway. Is she okay?"

In the darkness, he dodged the moving trucks.

"I dislocated her shoulder, and she passed out. Did you hear their Russian accents?"

"Yeah, I think we're compromised. The trailer door's unlocked. Move it, Mick."

Scanning the empty vicinity, Logan held her against his chest with one arm and climbed in. He barred the back doors. "We're in. Let's go."

"Hold on to something," Barrett replied.

Logan leaned against the door as the truck lurched forward. Then, he walked toward the only light coming from the computer screen in the front corner of the trailer. As Barrett maneuvered into traffic, Logan bumped into the long wooden crate that took up almost half of the space.

Midway, he laid her down on the cot. Kneeling beside her, he assessed her for other injuries. He removed her cap and ran his fingers through her soft curls feeling for bumps and blood. He touched her soft freckled cheek with the back of his finger. What was she thinking? Leaving her dislocated shoulder for last, he padded down her other arm and legs. Luckily, her only injury was her shoulder.

Glad that she was unconscious, Logan placed a hand below and above the joint. He quickly wrenched her arm to reset it. Her body twitched. How was she involved in this? Why were those Russians chasing her? Was she trying to kill herself?

Letting her rest, he pulled the computer chair closer. He waited. Barrett remained silent. While he scrubbed his hands over his face, she moaned in the darkness.

"Am I dead?" she whispered.

He set his hand on her shoulder to keep her from moving. "No, but you could have died. What possessed you to jump?"

"You were gone, and I wasn't going to go back."

He lightly caressed her sore shoulder. "Sam, you could have died. Nobody would have ever found your body in that ravine." The thought made him sick.

"This is bigger than just one person. Where are we?" she whispered.

"We're in the trailer of the truck. Sam, you need to explain this to me."

She sighed and pushed his hand away from her shoulder. "Those two Russians were looking for a military man who drives a truck. Other men are looking for me. The information I have is about the cargo you carry—a Russian spy satellite."

"Shit, how do you know that? The Russians don't even know we found their crashed satellite."

"But they do. I have a picture and the truck's route in my backpack."

"Hang on. I'm checking," Barrett said in his ear. "Damn it. It's all here."

"Get off the grid. We need a place to finish this discussion," Logan said.

"Logan, who are you talking to?" she asked.

"Sam, rest for now. Your shoulder's going to be sore for a while."

"Logan, why did you come for me?"

He touched her finger. "I just found out you're General Randall's daughter." She sniffed her nose, pulled her hand away, then shifted on the cot.

"You are such a dumbass," Barrett said. "No wonder you're single."

Logan sighed at hurting her again. He'd talk to her later. After sliding the chair back to the computer desk, he flipped a switch to disable their GPS.

"Will those men report back to their boss?" Barrett asked.

"No." Rubbing the back of his neck, Logan tried to understand what had happened and what he should do about it.

CHAPTER 9

IN THE SEMI'S TRAILER, SAM lay quietly on the cot and listened to Logan mumble and swear. Her stomach growled as she pretended to sleep. She realized she hadn't eaten since she left the embassy. She had no idea what time it was.

Her shoulder throbbed, but she resisted touching it. Feeling guilty, she didn't want Logan to know she was awake. She had made a big mess of things. The Russians found the cargo because of her.

Logan had checked her breathing and shoulder often. His gentle touch made her want to cry. She wanted him to hug her and reassure her that he didn't hate her for compromising his mission.

Once again, he knelt beside her. This time, he slid a hand behind her back and sat her up. His scruffy jaw pressed against her cheek. She found comfort in it. He placed something across the cot. After laying her back, he carefully folded her sore arm across her body. He had made a sling to protect her injury. Why was he being so sweet? She ruined everything.

The truck slowed to a stop. Logan opened the trailer door then retrieved her. He tried not to jostle her as he slid to the ground. His concern helped the ache in her shoulder.

While he held her close, she peeked past the bright sun to see that the semi had parked behind a rundown motel in a wooded area. She didn't hear any other cars along the road.

He carried her to the last room. In front of the door, he pressed his lips against her forehead. She sighed. Was he forgiving her? When someone yanked open the door, Logan quickly pulled his head away.

"Aw hell. Well, I'm taking over. Back to the truck, Major." She listened closely to the baritone voice.

"I should be here when she wakes up," Logan replied.

"No, you've done quite enough. Someone needs to stay with the truck. Right, Sir?"

Logan handed her over, and giant arms engulfed her. She opened her eyes.

Her grizzly Bear used his foot to slam the door on Logan. "Hey, Sammy, I like your hair. It suits you," he said, cradling her.

She cried. "Oh, Bear, I'm so glad to see you." She started to hug him and gasped at the pain.

"You need to be careful with your arm. It was dislocated."

"I only left you a message. How'd you find me?"

"You left chaos in your wake," he said, setting her on the bed next to the pile of snacks.

She leaned against the headboard. "I'm sorry. I thought I was doing the right thing. I don't know what to do now. I'm afraid to go back."

"First, you need to eat something. I got one of everything from the vending machine."

She reached for a bag of pretzels and struggled with it one-handed. Bear opened them and set a bottle of water on the bedside table.

"Where's Logan?" Sam asked.

"In the truck. I thought we should talk about your problem. Sammy, where'd you get the picture and truck route?"

She swallowed the pretzel and sighed. "Last week, I heard Karl talking on the phone in Russian. I looked up the words—два неделя до политическое убийство and уничтожать командировать чёрный цвет ящик спутник обломки. It translates *two weeks until assassination* and *destroy second black box on satellite wreckage.*"

Bear winced and rubbed his ear. "Sam's mother is married to Russian Ambassador Dmitri Demas. Sam lives at the Russian Embassy in D.C. Karl is Dmitri's assistant."

"Are you talking to Logan?" Sam asked.

"Yeah, through our coms," Bear said, turning his head to show her the tiny ear bud.

She moaned. "You heard our conversations ... and his rejection?"

"Let's stay on point. Shall we?" Bear said.

"Sorry," she whispered. She whimpered as she tried to unscrew the cap of her water bottle.

"Stop twisting your arm around or it'll dislocate again," Bear said.

After dropping the bottle on the bed, she pulled her knees to her chest and covered her face.

"Hey, don't cry." Bear bounced her on the bed as he sat down beside her. "Stay put, Major," he growled. He unscrewed her water bottle. Before she could ask what Logan was saying, he continued, "Sammy, tell me what happened next."

With the back of her good hand, she wiped her eyes. "I wanted to get more information so four days ago I snuck into Karl's office. He caught me and I tried to flirt." She paused. "Would you turn off your com for the rest?"

"Honey, I have to leave it on. The communication helps us protect the cargo."

"But it's embarrassing. I don't want him to hear."

"Say it quickly. Maybe that'll help," Bear replied, bouncing the bed again as he stood.

She moaned. "After laughing at me, Karl locked us in his office. When he bent me over his desk, I memorized the drawing of the satellite and the highlighted second black box from the scattered files."

Bear howled. "I'm sorry, Honey," he said, tugging the ear that held his com. "What happened next?"

"In my room, I, um, drew the picture and made a plan to warn the driver of the truck," she replied.

"Calm yourself, Major," Bear demanded. "Or you'll pop my eardrum."

"Is he angry with me?" she whispered.

"No, he's threatening to kill Karl."

She smiled. For some reason, it made her feel better. Bear sighed at her reaction and rolled his eyes as he listened to Logan.

"Can we continue please?" Bear asked.

"I snuck back into Karl's office two nights ago for the rest of the information."

Bear paced and growled again. "I'll ask her after you shut it. You're giving me a damn headache." He turned back to her. "He wants to know if you took the information or memorized it."

"I wrote it down on the pad from his desk," she said.

"You said other men were chasing you. Do you think they know you have the Intel?" Bear asked.

"I don't know for sure." She cringed. "Karl said he'd visit me in the morning, but I left the same night."

"Anything else we should know about?" Bear asked.

"Well, while I was on the balcony, I heard Karl talking to Colonel Williams about something important. The Colonel wasn't happy about a flash drive that Karl locked in his safe."

"Are you sure it was Colonel Williams?" Bear asked, stroking his grizzly gray beard.

"He has a limp, right? His daughter, Jillian, is a beautiful model," she replied.

"I know this is not good," Bear said to the ceiling.

Sam continued, "They've spent the last three months at the embassy. Karl told him he couldn't leave the grounds. He also said that the flash drive would keep the Colonel under his thumb."

"What does that mean?" Bear asked.

"I don't know. Bear, I tried to do the right thing. I can't go back there. I'm afraid," she whispered.

"I won't let anything happen to my Sammy. Now, eat something else."

She sipped her water and watched the caged Bear pace the length of the small room. For twenty minutes, he mumbled and growled. He and Logan were debating what to do next. They needed a secure place to open the crate and look for the second black box. They wanted to find it before they delivered the cargo. It would be safer in their hands especially if the Russians desperately wanted it back.

"Bear, what about the cabin? It's private and secure," Sam said.

"That's perfect. Yellow Springs is only a few hours from here," he replied.

CHAPTER 10

IN A RAGE INSIDE THE trailer, Logan had rammed the computer chair against the wall breaking the rollers, had stomped a hole in the cot, and had knocked over the flat-screen monitor. If he ever met this Karl, he'd seriously hurt him at best. Sam's sacrifice made him sick. It actually gave him chest pain. She did it all to protect their cargo.

While Barrett carried Sam to the cab of the truck, Logan grabbed his ringing cell. Knowing it couldn't be traced, he checked the caller ID.

"Who's calling you?" Barrett asked in his com. "The She-Devil?"

"Shut up and let me think." He answered it. "Yes, Sir?"

"Major, you missed your scheduled check-in time!"

"Colonel Williams, we ran into a bit of a problem," Logan said.

Barrett swore as the truck lurched forward.

"Have you been compromised?" Williams demanded.

"Our route has been delayed because of a car accident," Logan said.

"Why has your GPS been turned off?" Williams asked.

"I didn't realize it had been. There must be a glitch. I'll have Barrett check into it."

"How far behind are you? Where are you now?" Williams demanded.

"I'll check in as soon as we get there. Are you still at the Pentagon?"

"Yes, and I want updates on the hour until it's delivered."

"Yes, Sir," Logan replied before hanging up. "Did you get that? He assumed we were compromised."

Barrett growled. "Yeah, he knows something. He's not at the Pentagon either. Well, we'll backtrack for an hour and head south to Yellow Springs. The compound's a fortress."

"How's Sam? How's her arm? Any swelling?"

"God, you're a major pain. Just a minute."

Logan heard a crack of the com and then Barrett mumble. What the hell was going on up there?

80

"She doesn't want to talk to you right now. Get some rest," Barrett replied.

Logan sighed. Why wouldn't she want to talk to him? He hurt her shoulder, but he saved her. Was she upset about that? He didn't understand. He never understood Jillian either.

Now, Jillian was in danger because of her father. Should he warn her? He did tell her he'd call her back. He'd be breaking yet another protocol. He scrubbed both hands across his head. His instincts told him to wait until they knew more.

With the cot and chair broken, he laid the blanket on the cold hard floor. He stretched out and listened. Sam and Barrett discussed her father's cabin. Logan had been there years ago but didn't realize how high tech and secure it was. Sam knew the codes and could get them onto the grounds.

At a previous glance, the place had looked like a retired general's fifty-acre retreat. A rail fence surrounded the property. Cornfields, farms, and cattle extended the border of the compound. The thick wooded grounds had a one-story cabin, a large pole barn, and a gazebo beside a pond. Logan thought it was the perfect place to retire.

Now, he learned that the place had airtight security with electronic surveillance around the perimeter. Sam mentioned a safe room that observed the security cameras. The place even had satellite connections directly to the Pentagon and White House. Jeez, who knew?

After two agonizing hours on a hard floor, Logan felt the truck slow, pause, and finally stop. When Barrett turned off the engine, Logan opened the trailer door. He dropped down onto the cement floor inside the pole barn. As he turned the corner to check on Sam, he saw her hit a few buttons on the wall.

The whole truck and floor lowered to a room below the barn. Then another cement floor expanded across the space hiding the truck and basement. Barrett motioned him to another door and down the steps. Without looking at him, Sam hugged her arm in its sling. He needed to talk to her although he had no idea what he'd say.

"Sweet set-up, don't you think?" Barrett asked.

Logan nodded. They had more than enough room and light to dissect the satellite wreckage. Barrett pointed him to a lift. Who was the superior to whom on this assignment? Too tired to argue, Logan started it up and pulled out the crate. While Barrett unfolded the drawing, Sam picked up her backpack and left through another security door.

Logan tossed his com on a counter by the wall and rubbed his ear. Barrett added his and showed him the detailed sketch of the satellite and the black box. Sam's drawing also highlighted the area of a much smaller box. They'd have to sift through the mangled metal to find it.

"What do you think it is?" Logan asked.

"Something important enough that the Russians want it back," Barrett replied.

CHAPTER 11

AFTER LEAVING THE POLE BARN basement, Samantha walked down the corridor that connected to the cabin's lower level. She passed another security door, the general's conference room, and her large practice room with mirrored walls.

On the main floor of the cabin, she ignored her father's office and entered the living room. She approached the knotted pine wall and took off the cover of the thermostat. After tapping numbers into the hidden system, she stepped back as the wood panel retracted into the wall to show a steel door with a tiny square window.

She tapped more numbers into the pad. The steel door opened into the fortified room in the middle of the cabin.

With security cameras and computer consoles along two walls, a twin-sized bed, kitchenette, and bathroom took up the rest of the area. The panic room could lock someone inside or keep someone out depending on the circumstance.

After tossing her backpack on the bed, Sam sat behind the long desk. She typed in more codes and changed a few settings. Back at the entrance to the property, she had alerted the security company that she would be entering the compound and would manually take over while she enjoyed her stay. It was her place after all even though she hadn't been there since her father died three years ago. The military continued to pay a private company to protect the equipment inside the cabin and pole barn.

She had thirty minutes to type in the second set of codes to the company to prevent an Army siege. Bringing any more attention to Logan and his assignment would hurt her cause, too. While she waited for the transfer to take place, she flipped on the screens showing all the rooms in the house. Although everything had stayed the same, the cabin was stale and lifeless.

Sitting back, she watched Bear and Logan tear apart the wreckage. It looked like it would take a while. After typing in the last set of codes, she left the room and tapped the console button to lock the panic room doors.

Down the short hall, she entered her pale green bedroom across from her father's room. She spent the best ten years of her life here. After her dad died, her mother demanded she move in with her and Dmitri. Devastated by her father's heart attack, she complied. Hoping to snap her out of her depression, her mother sent her to Miss Martin's School. When that didn't work, she suggested Sam teach dance to some of the elementary students at the nearby school. It helped. She missed dancing. She had a chance to audition for Julliard once, but a broken leg prevented it.

Dismissing that emotional pain, she took a hot shower and changed into a pair of sweats and a t-shirt from her drawer. Leaving her makeshift sling on the bed, she tested the range of motion of her shoulder. The heat from the shower eased the ache.

She sighed when her stomach growled. The guys were probably hungry, too. She passed her father's bedroom and entered kitchen. Knowing the fridge would be empty, she opened the pantry. She took out two large cans of chicken noodle soup and a box of stale saltine crackers. Thirty minutes later, she balanced the tray on her hip as she opened the door to the pole barn basement.

Before the door shut behind her, Logan met her and took the tray. "You shouldn't be lifting anything heavy for a while," he said.

"I thought you'd be hungry."

With dirt smudges on his face, he smiled. "Starved. Thank you. Have you eaten?"

Sam nodded as he set the tray on the corner table. Bear quickly joined him. Logan and Bear attacked their big bowls.

Hugging her arm against her abdomen, she walked around the mangled mess. She had the drawing etched into her brain, not this giant piece of modern art. Bending over, she peeked into a hole where they had been yanking out pieces. Logan joined her while Bear crunched on more of the nasty cardboard crackers.

"We think that's the spot. We just have to enlarge the area," Logan said, kneeling beside her.

"Can you see it in there?" she asked.

"Yeah, but we can't reach it," he replied, aiming the flashlight deep into the metal cave two feet above the cement floor.

On her knees, she peered inside the wreckage again. "Is that square thing it? It's not black."

He laughed. "It's a figurative black box."

She faced Logan and stuck her arm slowly into the hole. Scrapping her flesh on the sharp metal, she finally touched the square with her fingertips. With her good shoulder pressed against the outside wreckage, she tried to loosen it.

On his knees in front her, Logan put his hands on her waist to keep her from falling into the sharp metal. A wave of heat raced to her face. She missed his touch.

"It's caught on something," she said, focusing back on the task.

"It may be plugged into a portal of some kind. Can you wiggle it free?"

She took a deep breath and pushed her arm in farther. "Got it."

"Great. Just pull your arm out slowly. Don't cut yourself."

With blood on her wrist and fingers, she produced the ring-sized box. Bear handed Logan a paper towel and took the box. Before they stood, Logan held her hand and blotted the blood off her arm. His intimate gesture sent another wave of heat to her toes this time.

"I'm fine," she whispered, looking into his green eyes.

"Thank you, Sam," he whispered back. He touched her cheek with his thumb and lifted her chin. She held her breath as he moved his head closer. Was he going to kiss her?

Bear yelled from the table, "There's a memory card inside. Sammy, we need computer access."

Startled, she lost her balance and fell toward the jagged metal. Logan grabbed her and slipped. The move pulled him backward and onto the cement floor. He hugged her as she lay on top of him.

Bear stood above them. "Stop messing around. We've got more work to do." He lifted her off Logan and cradled her.

"I can walk," Sam said.

Bear held the door open with his foot. "I know," Bear replied, scowling. Logan entered the corridor first and headed toward the end.

"Are you feeling neglected?" she whispered from Bear's arms.

"As a matter of fact, I am," Bear said. "Give me a little sugar, and I'll let you down."

"I kinda like being carried around," she replied, tugging on his beard.

"Just not by me," Bear said under his breath.

She giggled as Logan waited at the end of the hall. Bear carried her up the stairs and held her by the thermostat. He waited. When he didn't put her down, she laughed again.

She kissed his cheek. "I love you."

While Logan frowned, Bear grinned. "That's better," Bear said, standing her upright.

She opened the doors and stood back to let them work. Although Bear didn't know the security codes, he had been in there before to help the general on various occasions. She took her iPod from her bag and left the room. Her part was finished. She had given the information to the right people. She didn't know what would happen next, but she knew she couldn't go back to D.C. If Karl found out, he'd hurt her for sure.

CHAPTER 12

IN THE SAFE ROOM AT General Randall's cabin, Barrett sat in the only chair and shoved the memory card into a port. He had a computer background, so Logan let him mess with the card and the general's computer systems. It's easier to stay out of Barrett's way. They watched the screen upload the information.

"Can you read Russian?" Barrett asked.

He snorted. "No. Can Sam? I can find her."

Barrett clicked on a few icons checking the files. "Jesus, leave her alone."

"Why? You were all for it last night. I like her," Logan replied.

"She's my goddaughter, and you'll end up hurting her."

"I would not," Logan replied, watching her on the security monitor. She sat behind her father's desk in his office.

"She'd be your rebound," Barrett said, moving his chair closer to the computer screen.

"My rebound? I've been divorced for two years," Logan replied.

He glanced at him. "Have you dated anyone since then?"

Barrett knew he hadn't. Logan paced and stewed and ground his teeth. Pausing at one of the monitors, he saw Sam wipe her face. He touched the screen, which zeroed in on the tear on her freckled cheek.

Barrett sighed. "Oh, for God's sake, go. I can't concentrate on this with you in here, and this is going to take a while. If you're going to talk to her, take a shower first. You smell."

Logan practically ran from the room. After retrieving his duffle bag, he found a towel in the general's bathroom. He caught a whiff of himself and cringed.

With damp hair, he stood outside the general's office. She still sat in the desk chair. Her sore arm pressed against her body. When she pulled her knees to her chin, she wrapped her good arm around them. Her sadness hurt him. Literally. His chest tightened. As much as he wanted to kiss her, he needed to comfort her first.

"I wish you'd tell me what makes you so sad on that," he said just inside the room.

She set her iPod and ear buds on the desk. "I miss my father."

Logan wandered around and smiled at the pictures of a young blonde Sam fishing, dancing, and laughing with the general. "I met him a few times. The first time was here, in fact."

"Really? When was this?" she asked, putting her feet on the floor.

"Barrett brought me here before I received a medal. I think the general was working on his famous speech at the time."

Sam gasped and stared at him. "You're Major McCormick?"

He nodded as his cell rang. When Colonel Williams called early while they were stripping the wreckage, Logan had feigned a low signal. Expecting to see his boss's number, he saw his ex-wife's ID.

"Jillian, are you okay?" he asked. Sam stared with her mouth partially open. It looked as if someone had punched her in the gut.

"Mick, you promised to call me back. Where are you?"

"I'm still working. We ran into some delays," he replied.

"Are you giving me another chance?" Jillian asked.

Sam rubbed her shoulder. He caught a glimpse of something in her eyes—more pain? She lowered her gaze, and he saw that invisible shield surround her again. He thought Sam trusted him now.

Focusing on Sam, he absently replied, "I don't know. I told you I'm working. Listen, Hon, I gotta go, but I'll call you in a day or so."

He quickly hung up before she hijacked the conversation. Sam sniffed her nose. Why would talking to Jillian upset her? Sam had heard him talk to her before. Because he was affectionate? He groaned. Jillian continued to wreak havoc in his life. What the hell was he doing?

"The Colonel must have put her up to calling me," he said as a lame attempt to deflect.

Avoiding eye contact, she fidgeted with her iPod. "Jillian Williams is your ex-wife?"

"Yeah, but it's been over for a long time." Even he wasn't convinced by the statement.

Before he could continue, Barrett's voice boomed throughout the room. "Get in here. I've got the Intel."

Logan looked at the hidden security camera in the corner. He didn't realize Barrett could hear them, too. One more thing the Sergeant Major would harass him about. Logan was a Private all over again. Like a coward, he took a step toward the door.

Without a word, Sam followed. They stood behind Barrett and looked at the satellite images of specific U.S. landmarks.

"Look at this." Barrett clicked on the picture and a map with specific details of a building's floor plan and route around the area. "Each picture has the same details. Somebody already downloaded this information. This is residual. No wonder the Russians want it back. It seems to be the only link."

"If Sam heard *two weeks until the assassination*, it must be the sites where a political figure will be. Who's out and about in two weeks?" Logan asked.

"Well, it would be one week now," Sam said, standing beside Barrett, who leaned back in the chair. She slid her hand into her Bear's hand.

Logan wanted to be the one to reassure her. Instead, he scratched the back of his head. "The President is planning a tour to promote climate change legislation. Does that start in a week?"

"Why would the Russians want to assassinate the President?" Barrett asked. "His second term's up in November."

Sam tapped her finger to her lips. "Dmitri just had a party with the Vice President and Secretary of State for a goodwill fundraiser. They seemed to get along well enough."

"Makes me wonder how high up this goes," Logan said.

"We're speculating. We have no proof that the President is even stopping at these places," Barrett replied.

"If we know all the places, is there someone we could call to confirm it?" Sam asked.

"Good idea," Logan said. "Don't you know a guy on the President's security detail?"

Barrett smirked. "Yeah, but I don't trust him. We'll want to go higher. Who do we trust that wouldn't be in on this?"

"The obvious choice would be the President," Sam said.

"I like it," Barrett said.

"You know the President?" Logan asked.

"I met him at my father's funeral. When I slipped and broke my leg, he gave me a ride in his limo to the hospital. He respected my father's advice over the years, but I don't know if he'll take my call."

"It's worth a shot," Logan said. "You have his number?"

"Yeah," she said, pointing to the red phone next to the keyboard. "Dad's direct line."

"You're full of surprises," Logan said, smiling back like a fool with a crush.

Rolling his eyes, Barrett moved from the chair. Sam sat down while Logan set the phone closer to her. She took a deep breath and pressed the button.

"Hello, this is Samantha Randall, General Steven Randall's daughter. I'd like to speak with the President, please." She paused and then smiled. "Hello, Mr. President ... Yes Sir, my leg has healed nicely. Thank you for asking ... Sir, my father's most trusted friend Sergeant Major James Barrett, his colleague Major Logan McCormick, and I have come across some unsettling information that we believe is a national security risk. With your permission, I'd like to put the Sergeant Major on the line to explain it fully ... Yes Sir, and thank you for taking my call." She handed the phone to Barrett and blew out a breath.

"Thank you, Mr. President," Barrett said, standing at attention. "Here's what we've found..."

CHAPTER 13

IN THE LATE AFTERNOON, SAMANTHA left through the back slider in the living room. Needing fresh air, she strode down the narrow dirt footpath toward the woods. Her emotions flip-flopped over thoughts of Major McCormick talking to his wife and having met the general years ago. Her stomach ached more than her shoulder.

After a hundred yards of thick woods, the trail opened to a small meadow and pond. She smiled at the gazebo and skipped toward it. Bear and her father built it on her tenth birthday. The solid wood had weathered over the years. They had wanted to paint it, but she liked the natural roughness. Bear had given her a pocketknife, and her father let her carve designs on the railing and posts. She loved this place more than any other place on Earth. She should have returned sooner.

While she looked at her carved pictures in the wood, she thought about her father and his relationship with the President. The general had helped him win his first term, and she had inadvertently helped him win his second. She smiled again. It shouldn't have surprised her that he took her call.

Out of a deep respect for the general, the President had attended his funeral. It was happenstance that an ice storm hit in late October, which was a week before the Presidential Election in a tight race. With the chaos of camera crews, she had slipped on the sidewalk. The President had swept up the distraught daughter of the beloved general and had carried her to his limo. The media ate it up and public opinion rose twenty percent. He won by a landslide.

Sam sat on the railing facing the pond and leaned her good shoulder against the post. The setting sun sparkled across the pond as a few ducks chased after the bugs on the surface. She reminisced and found comfort in it. Maybe she should move back. Her mother couldn't argue about her safety—the place was definitely secure. She could teach dance in Yellow Springs. The possibilities made her smile.

With a new plan, she felt the weight lifting off her shoulders.

"Thank you, Daddy, for helping me find my way back," she whispered.

A throat cleared behind her, and she jumped. "Sorry to interrupt," Logan said.

Sighing, she straddled the railing and leaned back against the post. "How'd it go?"

"The President wants more proof before he'll act," Logan replied, rubbing the back of his neck.

"How much more proof does he need? We have the memory card and drawings."

"He agrees that there would be an assassination attempt, but he wants to know how high up it goes. Apparently, he and the Vice President have a difference of opinion about the Russian Oil Treaty. He's against it. With him out of the way, the V.P. would become the President and could sign it. He doesn't think that's the case though."

"Oh dear," she replied, pulling her sore arm closer to her body, "I see how that would create a problem. The treaty would buy more Russian oil and less Arab oil producing billions of dollars for Russia. It's all Dmitri and my mother discuss."

"They discuss it in front of you?"

"Not the details but how important he would look in the Russian president's eyes if he helped make it happen. Do you think my stepfather knows about this plot?"

Logan wandered around the gazebo and looked at her carvings. "Do you?"

Sam thought for a moment. "Dmitri doesn't seem the type to rock the boat. Karl would do it though." With his back to her, Logan clenched his fist at the mention of Karl. She smiled.

"How well do you know Dmitri?" he asked.

"He's been married to my mother for fifteen years. He and mother are socializers. I don't think he has a devious bone in his body. He likes America."

"I'll trust that assessment," he said, stopping at the post across from her. He chuckled and pointed at a heart with four initials. "S.R. is you, but who's M.M.? Who's the lucky guy?"

She covered her mouth as she laughed. She had forgotten about that. "At the time, he was a figment of my imagination." She watched him. He no longer wandered, he paced. "What haven't you told me?"

He stopped mid-stride and looked at her. "We need solid proof, and we're not sure how to get it."

"Do you think the flash drive in Karl's safe would have the proof we need?"

104

"Barrett thinks it would."

Sam blew out a breath. "I'll go back and get it."

"No, it's too dangerous," he replied. "Sam, you wanted to jump into a ravine to keep from going back."

"What other choice do we have? I've come this far. Let me help."

Logan picked up her hand and stared at her fingers. They warmed quickly. She gazed at his long lashes while he debated the issue in his head. He sighed and looked into her face.

"I'm sorry I got so angry at the last truck stop. I was too harsh," he said.

She slowly pulled her hand away and watched the sun lower halfway into the tree line across the pond. "I understand now. Jillian's beautiful."

"Jillian's a master manipulator," he replied with a clenched jaw.

"I'm sorry I tried to do it, too."

He sighed. "Why, Sam?"

She hugged her abdomen and stared at the weeds next to the gazebo. "I saw Sergei and Ivan at the gas pump at that truck stop, so I knew I had to leave. I thought they were chasing me, and I thought I could protect you. I was selfish though. I wanted you to kiss me. I wanted something to remember you by." She peeked up at him. She wasn't sure how he'd react to her confession.

"Why in the world?"

She flipped her leg over the railing to face him. "You are a great man, the kind my father's talked about. His famous speech was reflective of you. He told me so."

"That was before you knew who I was," he replied.

"*Some men think there's a choice between right and wrong. Great men know there is none,*" she said, quoting her father. "You saved me from that trucker before you knew who I was, didn't you?"

Standing between her knees, Logan slid his hand behind her head. Her hair rippled from his touch. He lowered his lips to hers. Excitement and comfort mingled with the warmth of his breath. She hummed.

She reached out to hug him, but the ache from her shoulder stopped her. Instead, she slipped her fingers through his belt loops and pulled him closer. She parted her lips letting him taste her. Her pain dissolved as his tongue found hers. Moments later, he pulled back slightly. Panting, she gasped.

"I've wanted to do that for a while," he said with a grin.

Lightheaded, she gulped for a breath. "Is kissing always that great or is it only with you?"

"You've never been kissed?"

She dropped her hands from his waistband. "In the fifth grade, Jeremy Betterly kissed me on the playground. In ninth grade, Scott Sullivan kissed me in the hallway at school. The principal called my dad."

Logan laughed and cupped her face with both hands. "That's all of them?"

She sighed. "Logan, my father was a Four-Star General who advised the President of the United States. He intimidated the boys without even trying."

"I'm sure he enjoyed it," he replied.

"Too much," she said with a smile. "Will you kiss me again? It was much nicer than kissing those boys."

"Why?"

"Why? You're a sexy, handsome, muscular, Army knight who has saved me twice. You're sweet and considerate, and you carry me around like a rag doll. Plus, you smell really good. Whenever you're near me, I tingle all over."

Logan tilted his head back and let out a deep hardy laugh. She wasn't joking, but she liked hearing him. He let down his guard, which she thought he rarely did.

"Something tells me you don't laugh enough. Now, what about that kiss, Major McCormick? Maybe I was wrong, and it was only a wonderful fluke. Maybe all this tingling is just the summer air."

He put his hands on the railing trapping in her place.

"That's a lot of trash talk for a woman who's only been kissed three times in her life."

"What are you going to do about it?"

"I'm going to call your bluff," he replied, leaning down so his nose touched hers.

"Good."

She closed her eyes and puckered her lips. He chuckled. She felt his warm breath on her cheek and then on her ear. When he nibbled her earlobe, she cried out and squeezed his biceps. He kissed her neck. She tilted her head back for easier access. Her whole body vibrated.

He whispered in her ear, "Is the summer air giving you the goose bumps?"

"No."

His lips moved along her jaw to her chin. He finally kissed her lips again, and she sighed in his mouth. She couldn't believe how great kissing was. She wanted to try more. She caressed his arms and moved closer. Through the darkness, a shield dissolved. Definitely hers. Possibly his? How could she not trust him after the last twenty-four hours? Would he trust her?

"Was it a fluke?" he asked.

Shaking her head, she slid her hands down his arms to cover his hands that gripped the railing. "Logan, make love to me."

He groaned. "Are you sure?"

"Show me what I've been missing out on."

With his hands at her waist, he lifted her. She wrapped her arms around his neck. He hugged her while she rubbed her cheek against his. Her legs around his waist formed to him.

"You feel so good even through your shirt," she said, wiggling against him. "I wonder how you'll feel naked."

He tripped down the gazebo's two steps. "When did it get so damn dark?"

She giggled. "Where are we going?"

"To the cabin," he said, stumbling. "I want you naked in a bed."

"I'd like that."

She kissed him as he walked. He tripped over a rock and fell to his knees. She continued to kiss his lips and run her fingers across his hair, his neck, and his shoulders. His hands roamed down her back to her butt. He squeezed her thighs, and she moaned loudly.

"I can't wait. Go back to the gazebo," she begged.

Standing, he caressed her low back and butt. "I want a bed," he growled. The meadow was dark; the path in the woods was darker. His steps were agonizingly slow. "I can't see a thing," he said. "Why don't you have any lights along the path? Someone could break their neck."

"I thought Army Rangers adapted. You need night vision goggles to maneuver?" she asked, trying not to laugh.

He snorted. "I usually don't have a woman leached onto me and distracting me with her loud moans. Are you a screamer in bed?"

"Do you want me to be?" She felt him walk faster.

"You're killing me, Sam," he said, stumbling again. "I'm going to impale us into a tree branch."

She giggled. "You don't want to impale me?"

In the middle of the woods, he stopped and kissed her again. Her hard nipples poked at his t-shirt. He touched her hair. With an unbearable arousal, she started to grind her hips into him. She whimpered and panted.

"Logan, please go back."

"God, Sam. We're half way there. I see a light," he replied, striding forward.

"I can't take it. You're making me crazy," she cried out.

He stopped. He, too, panted. "We gotta slow down. I won't last two seconds, and that's not how I want to do this," he whispered.

"No," she wailed. "You've changed your mind?" Sam dropped her forehead onto his shoulder and clawed her nails into his chest in defeat. She pushed away from him.

He held her tight. "Hell no, I haven't changed my mind. You are nuts. You had my attention the moment you paused at the lowering of the flag at that truck stop."

She hugged him and nuzzled his neck as he walked. "Is wanting sex supposed to be this intense?"

"Yes, it's supposed to be," he said. "Why do you think I'm walking so slowly? I'm so hard it hurts to walk." She giggled and squeezed her thighs tighter around him. He growled in her ear. "Do you want to make it to the cabin or not?" He groaned. "Tell me what you said to that attendant as he folded the flag?"

She harrumphed. "Did you see the condition of that flag? It was worn and shredded on the ends. It was a disgrace, and I told him so." He chuckled. "It's not funny, Logan. Do you know how many people have ratty flags? They want to be patriotic yet all they're doing is dishonoring the people who serve it," she ranted. "It's shameful."

"Do you confront all of them?" he asked with a laugh.

"When I can. Are you making fun of me?"

"I'm distracting myself from having my way with you on this path. It didn't seem like a long walk to the pond," he replied, stopping six feet from the tree line. "Sam, you're passionate and that's what I like about you. Will you kiss me now?"

She smiled. "If you insist," she said, sliding her fingers along his jaw. She turned his head toward her and kissed him lightly at first. With her tongue, she outlined his upper lip. When he opened his mouth, she deepened their kiss. She sucked his bottom lip as she pulled back. She liked kissing.

"Shit," he whispered. "That distraction didn't last very long. You know we'll have to be quiet, so we don't wake Barrett. He's in the General's bedroom."

"Mine is across the hall," she replied. "I don't want him to know."

"You think I do? What about the safe room?"

"Yes," she replied as he stepped out of the woods. "Move it, Major."

Grabbing her thighs, he hurried through the slider. She caressed his chest and wondered if it was hairy. She couldn't wait to see him naked.

CHAPTER 14

LOGAN HAD TURNED INTO A klutz. He had tripped, stumbled, and fallen because this woman preoccupied every cell of his being. What kind of Army Ranger can't maneuver in the dark? With the lack of blood to his brain, he couldn't think straight.

Samantha Randall confused the hell out of him. Her wildcat attitude amused him. Her passionate opinions aroused him, but her vulnerability made him weak. He wanted to be her Army knight.

"Can we lock the door? I don't want Bear walking in on us," she whispered.

He cringed. "The Sergeant Major would have my head for kissing his goddaughter."

From his arms, she tapped the key pad next to the steel door locking it behind them. With the security camera monitors dimly lighting the room, Logan smiled. He wanted to see and explore every inch of her sexy dancer body.

"What do you think he'll do when he finds out we had sex?" she asked.

"Are you going to tell him? 'Cause I'm not."

Smiling, she shook her head as he stood her on the bed. Only slightly taller, she leaned down and kissed him. His rough hands slid under her t-shirt and caressed her soft skin. He pushed her shirt up and over her head.

Her firm breasts begged to be tasted. Logan started with her neck; she gripped the front of his shirt. His hands glided around her ribs until his thumbs grazed her nipples.

She cried out and pulled his head against her. Her rose-scented skin made him lightheaded. As she tugged at his shirt, his lips found her nipple. Shivering, she let out a loud scream. He looked at her.

"What? What's the matter?" he asked.

"It feels so good."

"Do you want me to stop?"

She blew out a breath. "I can take it."

He laughed. "This room is sound proof, right?"

"Yes. Shall we begin again?"

While he chuckled, she pulled at his shirt. He helped her and tossed it on the floor. She launched herself at him. Her breasts against his chest were a taste of heaven. He laid her on the bed and quickly tugged off her sweatpants. Lying beside her, he traced his hand up her pale sleek leg to her white panties. She fidgeted to his touch.

"Your chest hair tickles," she said.

"How can I be romantic when you're so wiggly?" he asked.

"Okay, I'll hold perfectly still," she said, stiffening like a board.

He's had sex with a rigid board before, and he never liked it. Pushing the thought away, he hovered over her and licked her nipple. He smiled when she giggled and squirmed.

"I thought you were going to hold still," he said.

"It's boring. I need to feel you all over." She reached down and caressed his bulge. "Take off your pants."

"Yes, ma'am."

Logan rolled off the bed and onto the floor. Unceremoniously, he stripped down his jeans and then had to take off his Army boots. Smiling, she peeked over the edge and watched him struggle with his clothes. Sprawled out naked on the floor, he groaned and looked up at her.

She ogled him. He wasn't sure what was going on in her head. Reality hit him. He sat up, so his face met hers.

"We can't. I don't have any protection," he said.

"Oh," she said, looking around the room, "I have a condom in the front pocket of my bag."

He followed her eyes to her bag in the corner. As a major on a mission, he scrambled toward the bag. He overlooked reasons why she had one and stood.

"I was right. Yours isn't ugly; it's very nice," she said.

"Nice?"

"Pretty?" she replied.

"Nice and pretty? What kind of sex talk is that?"

She grinned. "When are you going to shoot me with your machine gun?"

He laughed and came after her on the bed. She squealed. As he kissed her, his hands roamed. She continued to wiggle, squirm, and cry out. He moaned from her aggressive touch. Her begging did him in. He couldn't wait any longer. He forgot everything but the sweet release with the wildcat.

Panting, they collapsed next to each other. Turning onto her side, she moved closer to him and tried to hide her yawn. Her hand rested on his chest as he caressed a soft lock of her hair between his fingers. He waited for her to say something. Her openness was so new to him. He liked when she shared her thoughts.

"What other positions do you know?" she asked.

He couldn't help but laugh. "Do you have any more condoms in your bag?"

She frowned. "No."

"You should rest your shoulder. We've been up for over twenty-four hours."

"You didn't like it?"

"You've shown me what I've been missing," he replied, kissing her temple. "I'll buy us a box of them later."

She grinned and moved even closer. He hugged her as she laid her head on his chest. She fell asleep cuddled against him—something Jillian had never done. He pulled up the blanket and gently massaged her sore shoulder. Before he passed out from exhaustion, he listened to her purr and enjoyed the contentment of the moment. Her radiance dissolved the heavy shadow that had hovered over his heart.

CHAPTER 15

IN THE SAFE ROOM'S BED, Logan reached out for Sam. Finding emptiness, he groggily sat up. With a red light blinking above one of the security cameras, Sam typed on the keyboard below it. At seven in the morning, she was already dressed. He watched her frantically slide the chair to another keyboard by the main computer screen.

"Sam, what's going on?"

She jumped from the chair and turned. The color had drained from her face. Alarmed, he threw back the sheet. She blocked the cameras, so he couldn't see past her.

"I'm sorry." With her backpack in her hand, she moved toward the closed door.

"For what?"

In his boxer briefs, he stood and tried to understand. Did he hurt her?

The doors opened, and she back-stepped into the living room. She pointed at the security camera. "Karl came for me. I'm going back. I can help with this."

Logan scrambled for his jeans. "No, it's too dangerous."

"Either he'll kill you or you'll kill him," she replied as the steel door closed.

Logan tapped the four-digit code he had seen her use into the key pad. Nothing happened. He pushed the buttons again. Still nothing.

"Samantha! Open the door! Now!" Logan said, staring at her through the square window.

Sam motioned that she couldn't hear him. He mouthed for her to open the door, and she shook her head. When she said she was sorry again, he heard her voice through one of the computer monitor on the table.

She continued, "Logan, I know you can hear me. There are enough supplies for a few days. You can't get out without the password. I'll have Bear come back for you. It's for your own protection. Before I shut the panel, I need to ask you something. I can't hear you so hold up one finger for *no* or two for *yes*."

His frustration increased as he waited for her question. She tossed her bag in the chair before she looked at him.

Her eyes pooled with tears. "Do you believe lovers can be best friends?" she asked.

What kind of question was that? He glanced at the monitor that overlooked the property entrance and road. A black sedan parked in front of the cabin. A man in an outdated brown suit got out of the back seat. The driver remained as the man with a black ponytail and gaudy gold chain stalked toward the front door.

Logan heard the door open. Sam bit her bottom lip and waited for his answer. Holding up one finger, he yelled again for her to let him out.

Sam shook her head sadly. "I thought you might think that way. Thank you for trusting me enough to be with me."

She pressed the buttons behind the thermostat. The panel door covered the metal one hiding any indication of a security room. Logan punched the door and swore. He helplessly watched her through the security camera.

Karl stormed into the room, grabbed her dislocated arm, and shook her. She barely winced while Logan wanted to jump through the screen and strangle him.

On another camera, Logan saw Barrett sleeping. He poked the intercom for that room. "Barrett, get your ass up. Sam needs help."

Barrett jumped from bed and reached for his gun.

"Where are you?"

"Sam locked me in the safe room. Karl's here. Get the password and let me out."

Logan watched Barrett leave the bedroom and stand in the hallway. They listened and observed Karl berate and manhandle her.

"Why did you run away?" Karl demanded, shaking her upper arms. "And what did you do to your hair. It looks ridiculous."

Logan clenched his hands into fists until they ached. Barrett had his cell phone in his hand and his gun in the other. What was Barrett waiting for?

"How'd you find me?" Sam whispered.

"Your mother thought you'd come here. Why did you run?" Karl demanded again.

Logan begged her to be careful. Although Barrett was right around the corner, she was still in danger, especially if this was an international issue. Karl's lackeys didn't seem to have a problem aiming a gun at Logan at the truck stop. Did Karl know Sam took the satellite information? Logan couldn't imagine what Karl'd do to her. Watching Sam, he held his breath and waited.

"I saw you with Jillian Friday night. You broke my heart and hurt my feelings," she said. Logan wondered if it was the truth or a lie. Either way, he felt a punch in the gut.

"That's the only reason you left?" Karl demanded.

"I gave myself to you, and you chose Jillian over me. You called me your странный кошка."

Logan growled. He didn't know what the Russian meant, but he now understood Sam's hurt look when he took the call from Jillian earlier. Sam thought he chose his ex over her, too. He shoved the chair away. Trapped in the damn room, he couldn't explain that it wasn't the case.

Karl laughed at her. "You're being childish. I told you she's a model. You can't compete with her."

Livid, Logan kicked the chair slamming it into the wall. He paced with his eyes on the screen. Sam cried and stepped away from Karl.

"Do you love her?" Sam asked.

Karl laughed again and tugged her ear, drawing her back to him. "She is a means to an end while you are my pet. Let's take the long way home."

Karl mashed his lips to hers. As Sam tried to push him away, Barrett finally stepped into the room with his gun drawn.

"Shoot him!" Logan yelled at the screen. Knowing they couldn't hear him, he ranted. "Kill the bastard! That's an order! Rip off his head! We'll bury him in the woods!"

"What are you doing here?" Karl demanded, keeping Sam between them.

123

Logan roared with anger. That bastard used her as a shield?

"Have you forgotten, Karl? I'm Samantha's godfather. After her mother called me, I knew she'd come here. I got in last night and have been trying to convince her to return home," he said, motioning Sam toward him. She broke away and cringed in pain at her sore shoulder.

"Well, you are no longer needed," Karl replied.

With Sam at his side, Barrett lowered his gun and held up his cell phone. "I already talked to Martha. I will accompany my goddaughter to her mother. Frankly, I don't trust your intentions."

Glaring, Karl reluctantly agreed. Knowing Barrett would be with her, Logan calmed himself slightly. He had to give Sam credit for locking him inside. He would have pummeled Karl and ruined their chance for more information on the assassination attempt. Given the chance when this was over, he'd still pound him for hurting her. Thinking about her abuse, he returned to his agitated state.

"Pet, retrieve your things," Karl stated. "We'll leave now, my freakish cat."

"Pet? Freakish cat? You've got to be kidding me!" Logan yelled at the screen. "You are dead!"

Plopping down in the wobbly chair, Logan scooted closer to the monitor. With her backpack in her hand, Sam hurried to her father's office. He wanted to hit the intercom, but he couldn't take the chance that Karl would overhear him. She scribbled a note at the desk. Logan needed her to acknowledge him with a word or a glance. She kept her head down. After propping the note in the chair, she rubbed her shoulder and left the room. Karl had dislocated it again.

Defeated, exhausted, and pissed, Logan leaned back in the chair and stared at the monitors. Barrett joined Samantha in the back seat. Scowling, Karl sat in the front next to his driver. Logan sighed as the car left the property. With Sam safe with Barrett, he pushed his emotions aside and focused on getting out of the room. He stared at the phone Sam had used for the President and wondered whom he would call for help.

Dismissing the phone, he searched for an emergency release button on the wall panel. With no luck, he rolled the chair to the computer and keyboard. He set the satellite's memory card aside. Since Barrett had already sent a copy to the President's secure e-mail, they didn't need it anymore.

Logan took a deep breath. For access to the computer system, he needed the main password. He started with words that the General might use. He typed SAMANTHA and was surprised when it didn't work. After typing variations of the General's daughter, he scrubbed his head and swore. Glancing at the monitor of the General's office, he sat forward and zoomed in on the note. She had propped it up enough for him to read.

SAMANTHA as a password was too easy, so I changed it. Bear will call you with the correct one. After I get the flash drive, I'm hiding. Thank you for ... everything.

As mad as he was, he smiled. She knew what he'd try. Now, he needed to get into her head. For an hour, he typed words he thought she'd use. His anger grew with each denied word and phrase. He didn't know her well enough.

He sprawled out on the bed and tried to think. His mind wandered to their earlier activities. He didn't want her to be his rebound. When the safe phone rang, he fell off the side of the bed and scrambled for it.

"Hello!"

"I only have a minute," Barrett said.

"What's the password?"

"She won't tell me."

"Make her!"

126

"Right. She's as thickheaded as her father was. Shut it and listen. Karl believes Sam's story, so she's out of the woods. She still wants to open the safe. Martha's planning some kind of party Monday night for some heads of state. I'm invited. Deliver the truck and call Colonel Williams."

"I'll call Jillian, too, and get invited. Tell Sam that I'll break into the safe. I don't want her doing anything dangerous. Now, what's the damn password?"

"She won't tell me until tonight. Get some rest. You're going to need it."

As Logan slammed the phone down, red lights flashed above four monitors. He retrieved the battered chair and focused on the screens. Four armed men in black combat gear and handguns approached the cabin from different directions. Using hand signals, they checked the perimeter and broke into the cabin.

Logan knew exactly why these men were there. They were the assault team looking for Samantha. He stewed as they checked each room. They met back in the living room.

"We're clear," the one said.

Logan swore. He immediately recognized Kyle O'Brien's voice. This was his former team, the team that he had led on many missions, his brothers. They had fought together. Although they each rose through the ranks, they remained a team because of their efficiency and special training used on covert assignments.

Colonel Williams sent them to find Samantha? That just pissed him off. His own team was working against him. Why? What was Williams going to do to her? Hurt her? Kill her? Logan needed to get out and find out what they were planning.

"I saw empty cans of soup, so she must have been here with someone," O'Brien said.

"How do you know she's still running with somebody?" Martinez asked.

"Williams said she might be held against her will," O'Brien replied. "And there were three bowls on the kitchen counter."

Cho sat on the couch. "I found a note about a password and a thank you."

"Who's she thanking?" Martinez asked.

"The General's bed is messed up. Maybe it's for a fun night as a threesome," Cho replied.

"Or not," Johnson replied, scowling.

They sobered as Logan fumed. He wanted to get on the intercom but resisted the urge. They didn't need to know about the safe room. Although he trusted his guys, he wanted details first. Instead of the intercom, he dialed his cell. Johnson answered his.

Logan got right to the point. "What are you guys up to?"

"Mick, hey man, what's new?"

"Answer the question," Logan demanded.

"What makes you think I'm with the guys?" Johnson asked.

"Colonel Williams has you, Martinez, O'Brien, and Cho on an assignment."

"Yes, Sir, search and rescue, but how'd you know? It's hush hush."

"Why is searching for General Randall's daughter a secret?" Logan demanded.

"She ran away from home. Colonel Williams wanted her found as a courtesy to her mother and Ambassador Demas. A sixteen-year-old girl is missing. Her Amber Alert photo was with five others. Out of respect for General Randall, we jumped at the chance to help."

"Who told you she was sixteen?" Logan asked.

"The colonel. What's going on?"

Logan paced. "Have you found her?" His cell beeped signaling a low battery.

"No, they're pretty sneaky and had us following dead ends, but we're getting closer."

"I know you're at the General's cabin. I'm on my way there. Barrett found her and is escorting her home to her mother."

"Okay, so we'll meet up for a beer in D.C.?"

"Stay put. Enjoy the stale crackers," Logan said.

"Sir?"

"Clean up the broken glass from your break-in and don't make a mess," he said just before his phone crapped out.

CHAPTER 16

HUGGING BEAR'S THICK UPPER ARM in the car, Samantha cringed. The one thing she never wanted to do was go back to D.C. She faked sleeping, so Karl wouldn't talk to her. They were returning to an airfield an hour away. Dmitri and his mother had chartered a small plane to bring her home. Karl had acted like the hero and had made suggestions as to how she could repay him. She had learned what sex was supposed to be like. Never again with Karl. With a sigh, she rubbed her shoulder.

While Karl talked on his phone, she whispered to Bear, "Can you fix my arm? A sharp pain goes all the way to my fingers."

"It'll hurt," Bear said.

"I know."

Karl glanced back at them and continued talking in Russian. She should have gotten the Russian Rosetta Stone software. He could be talking about the assassination plot right now. When Karl faced forward, Bear lifted her onto his lap. Without any pretense, he wrenched her arm back into the socket. She pressed her lips together, so she wouldn't cry out. Her shoulder throbbed.

While Bear cradled her, she quietly sobbed against his plaid flannel shirt. The stress was finally getting to her. She'd rather be cuddling with Logan. With a deep breath, she calmed herself.

Thoughts of Logan helped the pain. Through her circumstances, she had gone full circle with Major McCormick. Ironically, it started and ended at the cabin. She thanked her dad again.

As she wiped her eyes, Bear whispered his plan in her ear. She agreed and disagreed with its parts. After retrieving the flash drive from Karl's safe, she would return to her cabin in Yellow Springs. She had more happy memories to add to her collection. She'd even find her old pocketknife. The plan for her future helped her focus on the plan at hand. This was her moment to do the right thing. At the small municipal airport, Bear helped her out.

She walked away while Bear sighed and talked to the pilot. They would leave in an hour.

Next to the dirt parking lot and runway, the Fly Boy Diner doubled as the airport tower. Suddenly starving, she walked toward the building made of cement blocks. Karl talked on his cell and followed her. She couldn't outrun him.

"Ivan, where the hell are you and Sergei? Have you found it yet? Call me now!" Karl demanded into his cell phone.

After hanging up, Karl gripped her arm and shoved her into the tiny diner that had three booths and a five-stool counter. Not wanting to be trapped in a booth with Karl, she pulled her arm away and sat on a stool. Grease permeated the room and made her mouth water. She quickly reached for a menu between the sugar jar and napkin holder. She wanted to feast on a thick burger and fries.

She ordered one for her and another for Bear. Karl ordered coffee and continued to check his phone for text messages. She wondered what had happen to Sergei and Ivan. Logan never said.

With his mammoth size and grizzly beard, Bear rushed through the door and startled the waitress. "Did you order for me?" Bear asked.

133

Sam nodded as he sat beside her at the counter. She devoured everything, and Bear asked for two slices of apple pie. She forked a bite, but he wolfed down both pieces. She giggled when Bear's belch annoyed Karl.

After forty-five minutes, the pilot joined them and rung his hands. "Uh, Sir, we're having a problem with the engine and won't be able to get a mechanic out here until later tonight."

"So you're saying we don't leave until morning?" Bear asked.

"Yes, Sir," he replied before he rushed back out the door.

Karl mumbled to himself and started to pace along the empty booths. Bear pulled out his wallet and paid the waitress.

"Any motels nearby?" Bear asked her.

"Sure, the Eagle County Motel is about a mile south on Twenty-eighth Street. It's old but clean."

Karl stopped and smiled. "I'll spring for a couple of rooms," he said, eyeing her.

Sam trembled. Karl would try to break into her room even if she triple locked it. Nodding, Bear put his hand at her back and nudged her toward the door. Karl beat them to the car. She slowed and thought about making a run for it. Maybe she could sleep in the plane.

"Jeez, will you give me a little credit?" Bear whispered, shoving her toward the car. "I'm your roommate unless you snore."

She blew out a breath and leaned into him as they walked. Karl sat in the back seat and waited. She smiled when Bear opened the front passenger door for her then joined Karl in the back. She felt Karl's icy stare without looking.

At the long narrow one-story motel, Karl rushed to the office while she, Bear, and the driver stretched next to the car. A few minutes later, Karl strolled out with three keys. Bear took one and then tugged her hand. She gladly followed.

"Samantha has her own room," Karl called out.

"No, she'll stay with me." Bear turned away to dismiss him. "Your driver deserves his own room," he said over his shoulder.

Karl stormed after them. Bear casually opened their room door and gently pushed her inside. Taking up the entire doorway, he turned back to Karl. Bear dwarfed him.

"I paid for Samantha to have her own room," Karl stated again.

Bear stepped within a foot of him and stared him down. "No. I don't like you. I don't trust you. You will never touch my goddaughter again."

135

"Or what?" he asked with a smile. "With diplomatic immunity, I will continue to do whomever I please."

Bear bumped his chest against him. Karl stepped backward. "Or what?" Bear repeated with a deep baritone laugh. "Claiming diplomatic immunity may be hard with my fist down your throat. Don't poke the Bear, boy. They call me that for a reason. I could shred you into unidentifiable pieces."

Karl dropped his jaw slightly while Sam's eyes widened at the threat.

"Now, if you'll excuse me. I get grizzly without a nap." Bear slammed the door behind him and growled at the ceiling.

"Wow, you're my hero," Sam said, sitting on the edge of the only bed.

Standing by the door, Bear took up half of the tiny room. He snorted. "You're fickle. First Mick and then me. Sheesh, I don't like being second best."

She shook her head and covered her face. "I'm sorry."

He sighed and sat in the rickety desk chair. It creaked under his weight—a giant in a tot's chair. "Do you want to call him?" Bear asked.

She sniffed her nose. "No," she said, standing. "Sit on the bed before you break the chair."

He shrugged. "Why don't you want to talk to him?"

136

"He's angry with me for locking him in the room. I don't want him to yell. It would hurt too much," she said, rubbing her sore shoulder.

Bear stretched out on the bed taking up all but the edge. It would be a long night. At least, Karl wouldn't be lurking outside.

"What am I missing?" he asked, balling the pillow behind his head.

She sighed then blurted, "We had sex."

"What! When? Did he hurt you? 'Cause I'll kick his ass."

"It was wonderful," she replied, leaning back against the wall.

"God," he said, rubbing the bridge of his nose. "Without giving me details, why is that a problem?"

"I love him."

"You've only known him for a day and a half."

"I feel like I've known him longer."

Bear nodded and put his hand behind his head. "He's a good man, Samantha. Your father liked him."

"He still loves Jillian," she replied.

She jotted the password on the pad from the desk then handed it to him. He glanced at it, shook his head, and pulled his cell from his pocket. She quickly left for the bathroom.

CHAPTER 17

LOCKED IN THE SAFE ROOM, Logan had become a clock-watcher. Lying on the bed, he listened to his team discuss his brief and painful relationship with Jillian, his reluctance to date, his bitter attitude, his trust issues, and his need for a woman. He didn't like hearing the truth. They joked and jeered at his expense. He chuckled a couple times, not at their relentless ribbing, at their stupid brainstorming on how to help him.

Martinez thought he needed a beach vacation. O'Brien recommended a massage from a hooker. Cho wanted to knock some sense into him with a two by four, and Johnson suggested booze and a strip club. None of them suggested more work assignments.

Samantha Randall would help—had already helped. Logan would have ripped into those guys for their jokes at his expense. His attitude had lightened. He needed her, and it shocked him. In less than forty-eight hours, she had turned him upside down, and he liked it. His black and white life in Kansas became a Technicolor Oz.

Half listening to more of their idiotic ideas; he tried to understand his feelings for the young woman who had plowed into his life with a force that restarted his heart. When the safe room phone rang, he jumped for it. He dismissed his team's ramblings in the living room and listened.

"Did you call the Colonel?" Barrett asked.

"No, my cell charger's in the truck. How's Sam? You're not letting that bastard near her, are you?"

"Her arm's locking up. She'll need to see a doctor."

"Damn it, I didn't mean to hurt her," Logan replied, rubbing his hand over his head.

"But you did, and she's upset."

"Let me talk to her." He just needed to hear her voice.

"She doesn't want to talk to you. Do you want the password or not?" Barrett asked.

"Fine, and make sure you coach her. If she sees me at the party, she doesn't know me."

"That won't be a problem," Barrett stated.

"What the hell does that mean?" Logan demanded.

"Jesus, Mick, after all the sex talk and hearing her story, you still took advantage of her?"

"No, it wasn't like that."

"You still love Jillian."

"I do not!"

"That's the password," Barrett said.

Hearing the click of Barrett's phone, Logan swore. Before leaving the safe room, he sat in the chair and stared at the bed. Did he take advantage? They laughed; they cuddled afterward. It was the most fun he's ever had. He frowned at her password. He did not love Jillian. After last night, how could she think that?

Logan typed the insane words and watched the doors open. Sprawled out in the living room, the team jumped for their guns as he stood in the doorway. Shocked, they glimpsed past him to see the secure room. He smiled. They realized he had heard every comment.

"We knew you were in there," Cho said.

"Sure, you did," Logan replied.

Before leaving the room, Logan grabbed his cell. He punched in the code again, and the doors closed behind him. He leaned against the pine paneling and waited. They flinched.

"I don't understand," Martinez said, sliding his handgun back into its hip holster.

Logan folded his arms. "How'd you track her here?"

They relaxed as Johnson answered for them. "Well, we followed her to the Greyhound bus terminal. She stayed at a crap motel with her boyfriend."

"Boyfriend?" Logan asked.

"The clerk said she paid while her boyfriend waited outside," Johnson replied.

Logan smiled. "She lied, so he wouldn't think she was alone."

"Really? Well, we traced the GPS in her phone to Las Vegas," Johnson continued.

Cho laughed. "We almost gave a couple of old ladies heart attacks. Apparently, she ditched it into the woman's purse."

Logan smiled again. "So you went from D.C. to Vegas, then what?"

"The colonel gave us a possible route of another bus. We tracked it to a rest area where it had caught fire," Johnson said.

Logan remembered all too well. "And then?"

Johnson sat on the arm of the sofa. "The waitress said she was talking to a trucker. We assumed he gave her a ride. With the Amber Alert of her and five other teenage girls, we hurried to the next truck stop on the route and found that there was a ruckus next to a dumpster at about 0200 Saturday."

"And when were you there?" Logan asked.

"2000 Saturday. We rushed toward the next large truck stop," Johnson said. The guys nodded.

"The State Police had that place locked down because of an accident involving a sedan with diplomatic plates," O'Brien added. "The cops found the sedan but not the driver."

Johnson glared at O'Brien, who clamped his mouth shut. "We called Colonel Williams who gave us the address to the General's cabin," Johnson said.

"It looks like you beat us here. Have you seen her?" Martinez asked.

"Yeah, I have, and there's more to the story," Logan replied.

CHAPTER 18

MONDAY

LOGAN MOTIONED THE TEAM TOWARD the lower-level door of the General's cabin. Once in the pole barn basement with the wreckage, he explained his assignment, Samantha's copies of the wreckage, its secret memory card, and his truck route, which took them into the early morning hours. He didn't elaborate about their truck stop adventures but continued to discuss what he, Samantha, and Barrett found on the memory card.

"An assassination plot against the President?" Martinez asked.

"Yeah, and the President wants more proof," Logan replied.

"More? You already have proof," Johnson said.

Logan smiled. "Sam said the same thing. The President wants to know how high up this goes."

"So you call her *Sam*?" Cho asked with a grin.

Logan narrowed his eyes. "She's returning with Barrett to D.C. to obtain more information. I need to deliver the cargo and hurry back to help her."

"You're letting a sixteen-year-old help uncover an international assassination attempt?" Johnson asked.

"She's twenty-one," Logan said, gnashing his teeth. "And I'm not letting her. She's as stubborn as her father." Smiling, the men glance at each other. "Yeah, I care about her. Are you going to help me or not?"

"We'll help," O'Brien replied. "But we want more details."

"I told you everything I know until we see what's on the flash drive in the embassy safe," Logan replied.

"I'm referring to the twenty-one-year-old freckled blonde with one blue eye and one green eye. The one you call *Sam*," Cho said, standing next to the rest of the team. Smiling, they crossed their arms and waited.

"Well, first of all, she cut and dyed her hair to a reddish brown. Second, if you help me finish this and keep her safe, I'll tell you whatever you want to know," Logan said.

They eyed him. "You're not much on sharing details, Major," O'Brien said.

146

"If this ends the way I want it to, Sam can answer anything I don't. She's not one to hold back her feelings." That was an understatement.

The men put their heads together as they consider his statement. Logan tapped his foot while they took their time. He still had to deliver the cargo.

"Come on, guys. You really want to help? Those earlier idiotic ideas aren't going to cut it. I need her. Is that what you want to hear from me?" Logan asked.

They chuckled. "What do you want us to do first?" Johnson asked.

"We repack the cargo into the truck. I make a delivery while you guys call the Colonel and return to D.C. I need a layout of the Russian Embassy inside and out as well as any other Intel you can get about the grounds and its security. Use the computer at my apartment."

"Are we really going to storm the building? We could start an international incident," Johnson replied.

"We're not storming anything. I'm going to a party to get the flash drive. If I can't take the easy exit out the front door, I want to have a backup plan," Logan said.

The team crated the wreckage and loaded it back into the truck. After leaving separately, Logan plugged his phone into the charger and turned on the police frequency of the CB. He had two hours of backtracking and another three to Fort Reilly. Back on Highway 70, he accelerated and contemplated his next steps. When his cell rang, he took a deep breath and answered.

"Where the hell are you, Major?" Colonel Williams demanded.

"Highway 70 almost to Topeka," he replied.

"Where have you been? You should have arrived at Fort Reilly twelve hours ago."

"Yes, Sir. Barrett had a family emergency. We spent some time at a truck stop, so he could make some calls. I continued our assignment."

"Why is your GPS still off?"

"I didn't realize it still was. Barrett fixed it once. I'll have the techs check the truck after I complete the drop-off. I'm not sure if Barrett resolved his emergency," Logan said.

"He has, and he's on his way back to D.C. I want you back here for a full report. I'll call Fort Reilly to arrange your ride. There's a party at the Russian Embassy that I need to attend. I'll leave your name at the front gate."

"Yes, Sir." Logan smiled with relief. He wouldn't have to call Jillian, and he wasn't still in love with her.

CHAPTER 19

ON THE PLANE, BEAR RECEIVED a call from Martha. When he tried to hand his cell to her, Sam shook her head and pursed her lips. Her mother would lecture her soon enough; she wouldn't be happy about her disappearance.

Karl had been preoccupied with finding Sergei and Ivan, so she and Bear discussed the plan. It didn't seem that difficult. Sam would retrieve the drive from the safe, make a copy, return it to the safe, and give the copy to Bear. While arguing about Logan's part, they finally touched down in D.C. at one in the afternoon. Karl motioned them to his driver, but Bear said they'd take a taxi.

"Samantha will join me. You can take the taxi," Karl replied.

Bear frowned. "No. Sam will accompany me in the taxi. Martha invited me to her Memorial Day party this evening. I'm picking up a few things first and then we will arrive together."

"Her mother wants her home now," Karl said.

"You have no idea what her mother wants, so shut it or I'll shut it for you," Bear replied.

Karl stormed off with his driver while Bear flagged down a taxi. She slid her backpack over her shoulder and cringed, gingerly switching to the other. Bear helped her into the taxi.

"Do you like pissing him off?" she asked.

Bear chuckled. "He's not use to someone standing up to him. You should be proud of me. I controlled the urge to sucker punch him."

"Proud? I was hoping you'd pop him in the face."

After a short trip to his tiny apartment, they headed for the embassy. In the taxi, she fidgeted. She had hoped she could get in a nap before the party, but Karl had a master key to all of the rooms.

"I think if you sneak away early—" Bear said.

"Stop. I'm tired of talking about it. I don't understand why Logan has to be there."

150

"He doesn't want you to do it alone."

"You'll be there," she said.

"It's a two-man/one-woman job. Besides, your father and I have tried to get you both to the same party for years. Here's our chance."

"What do you mean *get us to the same party*?"

Bear sighed. "Your father had a fondness for the Major. You know that. He wanted you to meet him. That's all."

She snorted. "Yeah, he wanted me to meet a married man."

"That was two years ago, and he was only married for four months. You really think he still loves Jillian?"

She hugged her arms around her and frowned. "She's beautiful."

"God, I'm co-starring in a freaking soap opera," he mumbled.

The taxi pulled up to the front entrance to the Russian Embassy. She blew out her forty-second breath. The security guard looked into the back seat and nodded to the other guard who opened the gate. She groaned as her mother waited in the doorway.

Bear chuckled. "Go. Take your lumps. I'll escort you to the party later." With his suit bag and duffle, he led her to the door. She wanted to jump back into the taxi. "Martha, thanks for the invite," he said.

"Thank you, Bear," Martha said, touching his forearm. She stood aside and let him pass her.

"Hello, Mother," Sam whispered behind him.

"Oh Samantha, what did you do to your hair?" Martha asked, wrapping her arms around her.

"I like it," she said, smothered against her mother's breasts. "Can Bear stay for a few days? I wanted him to meet my students."

Martha looked at him. "Only if he shaves that horrid beard."

"But I've been working on this for three weeks," he replied.

Sam smiled when he acted crushed. Martha raised an eyebrow, and he relented.

Martha tugged her up the stairs and pointed Bear to the guest room down the hall. She pulled her into her and Dmitri's sitting room. As soon as the door shut, Martha launched into an interrogation.

"Why in God's name did you run away?"

"I went to the cabin; I missed him," Sam replied.

"Why didn't you tell me? I've been so worried. Do you know how many other young women have Amber Alerts out? I had heard there were five."

"I'm old enough to be on my own."

Ignoring the statement, Martha inspected Sam's reddish brown hair. "You're a ragamuffin." She tusked and handed her a silk robe. "Samantha, jeans with a flannel shirt? And why did you cut your beautiful hair?" Not waiting for an answer, she continued, "Well, I have my hairdresser, Karen, coming in an hour. I'll have her try and fix this mess."

Sam changed into the robe and sat in the chair.

"How could you be so selfish? How do you expect to find the right man wearing flannel and chopping off your hair? For goodness' sake, Samantha, you look like a boy."

"I like my hair," she said weakly.

Martha sighed and shook her head. "We'll do your makeup. That forest green strapless dress and matching heels will look nice," she said, tapping her thumb to her lips. "You can dance for the guests tonight. You are graceful. That'll attract the men."

"Mother, I don't—"

"Not a word, Samantha. General Yzemikov and General Stovall are here for the party, but there will be a number of single military men. Let's hope they don't hear about your selfish antics." Martha held up her hand, so Sam couldn't interrupt. "Do you think I want you to grow old and be alone like your father?"

"Please, don't push this."

"You won't, so I will. I hired a quartet for the ballroom. I think your ballet dancing will distract the men from arguing. I have to keep the peace with a few Russian and American hotheads. Don't hide behind Bear tonight. I expect you to mingle and dance when asked."

"I am not dancing with Karl or his goons," she replied with a little more energy.

Her mother cringed. "I'd prefer you stay away from him. Dmitri likes him, but I think he's disrespectful."

"And creepy," she added.

Martha nodded, and Sam sighed with relief. At least, her mother got that part right. While Martha continued to rant, the hairdresser tried to dye her hair back. Instead, it made it lighter brown with redder highlights. Sam smiled in the mirror; she liked it even better. Karen trimmed her waves and slicked it back. She kept wondering what Logan would think. He might not recognize her.

Sam finally found her spine when her mother wanted to do her makeup. Martha liked blue eye shadow. While her mother could blend blues to look attractive, it always looked odd on her. Martha gave in, and Sam ran from the room.

In front of the mirror in her bedroom, Sam picked out neutral and brown tones. She added a hint of deep green to her eyelids to match her dress. Again, she wondered what Logan would think, but it made her mad and a little sad.

Jillian would be at the party and would be the center of attention, like usual. She knew all about hair, makeup, and stylish clothes. She easily charmed the men, and they fawned over her. They drooled really. The fact that Jillian called Logan twice didn't bode well for Sam. Jillian wanted her husband back. It shouldn't matter though. What happened at the cabin stayed at the cabin.

In her mother's robe, Sam sank into the chair. She would not cry and wreck her makeup. Jumping at the knock at the door, she peeked through the crack. The maid held a tray of food. At eighteen, Lara looked matronly with her large bosom and wide hips.

Smiling, Sam opened it. "Thank you. I'm starving."

"Welcome, Ms. Sam," Lara said with a curtsy.

After looking up and down the empty hallway, Sam pulled her inside. Lara set the tray on the desk. Forgetting etiquette, Sam stuffed a slice of chicken breast into her mouth and moaned. She motioned for Lara to help herself.

When Lara snitched a piece of cheese from the tray, Sam saw her upper arm. She reached out and gently held her bruised arm.

"Who did that?" Sam demanded.

Lara looked away. "I am clumsy."

She saw the other arm with the same bruise. "Oh Lara, did Karl do this?" she asked, sitting her in the desk chair. She knelt beside her.

"He so angry when he not find you. I got in his way," Lara replied, rubbing her abdomen. "He, um, locked us in his office."

"I am so sorry. I'll tell my mother."

Lara jumped from the chair. "No, I don't want to go back to Russia."

Sam sighed and paced. Karl would find a way to blame Lara for something and have her deported. "Okay, but stay away from him." Lara nodded. "How many are coming tonight?"

"About fifty, a mix of Americas and Russias, Ms. Martha opened the great room, the ballroom, and the patio. She already told the musicians about your ballet dancing."

Sam groaned and looked in her closet. "What color dress should I wear for the ballet?"

"I pick the dark blue one with your feather blue headband. Very pretty."

Sam nodded. "And it's easy to slip into," she mumbled.

Lara checked the hall before stepping out. "Good luck, Ms. Sam."

"Be careful," she called out as the door shut.

While she munched on another piece of chicken, Sam set her toe shoes and iPod next to her laptop on her desk. Later in the evening, she'd returned to her room, change, sneak over, and grab the flash drive. Her nervousness left. She would not let Karl get away with this assassination plot or hurt any more women in the household.

For an hour, Sam practiced walking in heels. She was more nervous at seeing Logan again than grabbing the flash drive. She didn't want to trip and wanted to appear sophisticated like Jillian. When someone knocked on her bedroom door, she wobbled in her heels then growled. She needed to calm down.

At the door, Bear frowned. Shaven with his hair trimmed, he wore his dress green uniform. Her mother must have offered the services of her hairdresser. Martha had tamed the grizzly Bear into a distinguished service man with a chest full of medals and ribbons.

Sam grinned. "Sergeant Major, you clean up rather well."

He snorted. "That woman kept cutting and cutting," he said, smoothing down the graying brown hair above his ears. "Are you ready for this?"

"Yes, Karl is going down," she said as she took his arm.

"What's with the harsh tone?"

She stopped in the middle of the corridor. Hearing the music and banter at the end of the hallway below, she looked up at him and poked the center button on his uniform. "Karl may have hurt me, but he also hurt our maid, who's my friend. I won't stand for it. She's barely eighteen."

"Did you tell Martha?"

"Lara didn't want me to. If you get the chance to shred him, do it. Otherwise, I will. I've sharpened my claws," she replied, scratching his uniform with her nails.

"Is that an order, Ms. Randall?"

"It is, Sergeant Major Barrett. Don't disappoint me."

Bear's laugh was a deep baritone rumble. Sam smiled back, and they continued down the hallway to the staircase that descended into the ballroom at the west end of the embassy. Before they stepped onto the open balcony, she scanned the crowd that mingled along the edge of the dance floor.

Russian dignitaries had on their shiny uniforms with sashes while Army officers wore their dress green uniforms. She even saw Marines in their dress blues. On the arms of their husbands, the women laughed within the small groups. Their garb ranged from black, gray, and Navy blue. Martha opted for a peach silk gown. A group of single daughters of elder officers eyed the young military men drinking at the bar in the corner.

While the quartet played in the corner, Sam sighed. She wasn't in the mood to dance. Bear urged her forward, and they descended the stairs. She paused on the vivid green eyes of Major Logan McCormick. He, too, wore his dress green uniform with his many ribbons and medals that matched Bear's decorations. She caught her breath and groaned. She wished he hadn't come. This was going to be painful.

"Stop staring," Bear whispered.

"How can I not? He's the most handsome man in the room," Sam replied.

"Hey, I'm right here. Once again, I'm second best," Bear mumbled.

As she smiled at Logan, Jillian came out of nowhere and launched herself at him. In a slinky red gown with a slit to the hip, Jillian practically molested him in the middle of the crowd. Could she get any closer? Sam blew out a breath. The handsome couple belonged together.

Bear moved her away from the She-Devil and introduced her to a Marine Lieutenant and two Army Captains. After another group of wives rudely stared at her heterochromia, Sam avoided any more eye contact. She sighed as her stepfather approached them. Looking like

Humpty Dumpty in a tailored black suit, Dmitri greeted Bear.

"Sergeant Major, we owe you many thanks for escorting Samantha home safely. Her mother worried although I believe she was smart enough to take care of herself. In Russia, women Samantha's age already have two and three children."

She snorted. "Thank you, Dmitri, for the backhanded compliment."

Bear laughed as Dmitri smiled and added, "Maybe I listen to your mother a bit too much. I apologize, Samantha."

"Accepted," she replied, touching his forearm. "And you're right. I am smart enough to take care of myself."

"Dmitri, is this the young woman that disappeared and caused the chaos in your household?" General Yzemikov asked, crossing his arms. With a black patch covering his left eye, he honed in on Sam with his right.

She stiffened at the abrupt question. Before Bear could come to her defense, Dmitri patted her hand still left on his forearm. "Chaos? Of course not. My daughter may come and go as she pleases. She doesn't need anyone's permission to leave the embassy." Nodding at someone across the room, the general left in a huff, and Dmitri continued, "Although next time, if you're too cowardly to let your mother know, I hope you'll, at least, let me know."

With a smile, she kissed his chubby cheek. "Thank you, Father Dmitri, and I will."

Dmitri laughed and moved toward General Stovall, who glowered at her from the bar area. She shivered at the deep curved scar from the general's right temple to his chin.

"I don't like General Yzemikov's attitude toward you. It makes me wonder about his part in this," Bear mumbled. "Do you really think Dmitri knows nothing?"

"I don't know," she said with a sigh. "He's smarter than people realize."

"You always call him *Father Dmitri*? It makes him sound like a priest."

She laughed. "No, not always. Mother has wanted me to call him *Father* or *Dad* since they married. He told me he understood that I had only one father, but he hoped I understood he cared just as much. When he's extra sweet to me, I throw it in to please him."

CHAPTER 20

IN THE BALLROOM AT THE Russian Embassy, Logan spotted Sam and Barrett at the top of the stairway. He tried not to stare as they descended. Her dark green dress accentuated her feminine curves and strawberry blonde locks. She was definitely not sixteen. He held his breath while she searched the crowd and paused on him. When she smiled, he wanted to race to her and kiss her glossy lips.

Before he could return a smile, Jillian launched herself at him. She had always been a good kisser. Keyword: good. Sam had playful sensual lips. He wanted those lips again.

Logan gently pressed Jillian back and looked her over. He wasn't sure how he'd react. He hadn't seen her since their split. She still had a fabulous body with the help of enhancements. He saw a hint of wrinkles around her eyes probably from partying too much. Botox hadn't helped the thinner creases around her mouth.

He could be critical; he'd seen her raw. The skilled artist of makeup had flaws. It had just taken him a while to see them. He had kept this goddess high above him. Realizing he was immune now, he smiled at her.

"Hello, Jillian," Logan said, casually caressing her upper arm. He could play her game.

She grinned back. "I've missed you, Mick. I've forgotten how sexy you are in uniform."

"What about out of uniform?" he asked, waiting for more of her fake compliments.

She squeezed his bicep. "That can be arranged."

"What have you been up to?" Logan asked, wishing she'd get to her point.

While Jillian rambled about her modeling gigs, he scanned the crowd for Samantha. Barrett escorted her around the room where they chatted briefly with various people. Feigning interest in Jillian's life, he continued to nod.

"What brings you and Barrett here now that your assignment's completed?" Jillian asked.

"I don't know why he's here, but I was invited by the Colonel. Have you seen him?" he asked.

"He's talking to General Yzemikov," she said, nodding in their direction. "Why is she with Barrett?"

"Who is she?" Logan asked.

Before Jillian answered, Barrett greeted them. "Hello Jilly," Barrett said in a gruff voice. Hiding his smile, Logan knew Barrett had always irritated her. Glaring, she started to reply, but Barrett cut her off. "Samantha Randall, this is Major McCormick. Mick, Sam is General Randall's daughter," he said with his hand at his goddaughter's back.

"I have a great respect for him," Logan replied, taking her hand. Jillian eyed his warm reaction.

Sam smiled and politely lowered her hand from his. "Thank you, Major. I miss him."

Jillian tugged on his uniform sleeve. "Mick, let's dance."

"Right now? It's a bit rude. Don't you think?"

Jillian pouted as Karl joined the group. He sneered at Barrett, ignored Logan, and ogled Samantha. Logan tightened his fists behind his back. Karl turned to Jillian and held out his hand. Hoping to make Logan jealous, Jillian latched onto it.

"You had your chance," she called out over her shoulder.

"The She-Devil is showing too much cleavage. A tit's going to pop out," Barrett said.

Sam covered her giggle with her hand as Mrs. Demas joined them. She waited for Sam to introduce him. Sam flinched at her mother's smile. They had a discussion without ever talking.

"Mother, this is Major McCormick. He works with Bear. Major, this is Martha Demas, Ambassador Demas's wife."

"Major, so nice to meet you." Martha turned back to Barrett and patted his cheek. "Sergeant Major, you clean up rather well. That beard was dreadful. You look ten years younger now."

Barrett laughed. "I only did it, so you'd dance with me. How about it, Martha? For old time's sake?" Martha smiled at Sam and took Barrett's arm.

Standing alone together, Logan reached for her hand. From the dance floor, Jillian and Karl shot them venomous glares. "Dance with me, Sam," he whispered. She nodded.

Logan escorted her to the other end of the floor and away from prying eyes. He gently pulled her close. They waltzed around the room within the large circle of dancers. Even with her heels, she fit perfectly in his arms.

"You decided to slick back your hair and change its color again?"

166

Stiff and proper, she followed his lead. "My mother's idea. I prefer my spikes."

"The curls are more my wildcat's style," he said, twirling her around with ease.

She frowned. "I'm your pet, too?"

He mentally cringed. "That's not what I meant." Jillian and Karl scrutinized their every move. "You're pretty light on your feet. All those dance lessons paid off."

Twirling her again, he tried to out dance Karl who moved closer. Jillian always had a hard time following any lead. Sam gracefully kept pace with his countermeasures to avoid the other couple's interference.

"Karl's getting his feet stepped on," he whispered.

Logan had missed her smile. He wanted to pick her up and hold her again. He felt pain in his chest that he couldn't. Not yet, he thought. Away from oglers, he touched her shoulder. When she winced, he looked closer at the swelling. Makeup covered the deeper bruising.

"God. Sam. How bad does it hurt?"

She shrugged. "It aches, but I can handle it. Are you still mad at me?"

"I didn't agree with your password."

She tensed at Jillian's glare. "She's your standard. You compare every woman to her."

"I'm not talking about her. We have a couple minutes left. Which room is the safe in?"

"It's on the patio side, but I'm doing it," Sam replied.

"No, you're not. It's too dangerous."

"I have to change into my dance outfit soon. Mother wants me to entertain the guests. I'll do it then."

"I'll go with you."

She shook her head. "You'll need to help Bear keep an eye on Karl and Colonel Williams. Nobody suspects me."

While they danced, they stared at each other, waiting for the other to give in. Sam was right. He had compared Jillian to her, but Sam was so much more. Why couldn't he just tell her?

"Fine," he said. "I'll be on the terrace watching. Be careful." As the song ended, she turned to go. "Sam, I've missed you."

She smiled. "You, too, Logan."

Barrett joined him as they watched Jillian stop Samantha by the stairs. Logan casually pushed Barrett backward, so he could hear them. When the Sergeant Major started to talk, Logan told him to shut it.

Jillian flipped her long blond hair off her shoulder. "Mick is out of your league. He adores me. I like being on his pedestal."

"I bet you do," Sam said, stepping closer. In her F-me pumps, Jillian towered over her.

"Is there going to be a cat fight?" Barrett asked. "My money's on Sam." Logan growled, and Barrett laughed.

"Stick to being Karl's pet. You won't win against me, Freak," Jillian said.

"I have no intention of competing with the Ice Queen."

Jillian looked surprised that Sam was talking to her like that. As Jillian raised her hand to slap her, Sam hissed and scratched her claws in the air. Jillian took a step back. When Sam glanced at him, he raised an eyebrow at her toughness. She flinched and dropped her head. Turning on her heels, Sam escaped up the staircase. Logan groaned. He wanted to appear reassuring.

"You're single for this very reason, dumbass," Barrett mumbled. "What are you trying to do?"

Logan snapped his head toward him and glowered. "We have work to do."

Colonel Williams limped toward them. He scowled as he leaned on his cane. "Sergeant Major Barrett, why are you here?"

Moving to the corner of the ballroom, Barrett stood straighter. "Samantha Randall is my goddaughter. Her mother left a voicemail that she was missing. I thought she might return to her father's cabin, well, her cabin. I found her and escorted her home. Grateful, Mrs. Demas asked me to stay. I am here as her guest."

"You're dismissed," Williams said.

Barrett stalked toward the bar.

"Major McCormick, fill me in on the timeline."

"Yes, Sir," Logan replied. "Like I mentioned before, we were delayed by a car accident. At that time, Barrett received a voicemail about a family emergency. I dropped him off at the next truck plaza. After he made some calls, he left. I rested before I continued to drive."

"Sleeping on an assignment?" Williams asked.

"I thought being clear-headed was more important than a time constraint. Nobody knew about our cargo, so driving safely took precedence."

The Colonel nodded as Jillian laughed with the men who surrounded her. He and Williams turned toward her phoniness. She glanced at him and smiled that her plan for his attention worked.

Colonel Williams sighed. "I spoiled her too much."

"Yes, you did and so did I," Logan replied.

"She's out of control. I think you're the only one who can stand up to her now. She has a soft spot for you," Williams said.

"With respect, Sir, she is not my problem."

"Mick, I was proud to have had you as a son-in-law even if it was brief. You were a good influence on her."

He snorted. "Not good enough. Sir, I'm uncomfortable talking about this."

The Colonel nodded. "I know we agreed a long time ago to keep things professional. Soon, you'll realize that this is professional. Talk to her before someone gets hurt."

Logan sighed and nodded. He knew the Colonel was into something dangerous and wanted her shielded. Damn it. Jillian would need protection. Barrett wouldn't like it. Hell, he didn't like it.

After Williams left, Logan watched Jillian smile and slink toward him. He didn't have to suggest the patio terrace. She tugged him in that direction and talking wasn't on her mind. What did she really want from him?

CHAPTER 21

LEANING AGAINST THE DOOR IN her bedroom, Samantha blew out a breath. She couldn't think straight. The dancing had been amazing and made her think about the other wonderful pursuit with him. She winced again as she remembered Logan's disappointing glance before she left. While she tried to focus, someone knocked on her door. Praying that it wasn't Karl or Logan, she opened it. Her mother smiled.

"Do you need help getting ready?" Martha asked, pushing open the door.

"No, I can do it. I wanted a few extra minutes to go over my routine."

Martha looked at the dance outfit she had chosen and nodded. "Major McCormick is very handsome. You followed his lead around the dance floor nicely. A natural fit. He seems interested, and I can tell you like him."

Sam loved him, and she thought it was a natural fit, too, but she frowned. "He's Jillian's ex-husband."

"So. Are you jealous of her?" Martha asked.

"Yes," she replied, slipping off her heels.

"You are a catch, Samantha. Smart, pretty, and graceful. Jillian was the one jealous of you and the Major dancing. Besides, Jillian's a whore, and that's probably why she's his ex."

"Mother!"

"What? You are a far better woman and if he can't see it then to hell with him."

"Mother!"

"If you want something, you fight for it. Didn't your father teach you anything?"

"Mother, please. I have to think about my routine."

Martha nodded. "Okay, just promise to talk with him again before the party's over. I'll run interference with Jillian, if you'd like. I'm sick of her whiny princess attitude. She needs to grow up."

Sam sighed again. "I'll promise if you leave him alone."

"Agreed. How much time do you need?"

174

"Twenty minutes to change and touch up my makeup and thirty minutes in the practice room to run through my routine. It's been a while since I've danced it."

"Thank you, Honey. I'll have Dmitri make an announcement in an hour."

Sam locked her door and hurried to dress. Skipping her makeup, she opened the French doors of her balcony. In her dark blue halter dance dress and her leather dance slippers, she climbed onto the ledge and jumped to the middle balcony. She mistakenly glanced below. Jillian was groping Logan.

Sam leaped for Karl's balcony and lost her footing. She slipped and scraped her shin giving her a gaping hole in her nylons. Mad at the distraction, she climbed over the railing and slid into the room.

The dog growled at her from his cage next to Karl's desk. She shushed him and punched in the code to the safe. Under a stack of files, she found the flash drive then quickly slid into his chair behind his desk. Locked out of Karl's computer, she stuck the drive into her bra and shut the safe.

On the balcony, she glanced below once more to make sure nobody saw her. Logan scowled at her as he hugged his She-Devil. Shouldn't he be watching Karl and Colonel Williams?

Sam leaped back to her room. They had a mission to finish. After that, she'd return to the cabin. The sooner, the better.

While she waited for her laptop to turn on, she changed her nylons to heavier tights to cover her scrapes. Realizing the flash drive had only one audio file, she quickly downloaded it onto her iPod. She listened and groaned. The information was more horrible than she thought.

When someone knocked on her door, she stuck the flash drive back into her bra and turned off her computer. With her iPod, ear buds, and toe shoes, she answered.

Karl smirked. "I'm here to escort you to the ballroom."

"I'm going to the practice room first. I want to stretch and run through my routine."

"The practice room it is then," he said, offering his arm.

She ignored him and left for the other set of stairs to the main floor. Karl chuckled and followed. He gripped her upper arm and shoved her down the last two steps. The pain shot to her fingers. She gasped aloud. He laughed again. She quickly opened the door to the room directly below hers.

"Would you like me to hold your iPod?" he asked.

"No, my iPod has my song on it."

"I'll wait outside the door until you're ready," he said.

She shut the door and paced. She didn't care about her routine. She'd make something up. As she bit her hangnail, she heard Bear, talking to Karl outside the room's door. What was she supposed to do now? Karl wasn't letting Bear see her. Hearing a tap on the French doors to the terrace, she jumped as Logan let himself inside.

"God," he said, straightening his uniform jacket. "Were you trying to make me mental?"

"What are you talking about?" she whispered, glancing at the unlocked door where Karl and Bear argued.

"You almost fell and broke your neck," he whispered as he looked at the red marks on her sore arm. "What happened?"

"Karl escorted me here."

Logan growled and mumbled incoherently. He lifted her chin. With a tissue from his pocket, he dabbed the wetness under her eyes. "Stop it or your mascara will run. It doesn't look water-proof."

She smiled. "You know about water-proof mascara?"

He lowered his face to just inches from hers. "Can't you tell?" he asked, batting his naturally long lashes.

She giggled and then sighed. "I downloaded a copy onto my iPod," she said, setting it and the ear buds in his hand. "I'm sorry, Logan."

177

"Did you hear it?" he asked.

She nodded. "You should listen to it before you leave the party," she said, sitting in the corner chair to put on her toe shoes.

"Why? What's on it?" he demanded.

"It may change your mission depending on how you feel about her."

The knock on the door stopped him from more questions. He paused as if to say something but changed his mind and ducked back out the door. Karl and Bear fought to enter first. To distract Karl from seeing the patio door close, she spiraled in her toe shoes and leapt across the room. God, her arm throbbed.

CHAPTER 22

DEPENDING ON HOW HE FELT about Jillian? What the hell did that mean? Logan stalked from the shadowed part of the patio and entered the ballroom. Ambassador Demas made an announcement and had everyone stand back from the dance floor.

For a better view, Logan found a spot on the staircase halfway up. He stuck a bud in his ear and scrolled through her playlist that consisted of only two items—*Daddy* and *Logan*. He pressed the *Logan* playlist. The shock made him dizzy. He gripped the banister.

Jillian, not the Colonel, was the one selling secrets to Karl and the Russian Generals. She admitted to the offense on tape. His ex-wife was committing treason. Colonel

Williams wanted to take the blame to protect her. Instead, Karl used the leverage to find out where the wreckage was, so he could retrieve the only evidence connecting Russia to the assassination of the President of the United States.

Karl planned to blame Samantha if the investigation headed in their direction. That's why they searched for her. They couldn't put her in a place unless they found out where she really was.

As the quartet played, Logan reeled. He watched Samantha's graceful ballet even though she favored her arm. The truck stop tomboy with the fire extinguisher transformed into an artistic woman with perfect posture and smooth gliding moves. Her sadness reflected in the haunting rendition of the Russian ballad. He caught her eye. Pain reflected back. Did Sam think he'd cover for his ex?

Logan slipped the iPod into his pocket as Jillian joined him on the stairs. With her back to Sam, she placed her hand on his chest. He put his arm around her waist to lull her. His thumb caressed her smooth skin through the open back of her trashy red dress.

"I talked to your father. What have you done, Jillian?" he demanded.

She shrugged. "Men adore me and tell me things. Why shouldn't I cash in on that?"

"You really think you're Mata Hari?" he whispered.

She smiled. "I'll go down in history like her. Every man wants me, including you, Mick," she said, playing with his ear. "I'm safe here. This is Russian soil."

Everyone except Barrett was riveted with the ballet. Confused, Barrett watched him from the corner of the room. He gestured with his hand, and Bear nodded. He hoped he understood that he revised the plan.

"What about your father? Are you throwing him to the wolves?" Logan asked.

"I'm not worried. He'll do anything for me, just like you will."

He drew her closer. "Jillian, leave with me now, and we'll disappear."

He kissed her passionately to prove it. Jillian finally nodded. With his arm around her waist, he escorted her down the steps. He turned to Sam as she finished. Tears glistened in her eyes. He psychically tried to tell her that he hadn't chosen Jillian over her.

Jillian peeked around him and smiled at the dancer. Distracted, Sam tripped and fell onto her shoulder. Something slid across the floor. As the guests gasped at her collapse, Karl narrowed in on the flash drive. Shit!

Karl rushed toward her. "Samantha, are you all right?"

Sam scrambled for the flash drive while Logan helped Jillian down the stairs. Holding the drive in her palm, she cried out as Karl squeezed her hand in anger. Damn it! Sam kept the original. Logan searched for Bear who worked his way through the crowd.

"I'll let Bear know I'm leaving, so he can work with someone else on the next assignment," Logan said casually.

Before Jillian answered, Logan hurried toward the chaos. Karl picked up Sam and carried her off the dance floor. Most of the guests chatted quietly and stared. The Russian Generals scowled and put their heads together. At the thick double oak doors to the hallway, Karl stopped and spoke to two bulky men in black ill-fitting suit coats. Karl nodded in his direction. Barrett ducked through a side door. Karl's security team blocked him from following.

"Major, you are no longer welcome here," the biggest one said.

"Why?" Logan demanded. "I'm a guest."

Shrugging, the security man glanced at Jillian near the staircase. "I'm guessing you're moving in on Karl's woman."

Hoping he meant Jillian and not Samantha, Logan turned back to the staircase. Jillian frowned and left the area. Shit! As Mrs. Demas motioned for the quartet to continue with the music, the crowd dismissed the incident and resumed their dancing and conversing. Security corralled Logan toward the front door.

"What's going on?" Colonel Williams asked, limping after them. Security stepped back but remained ready to escort Logan off the compound.

With his arms crossed, Logan faced him. "You know exactly what's going on. You're a traitor to your country. How could you be a part of this?"

"I am a father first."

Logan sneered. "This could have been prevented, and what about Samantha Randall?"

"I sent your team to protect her from the blame of the Russians' plan and from Karl. I know him, and I didn't want him to find her first." Williams said.

"You know you're finished?" Logan said.

"I do. If Barrett's not careful, he'll be kicked out of the embassy, too. I can't help him."

"You can't hide here forever and neither can Jillian," Logan replied.

Williams nodded again. "I'd gladly accept the death penalty to protect my daughter."

"So much for making her take responsibility for her actions. Daddy will fix it. You disgust me."

Logan stormed from the building with security at his heels. In the small parking area at the side of the building, he jumped into his Dodge Charger and punched his steering wheel. With hands on their side arms, they waited at the edge of the walkway. He floored it toward the open gate and peeled out onto the street. He didn't feel any better.

Logan fumbled for his ringing cell. "How's Sam?"

"I can't get near her," Barrett replied. "What the hell is going on?"

"Karl knows she took the flash drive from the safe."

"Shit! What's on it?" Barrett demanded.

"This is all on Jillian. She seduced men for information that she sold to the Russians."

"Jesus, and she's protected here. What's your plan?"

"I'm working on it. Stay put!" Logan replied.

"Well, hurry the hell up!"

Logan dialed his cell. "Are you guys at my apartment?"

"When was the last time you stocked your refrigerator?" Johnson asked.

"I've got a big problem. I'll be there in ten."

God, what was Karl doing to her? Logan wanted to puke. Inhaling slowly, he listened to the iPod recording again and hoped he misheard the information. He hadn't.

Before he hyperventilated, he thought about the other recording that Sam had listened to throughout their trip.

Curiosity got the best of him. He needed to know what made her so sad.

As he listened, he drove through two stoplights and almost clipped a taxi. He chuckled and then sobered.

He now understood every action and decision she had made. Everything. From approaching him at the diner, her crazy questions about best friends and lovers, her state of mind, and, most of all, her motive for searching for the truck and driver.

Logan smiled. He knew her so much better now, and he would not let her down again. He parked in the first available space close to his apartment building.

With her iPod, he took the stairs three at a time to the fourth floor. He flew through his door so quickly that his men jumped from the dining room table.

Seeing that it was only him, they returned to the pages cluttering the table. While he explained what had happened, he searched his kitchen drawers. After slamming the last one, he set a small iPod speaker on the table.

As he unbuttoned his uniform jacket, he continued, "Sam risked her life to bring this information to us. You guys need to hear her motive. It's also one of the reasons why I care about her." Logan pushed *play* and General Randall's voice boomed through the speaker.

CHAPTER 23

"THIS IS FOR THE JUNE 4th commencement. I want to talk about the men and women of our country—those heroes and their patriotic duty to a bigger cause." After a long pause, General Randall sighed.

"Daddy, are you working on your speech?" Sam's voice asked.

"Samantha, come in. I could use some inspiration."

"How can I help?"

"I'm trying to find the right words. I want the graduates to understand that we have a calling to look after the day-to-day problems and the big picture. Who else will do it if we don't?"

"What's the big picture?" she asked.

"To protect the United States and its people. You and I are alike, Sam. We have the strength to overcome diversity like the other great men and women who serve."

"How do I recognize a great man?"

"Some men think there's a choice between right and wrong. Great men know there is none. He will act selflessly for the greater good."

"If the common goal is to protect the United States, how will I know when to act?"

"Samantha, you will live your life by going to Juilliard, by marrying your best friend, and by having a family. However, there may be a time when you see that you have no choice but to act."

"How will I know what to do?"

"You'll know, and you'll have to trust that like-minded people will be there to help you. For instance, the medals and awards that individuals receive are through a group effort with that common goal in mind."

"I don't know if I'm brave enough," she said.

"You'll find the strength. I truly believe that. There are brave men and women out there who think of others first. In fact, Bear and Major McCormick are stopping by soon. Mick is getting a medal for bravery in the field. He saved a civilian family and two men from his team."

"Wow, how'd he do that?"

"His team was ambushed helping a family from a danger zone and two of his men were shot. After helping the family escape from a group of insurgents, he raced back in and pulled his men to safety."

"How many on the team?"

"Five."

"Are the others getting medals?"

"No."

She snorted. "That doesn't seem fair. I imagine they covered him while he helped the men."

"Yes, but he's the one who ran in."

"Because he knew the others would have his back. You just said the team works together. Apparently, only until the medals are handed out."

They heard the doorbell at the front door.

"Stay and meet him," the General said.

"I'll see Bear later. I have dance practice. I love you, Daddy."

"I love you, too. Don't ever forget that." While the General shuffled papers, someone knocked on the door. "Bear, good to see you."

"Where's my Sammy?" Barrett asked.

"Practice. Major McCormick, nice to finally meet you."

"Likewise, Sir, it's an honor," Logan said.

"Come in and have a seat. We'll fly in for the commencement. Then, after I give a brief speech, the awards ceremony will follow," General Randall replied.

"Uh, Sir, that's what I'd like to talk to you about. I don't want or deserve the medal," Logan said.

"I'm sorry. I don't follow. Was the report wrong?" Randall asked.

"No, Sir. My men gave me the opportunity to retrieve part of our team. They should be honored, too," Logan said.

The General laughed. "My daughter would like you, Major. Bear, find the other team members and make sure they're at commencement as well."

"Thank you, Sir. That's extremely generous," Logan replied.

"My daughter would give me hell if I didn't."

CHAPTER 24

TUESDAY

AFTER MIDNIGHT AT LOGAN'S APARTMENT, the team sat around the table and stared at Sam's iPod. "Whoa, she's the reason we received medals?" Cho asked.

"You've never met her before this?" Johnson asked.

"I've met the General a few times, but she wasn't with him. She's Barrett's goddaughter," Logan said.

"What a coincidence," Cho said.

Or fate, he thought. The General told her like-minded people would help her. She identified him as military. God, it all made sense.

"Wow, because of that speech, I signed on for another tour," O'Brien replied.

"She's in trouble and needs our help," Logan said.

"Of course, whatever it takes. Besides, we still want details," Cho said as the others nodded.

"Okay, here's what we'll do," Logan said, reaching for the layout of the embassy grounds.

After changing into black fatigues, they loaded their guns, ropes, and anything else they thought they needed into a full-size white van that O'Brien used for local jobs.

By the south stonewall at the Russian Embassy, Logan checked his watch. It had only been two hours; it just seemed like a lifetime. He had no idea what he'd find.

CHAPTER 25

FEIGNING CONCERN AFTER HER FALL, Karl picked Samantha up off the dance floor. With pain shooting down her arm, she couldn't move her fingers. Karl paused at the double doors of the ballroom and spoke to the new security men.

"Escort Major McCormick and Sergeant Major Barrett off the premises. Now."

Karl seethed as he carried her roughly to his office. Once inside, he tossed her on the leather couch. Her blue feather headpiece flew off. After ripping the flash drive from her hand, he locked the office door. He scowled and rubbed the back of his neck while he paced. She tried to stretch her shoulder to reset it. It wouldn't move, so she pulled her lifeless arm against her abdomen, hoping to protect it.

Karl stared at her. "How did you get this?"

"I wanted to hurt you for liking Jillian more than me," Sam said.

"Who were you going to give this to?"

"I was going to give it to Bear, but you wouldn't let him in the practice room. I saved it for after my dance."

"How do you know Major McCormick?" Karl demanded.

She pulled her legs closer to her body. "I just met him. He works with Bear. I'm sorry. I don't even know what's on it."

Her mother knocked on the door. "Samantha, are you all right?"

"Send her away or you will really feel my wrath," Karl whispered.

Cradling her arm, she limped to the door and opened it a crack. "Mother, I'm fine. I'm sorry I embarrassed you."

"Well, stay out of sight, and I'll make up an excuse for the guests."

"Thank you, Mother."

Sam slowly shut the door. She wanted to run from the office, but where would she go? Logan was with Jillian, and Bear disappeared. She tensed and turned back to Karl. He let Bruno out of his cage. When the Doberman bore his teeth, she shivered.

"Until this party is over and I decide what to do with you, you will truly be my pet," Karl said, pointing to the cage.

With tears in her eyes, she crawled backward into the smelly tight-fitting box.

"If I hear any word or noise from you, your mother will have an unfortunate fall down the staircase and your precious Bear will die from a bullet in his head. Do you understand?" he asked, locking her inside.

Through the bars, she looked up at him and nodded. While he called for his new minion to take the dog, she struggled to get comfortable. Her toe shoes kept her from flexing her ankles and her dislocated shoulder seized in pain. She wiped her tears, smearing her mascara.

What was she going to do now? Logan had chosen Jillian. Sam had hoped he wouldn't have, but she understood. Maybe Bear could still help her. She didn't know how. Karl kicked them both out. How had this gone so wrong? Would the President take precautions now without any other proof?

"Oh, Daddy, I've disappointed you again—first with Juilliard and then not having a best friend and a family. I'm not strong enough to do this," she thought.

While she tried not to sob, Karl talked in Russian on his phone. He sounded pissed with the first call and apologetic with the second. He slammed the receiver down and kicked the cage. It flipped onto its side, and she landed on her sore shoulder. The movement popped it halfway back into the socket causing a nervy buzz from her neck to her fingers. Her arm still throbbed and her fingers became numb. She couldn't shift, so she remained twisted like a pretzel.

When someone knocked, Karl kicked the other side of the cage to turn it upright. It didn't help her back or her legs. He covered the cage with a blanket, but she could still see out the corner of the cage door.

"Where is she?" Jillian demanded.

"In her appropriate place," Karl replied. Jillian cackled. "What did he want?"

"He wants me, of course," she said. "How safe am I here?"

Karl snorted. "Safer than I am. General Yzemikov wants to know how she got the drive. I have to meet with him. He wants an update on the satellite wreckage and its black box, too."

"What update?" Jillian asked.

"Exactly! Ivan and Sergei failed to retrieve it. They know better than to return empty-handed. The cowards."

"Mick hadn't a clue about his cargo. Maybe the Army will destroy the whole thing without looking for it."

Logan didn't trust Jillian enough to give her any details. Could he love Jillian without trusting her? Sam had asked him before, but she didn't believe his answer.

Pet-sitting, Jillian lifted the corner of the blanket and smiled at her. "Did you really think he'd enjoy your company over mine?" Not waiting for a reply, she paced and mumbled to herself. "He's never danced me around the floor like that. Maybe he took lessons for me. Of course, he did ..."

While Jillian continued her psychobabble, Sam smiled. Her mother was right. Jillian was jealous of her. The fact helped her pain.

CHAPTER 26

AT TWO-THIRTY IN THE MORNING, Logan and the men scaled the outer stonewall of the Russian Embassy. Staying out of the cameras' views, they watched the last of the guests leave the party. Security would let down their guard after the long night.

Having seen Sam jump the balconies earlier, Logan knew where her bedroom and Karl's office were. Logan and the team climbed the twenty feet to Sam's room. He was hoping this would be easy and he'd find her there sleeping. Not so.

In the darkness, he gave Martinez the iPod and ear buds. The men already knew their assignments. Martinez and Johnson quickly left through her door to find Barrett down the hallway. Cho and O'Brien remained in Sam's room until they were needed.

Logan checked the grounds below and jumped to the middle balcony. It was farther than he thought. Dismissing thoughts of Sam's earlier slip, he sprang to Karl's balcony. A soft glow from the desk lamp lit the room.

Logan listened to Jillian talk to someone, who remained silent. Sliding the curtain aside, he saw Jillian and her slinky red dress in the empty room. He entered as she kicked the dog cage.

"You're a dirty stray cat that should drown in the river," Jillian said.

"Jillian," Logan whispered, "I've come back for you."

"Mick, what are you doing here?"

Before Jillian covered the cage with a blanket, he saw Sam's smeared mascara face between the bars of the cage door. His heart stopped, but he pushed on.

"I've come to whisk you away. I've realized I've never stopped loving you," he said. "The U.S. government is going to make the ambassador hand you over. An international incident will ensue if he doesn't. I'm here to protect you." He was glad he couldn't see Sam's disappointment. Instead, he felt her thoughts of betrayal.

"Why should I trust you?" Jillian asked.

"I've risked everything. You're my world, Jillian. I need you."

Jillian flipped her hair off her shoulder. "You'd turn your back on the Army for me?"

"I'm here, aren't I? I was wrong not to put you first," he said, opening his arms for her.

She hugged him. "Oh, Mick, I knew you still cared."

As he held Jillian, Logan stared at the blanket-covered dog cage. "I believe now that lovers can be best friends."

Two of Sam's fingers poked out from under the blanket and wiggled. The relief made him more determined. He prayed that her father's memory would keep her tough for a little while longer.

Jillian stepped back. "I don't want a best friend. I deserve to be worshipped."

He kissed her finger and tried not to choke on his words. "I'm your servant."

With Jillian satisfied with his answer, he checked the hallway and quickly escorted her to Sam's room where Cho and O'Brien waited. They had already rigged a device to lower Jillian safely to the ground. He gripped Cho by the front of his shirt and barked for him to handle his woman with care.

"Don't let her feet touch the ground," Logan added to O'Brien.

Basking in the glow of her adoration and delusion, Jillian let him fasten the harness and lower her to the patio below. O'Brien held her in his arms until Logan untied the ropes and climbed down after them. He handed Cho the gear and took Jillian back from O'Brien. He couldn't get rid of her quick enough. This ploy made him nauseated.

Cho took point while O'Brien followed. They gently helped her over the outer wall. Leaning back against the outside of the van, Johnson saw them coming and slid open the side door.

Sitting on the floor of the van, Colonel Williams saluted Logan with his cuffed hands. Martinez slid out to stand next to Johnson.

Logan smiled and unceremoniously set Jillian to the ground. Her heels sank into the grass by the curb. He motioned for Johnson to cuff her, too.

"Mick, what are you doing?" she asked, struggling against Johnson.

Logan squeezed the cuffs around her wrist behind her back. "It's called Karma. I've learned the art of manipulation from you," he seethed.

As the guys smiled, Johnson picked her up and stuffed her in the back next to her father. Cho slid the door shut to muffle her screams.

"Was that as satisfying as it looked?" Cho asked.

202

"Yeah," Logan replied. "But I'm not done yet."

"Are you sure you don't need all of us?" Cho asked.

"I'd rather have you guys deal with them," Logan replied. Out of habit, he double checked the clip in his sidearm.

"Good luck. We'll meet you and Samantha at your apartment," Cho replied.

Logan nodded. He could hear Jillian's angry screams as Cho climbed into the driver's seat. She would get everything she deserved. Now, he prayed for Sam's safety and forgiveness.

Behind a tree inside the compound, Logan watched one of the security men, who grumbled to Bruno about choosing the short stick while the others slept. The man walked toward the other side of the perimeter until the Doberman growled in his direction and broke free. When it ran toward him, Logan sprinted for the latticework next to Sam's balcony.

Bruno barked below the balcony like Romeo calling for Juliet. Logan waited inside Sam's room while the security man shushed the dog and pulled him toward the side of the building. Logan quickly leaped to the second and then the third balcony. He pushed the curtain aside.

Behind his desk, Karl had his feet propped on top of the dog crate. Without the blanket covering the cage, Logan

203

saw how cramped she was. He clenched his jaw as he remembered how she hated enclosed spaces.

When Karl leaned back in his chair, Logan stepped beyond the curtain and aimed his gun at the bastard. Karl smiled and set his feet on the carpet. His Makarov pistol pointed at Samantha.

"I only came for the girl," Logan said.

"She stays with me or she dies. You choose," Karl replied.

Logan lowered his gun but kept his finger on the trigger. "Why do you care? I came for Samantha that's all."

Karl laughed. "It's the principle of it. Why do you want her?"

"She's a General's daughter. She doesn't deserve to be in a dog cage."

Before Karl could reply, they heard the handle of the office door. Wearing a red paisley silk robe, Ambassador Demas entered holding a set of keys. He shut the door behind him. The gold tie around his waist loosened from his rotund girth.

"Karl, what is the meaning of this? What have you done? And why is Samantha in the dog's crate?" Dmitri demanded without acknowledging Logan's presence.

The fact that the ambassador skipped over the reason Logan was in a black t-shirt and fatigues with a sidearm at the ready gave him hope.

Karl stood behind the desk and kept the gun on Sam. "You don't have a clue, Dmitri. I am sick of living on the coattails of you and the U.S. government. Generals Yzemikov and Stovall will assassinate their President."

"Are you saying our president sanctioned this act?" Dmitri asked with his hands in his robe pockets.

"He's as clueless as you are," Karl sneered.

"We've come so far. Why would you do this?" Dmitri asked.

"So their Vice President will buy more Russian oil. Isn't that obvious?"

The ambassador tightened his robe belt. "Their election is in a few months. Why not wait for the V.P. to enter into the executive office."

"Because he may not win! You think we want to wait for the outcome? No! We are active in our pursuits. In fact, it's too bad this U.S. soldier entered the embassy unlawfully and shot you. I'll happily take over your position."

Karl raised his gun toward the ambassador. Logan shot him in the shoulder. The noise sent a shockwave throughout the house. When Karl lowered the weapon back to Sam, Logan shot him in the forehead. Karl fell backward into his chair.

Ambassador Demas stepped forward. "Thank you, Major. Give me your firearm and get Samantha out of there. Please return her to her room before security arrives."

"Yes, Sir." Logan practically ripped the cage apart. He gently lifted out his raccoon-faced wildcat. Careful of her shoulder, he cradled her in his arms and hurried to the balcony. "We've got to jump. Can you hang on?"

She wrapped her good arm around his neck. "I'll try," she whispered, squeezing her legs against his sides.

He leapt for the middle balcony and raced to the other side. "I've missed you in my arms," he whispered against her cheek.

"Me, too. Please fix my arm again."

"As soon as we're in your room." He jumped for her balcony and teetered on the edge of the railing. He lost his balance, and they fell backward. Out of nowhere, a huge hand reached out, gripped his arm, and yanked him forward.

"Saving your ass again," Barrett mumbled. "What happened?"

Logan rushed into the dark room. "The short version: the bastard kept her in a dog cage and now he's dead. The ambassador has my gun, and we need to get out of here," he said, setting Samantha on the bed. He sat next to her. She nodded, and he quickly wrenched her arm. She gasped as it reset.

Meanwhile, Barrett entered Samantha's bathroom, reappearing with a wet washcloth. "You won't make it past security dressed like that," he replied. "You need a reason to be here."

Logan took the warm cloth. "What about you?" He wiped Sam's face while she hugged her arm against her.

"I'm covered. I was visiting with Dmitri," Barrett said.

"How'd the ambassador react to the recording?" Logan asked.

Barrett rubbed the back of his head. "Surprised and appalled. Sammy, are you all right?"

She took the washcloth and scrubbed her face. "Yeah," she whispered.

"You have ten minutes to get presentable," Barrett said, striding toward the door.

Logan unlaced Sam's toe shoes. He tossed them aside and quickly stuffed his t-shirt under her pillow. She watched him move in the moonlight.

"What happens now?" she whispered.

"I'm going to scandalize your reputation."

With a smile, he pulled down the sheet and comforter. After tucking her in, he climbed in beside her with his boots still on. While she lay on her back, he moved onto his side and checked her shoulder. With tears in her eyes, she watched him, saying nothing.

"I'm sorry I hurt you," he said, gently massaging her arm. "Will you let me make it up to you?"

She wiped her face and looked away. Moving closer, he played a lock of her hair. She remained silent.

"Sam. Please," he begged. "Please, tell me what you're thinking."

She shook her head.

Alarm shot through him. "I didn't mean any of that with Jillian. I had to get her off the property. The team has her in custody. Please, talk to me."

"You don't still love her?" she asked.

"No. After everything we've been through together, how can you think that?" He touched her chin to make her look at him. "I care about you."

She smiled through her tears and placed her hand over his heart. His thumb pushed her tears across her cheek. As he leaned in to kiss her, the door flung open. The hallway light blinded them.

"Samantha, are you okay?" Mrs. Demas abruptly stopped and stared. "Oh. My."

"I'm fine, Mother," she replied, leaving her hand on his bare chest.

Mrs. Demas smiled as he played with Sam's hair. "See. I knew Miss Martin's School would help you find a man."

"They didn't cover sex at the School for the Proper Lady," Sam replied.

"Samantha, can we at least call it lovemaking?" Mrs. Demas asked with a sigh. "Major, will you be here for breakfast?"

He looked at Sam and grinned. "Yes, ma'am."

Mrs. Demas nodded. "So what was it? The hair? The etiquette? The waltzing? The ballet?"

"The smile," he replied.

Mrs. Demas gave him an approving nod. "Very well, I'll have two breakfasts brought up in the morning."

"Thank you, Mother."

Before she left, Logan called out, "Ma'am, was that a gunshot earlier? Is everything all right?"

Mrs. Demas turned back from the door. "It was. It's a rather ugly incident, so please remain in the room until the investigation is finished."

"Yes, ma'am," he replied as she closed the door. "Are you going to tell her the truth about all of this?"

"I'll let Bear do it. I'd only upset her," Sam replied.

"I'm not sorry I killed him," he said.

"Thank you for coming back."

"Thank you for trusting that I would."

With a quiet mew, Sam shifted away from him. He tried to pull her body back, but she pushed him away. Slipping out of the bed, she limped to the balcony doors.

In the moonlight, he stared at her in her dance dress. Had Karl hurt her again besides shoving her in the cage? Was he too late? He had tasted a small morsel of happiness. Did he destroy his chance for her friendship because he dealt with Jillian first?

Leaving the blankets rumpled, Logan slowly approached her. With her good hand over her face, she sobbed. His heart ached. What could he do? He stopped a few inches from her back. He wanted to reach out for her but resisted.

"Sam, please talk to me. I swear I'll find a way to make it better."

"I'm sorry."

He barely heard her speak. He moved around to face her. "Sorry? You have nothing to be sorry about. I should have insisted that I retrieve the flash drive. I'm the one who put you in more danger."

She stepped closer and rested her forehead on his bare chest. What wasn't she saying? She usually blurted out everything. He couldn't take the silence. With his hands against her wet cheeks, he tilted her head to look at him.

"Samantha Randall, I need you as a best friend. Please, talk to me."

"I doubted you."

"The hurt I put you through made me crazy, but it was necessary to finish our mission. I had hoped you'd have understood that," he said.

"You just thanked me for trusting that you'd come back, but I didn't trust you. I thought you chose Jillian on the staircase. I thought you left me. I lost hope."

"Sam, it's over. You know now that I'll always have your back."

"I love you yet I doubted you. It was wrong of me," she whispered.

He stared at her. She loved him? She knew him for only three days. He froze at the one and only similarity Sam had with Jillian—a whirlwind relationship.

CHAPTER 27

THE SECOND SAM SAID IT, she regretted it. She had known Logan for only three days, but she had known Major McCormick a lot longer through her father's recording. Before she could explain, they heard the doorknob click.

A stream of light shone on the bed as a hand with a gun and silencer slid through the crack. Four thuds into the bed froze her in her spot. Pillow feathers flew. She slowly reached out for Logan, but he had already raced to the door.

Logan grabbed the gun with one hand and slammed the door on the mysterious hand with the other. The gun flew across the room as the figure rammed the door open shoving Logan backward. The man in camouflage pants swiped a knife at Logan, who blocked the hand with his forearm. Logan head-butted the man and kneed him in the solar plexus. When the man threw a punch connecting with Logan's jaw, Sam scrambled for the gun by her bathroom door.

Before she turned back, she heard a sickening snap. Her body shook as she prayed it wasn't Logan's neck. Holding the gun in both hands, she aimed it toward the noise.

"Sam, change your clothes. We gotta to leave," Logan said, grabbing the gun from her.

After blowing out a breath, she raced for her dresser. The adrenaline helped her ignore the pain. In a t-shirt and jeans, she struggled to tie her tennis shoes while Logan tossed the body in the bed. He covered it with the hole-covered comforter. She would never sleep in that bed again.

Turning away from it, Sam put a few things into her backpack. As Logan slipped on his black shirt, the door opened again. Blocking her against the wall, he blended in with the shadows. The hall light showed the beaten body on her bed.

"Oh, no," the voice whispered, stepping into the room.

Logan moved toward the door and the voice. She crept toward her desk lamp. Just as Logan neared the door, she flipped on the light. In his red robe, Dmitri held Logan's gun while Logan aimed the gun and silencer at Dmitri.

Dmitri immediately lowered his weapon and sighed with relief. "Oh, Samantha, thank God."

"Who is he?" Logan demanded as he shut the door.

"Russian Spetsnaz under General Stovall," Dmitri replied.

"Shit. How many men of the special forces team are here?" Logan demanded.

"Ten, well, nine now. Major, we haven't much time. Bear and Martha have left already and will go directly to the White House. They will tell your President that this assassination plot is the work of two generals and my former assistant not my beloved Russia. Please, take Samantha and hide. Please, Major, protect Samantha," he said, urging them toward the balcony.

"What about you? You can't stay. You're in danger, too," Sam said as Logan swung her bag onto his back.

"I must stay. It'll give you time to leave. Дочь, you have done a great service to your country and mine. You, your Bear, and the Major must finish this."

She hugged him. "I love you, Отец. We will meet again soon."

"Yes, now hurry." Dmitri gave Logan his gun back. "They don't know you're here, Major. I took the blame. This Spetsnaz had come for Samantha because she knows of Karl's flash drive," he said before he disappeared into the hallway.

Logan slid his gun into its holster at his side. With the Russian gun and silencer in his hand, he turned off the light and opened the balcony door. He scanned the area below while she wiped her face on her shirt.

"I'll go first. Do your best to climb down. I'll catch you if you can't," Logan whispered before dropping over the side.

With a deep breath, she climbed onto the ivy-covered latticework. Since her right arm had no strength, her left hand did most of the work. She had a hard time descending. When she heard men's voices in her room, she stopped halfway.

Holding out his arms, Logan motioned for her to jump. She fell backward as the balcony doors swung open. With his arms full, he stepped under the balcony while the men scanned the area.

He hugged her against his chest and whispered in her ear, "Can you hang on while I run for it?"

She kissed his cheek and wrapped her good arm around his neck. "We've done it before," she replied, squeezing her thighs against his side. Her left leg rested on his gun as the heels of her tennis shoes pressed into his back.

"I need you to be my eyes behind me. Ready?" he whispered in her ear.

She nodded as the noise above them quieted. In the shadows, he raced across the patio and into the wooded area along the perimeter wall. She told him about the tree branch that she had used. He knew exactly where it was since he and his team had used it before. She scanned the dark woods behind them and saw a glint of a knife blade.

"On your eight," she whispered in his ear.

He stopped, turned, and shot at his eight o'clock position where a man had started to step around an elm tree. She gasped as a man with a bullet through his forehead dropped to the ground.

At the large tree with the branch that extended across the wall, Logan tossed her up and onto the top of the wall. Before she blinked, he was on the other side. She dropped down into his arms again. He held her close as they looked down the dark empty street.

"The bus stop is a block that way," she suggested with a nod to the left.

"You don't happen to have a bus pass, do you?" he asked, walking quickly in that direction. "My ID and wallet are at my apartment."

"I have sixty dollars in my backpack," she replied, gripping his neck.

With his arm around her waist, he squeezed her. "Thank you."

"Are you going to carry me onto the bus, too?" she asked.

He laughed and set her down next to the bus sign. It had been a while since she heard him laugh. She missed it. On one knee, he put the two guns and a knife in her bag. She saw a man stalk toward them in the shadow along the wall.

"Logan, another at your six," she whispered.

When she turned to check the status of the bus from the other direction, Logan stood and casually put her backpack over his shoulder. She looked behind him and saw the lump on the ground next to the wall. She never heard the shot.

"I guess that's three down," she said as the early morning bus slowed to a stop.

Sighing, he checked the area. "And seven to go," he said, following her up the steps.

At five in the morning, Logan eyed the group on the partially full bus then pointed her to the back. With the Memorial Day holiday over, it was back to work for many. The only guy who stared at her was a teenager. When she slid onto the seat behind him, the teen turned to her and grinned with a mouth full of braces.

Logan sat next to her. "Turn around, Boy," he growled in a low voice.

The teen rigidly flipped around in his seat. Logan smiled at her. She thought it was a bit mean but let it go. Constantly checking the back window, Logan sat just as tensely as the boy did.

"Where are we going?" she asked.

He gave her hand a squeeze. "We can't go back to my apartment yet. They may have identified me. How about that motel by the bus terminal?"

She sighed. "Déjà vu."

"Can I be the boyfriend who joins you there?"

"How'd you know about that?" she asked.

"I know a lot about your travels," Logan replied, placing his hand on the gun in the backpack.

After four stops, they stood in front of the dark motel. With money in her hand, Sam entered the office. Logan kept an eye on the area just outside the door. She dinged the bell and waited. The scary old hippy with the long bushy mustache came out of the backroom and scowled. He cleaned his reading glasses as he shuffled closer.

"What the hell do you want so early?" he demanded behind the bulletproof glass over the top of the counter.

"I'd like a room please," she replied, sliding two twenties between the glass and counter.

He eyed her. "I remember you. Did your boyfriend come, too?" She nodded and waited. "I think that's a load of bull. You don't need to make up a boyfriend. I'll be your man."

She shivered as the front door opened. Logan stuck his head inside. "Baby, is there a problem?"

She smiled at the sexy way he called her *Baby*. She turned back to the manager and raised an eyebrow. He sighed and slid the key on the lime green fob toward her. She hurried out the door as the manager mumbled about the broken ice machine.

The sun rose and the traffic increased. Inside the room, Logan leaned on the door and blew out a breath. This room looked just as dirty as the other one. She lifted the bedspread and smiled at the crisp sheets. Suddenly exhausted, she pulled the top sheet down and sat on the bed. After flipping off her shoes, she slid between them.

Logan pulled a cell out of his pocket. She couldn't keep her eyes open any longer. His voice soothed her to sleep. Suddenly awake, she froze from fright at the men talking over each other in the room. Logan had his back to her. He blocked four men at the foot of the bed.

"No," Logan growled.

Thinking he was in danger, she sat up and screamed like a banshee.

Logan jumped while the men stepped closer. He crawled across the bed toward her. "Sam! Sam, what's wrong?"

The men surrounded her, and she scrambled from the bed. Tangled in the sheets, she fell to the floor. She cried out from the tightness in her shoulder.

Logan hurried to help her. "Did you have a nightmare?"

"Who are they?" she whispered.

"Guys from my team. They came to help."

She looked closer. Wearing black fatigues with guns at their hips, they had the same haircut and rigid military stance. "They watched me sleep?" she asked, pushing his hand away from her sore shoulder.

"No," Logan replied.

"Yeah, we kinda did," the shorter one said.

"Shut it, Cho," Logan said.

"She looks older awake," Cho said.

The others nodded. "Maybe fifteen while sleeping," another said.

She scowled as the manager pounded on the door. "What the hell is going on in there?"

"Sam, talk to him. Let him know you're all right," Logan whispered.

"No," she replied. The guys chuckled and stepped backward to the corner of the room.

Logan groaned. "Please," he whispered. "Then, I'll explain why they're here."

The guys silenced their smirks, and she cracked open the door. "I'm fine," she said.

"What's with the screaming?" the hippy manager demanded.

She motioned him closer to the door. "He likes it when I act afraid of his penis. It's not very big. When I pretend to be scared, the sex is better."

The manager snorted. "Well, keep it down or I'll call the cops."

She smiled and nodded. After she shut the door, the guys laughed. Logan narrowed his eyes. "That's not true and it's not funny."

"Yeah, it's funny," Cho replied.

Logan met her at the door. "Do you feel better now?" he asked.

"Yes, and you should have woke me," she replied.

I'm sorry." He leaned down and rubbed his stubbled face against her cheek. "This nice and pretty machine gun will shoot you whenever you're ready," he whispered before nibbling her earlobe.

Blushing, she grinned. "How about now?"

Logan laughed as Cho cleared his throat. "You know it's rude to whisper in front of the group," Cho said.

Smiling, Logan turned back to her. "We'll finish that discussion later. Right now, I'd like to fill everyone in on Barrett's call."

After a brief introduction, Cho and O'Brien sprawled out in the two chairs. She sat in the middle of the bed leaning against the headboard. Martinez and Johnson bounced her as they plopped down beside her. Logan paced.

Martinez smiled at her. "Did he tell you that we expect details?"

She blushed again. "What kind of details?"

"The juicy kind," Cho replied.

"Not juicy," Logan replied with a sigh. "About how we met?"

"Everything?" she asked.

"Everything!" the men replied in unison.

"Later," Logan growled. "Barrett and Mrs. Demas are hiding until Secret Service can escort them to safety. Apparently, the President never received the e-mail with the satellite information attached."

Sam pulled her knees to her chest. "Someone intercepted it?"

"So it's someone who works at the White House and has access," Johnson said.

"There's a mole close to the President," Logan said. "My guess it's anyone Jillian's talked to."

O'Brien spoke, "Jillian and the Colonel are being interrogated by Homeland Security, Secret Service, the FBI, and the CIA. They should get the names of the Russians involved as well as the Americans who gave up the Intel."

"To top this off, whoever deleted the info knows it was sent from General Randall's cabin," Logan said.

"Are we going to retrieve the black box memory card?" she asked.

Logan nodded. "There are seven Spetsnaz on our trail."

"But Dmitri said he didn't tell anyone that you and the team were at the embassy," she said.

"Word gets out," Logan replied.

"So that's who tried to break into your apartment," Cho said.

"When?" Logan demanded.

"After you called, we packed our gear and heard someone at the door," Cho said.

O'Brien continued, "We jumped them and tied them up. So, now we're down to five. That's doable."

"You left them in my apartment?" Logan asked.

224

"Yeah, but we called Secret Service first," Martinez replied.

Logan continued to pace. "Great, those guys will trash my place."

"What's to trash? Your refrigerator and cupboards are bare," Cho replied. "Samantha, have you been there?" She shook her head. "He still lives out of a suitcase."

"It needs a woman's touch," Martinez whispered.

She smiled at Logan, who clenched his jaw. "Can we focus on this national security issue?" Logan asked.

"It doesn't sound too tough. We catch a plane to the cabin and fly back to D.C.," O'Brien said.

"Not quite. Since we don't know who's involved, we're off the grid," Logan replied.

"Road trip," Cho yelled. "Dibs in the car with Samantha."

Logan kicked Cho's chair. "I don't want you and your flatulence anywhere near us."

The guys chuckled. Without another word, they put their duffle bags on the bed. She waited in the bathroom while they changed to street clothes.

Afterward, Logan pulled out an arm sling and helped her put it on to protect her shoulder. Johnson passed out the earpieces. When he handed one to her, she looked at Logan.

"Are you part of the team?" Logan asked.

She grinned. When they paused and stared at her, she quickly lowered her eyes. Logan smiled, but she didn't understand why. He sat next to her and showed her how to work it. His lingering touch warmed her. Wanting sex was one thing. Could he forgive her for not trusting him? She wanted that more than anything.

Within the hour, they left the motel in two minivans that O'Brien somehow appropriated. She had learned that they had extensive combat training and that each had excelled in different areas.

Skilled in hand-to-hand combat, Logan, their leader, strategized. O'Brien was the always-hungry scrounger, Cho was the smart-ass sniper, Johnson was the serious electronic tech and medic, and sweet-talking Martinez handled explosives. Logan had been right. He hadn't needed her help with the Ugly Penis Man by the truck stop dumpster.

While Logan drove her in the black minivan, Johnson and the rest followed in the white one. With their cell phones off, their only communication was their earwig coms, which had a one-mile radius.

She and Logan listened to their banter. O'Brien complained that they had no snacks. Cho and Martinez needed a pillow to snooze and Johnson wanted coffee. She watched Logan smile without comment.

"Logan, when was the last time you slept?" she asked. The guys stopped talking.

"She calls him *Logan*?" Cho asked.

Logan ignored him. "After you locked me in the safe room, I couldn't do anything but rest. I also caught a few hours of sleep on the cargo plane back from Fort Riley."

"Sorry, but I did it so you wouldn't get hurt. Did you change the password?" she asked.

"Hell yeah," he replied. "Have you noticed the team has gotten very quiet?"

"Do you think they're hoping we'd forget they were there, so you'd get sappy sweet with me again?" When he narrowed his eyes and snorted, she smiled.

"Mick gets sappy?" Cho asked.

"Oh yes," she replied. "And he likes to carry me around."

"I bet he does," Martinez replied. "I would."

"Leave it alone," Logan said.

"Hey, what about your promise?" Cho asked.

"Oh right, details about how we met," she said. "Well, I guessed he was an Army Major right off the bat."

"Can you believe she thought I had the superior air of an officer and a nickname like Mac?"

They snickered. "Then what?" Cho asked.

"Then she put her foot in my crotch to get my attention," Logan replied.

"Whoa, nice," Martinez replied.

"I take it she got your attention," Cho said.

"No," she replied with a sigh. "He sent me away, but later he saved me from Ugly Penis Man."

"Who?" they asked as one.

Groaning, she covered the com in her ear with her hand. Biting her lip, she looked at Logan. "That just slipped out," she whispered.

Logan reached for her hand. "I know, and you don't have to talk about it."

She looked out the window and pulled her knees to her chest. "But you made a promise to them," she said not bothering to cover her ear. They had heard her through Logan's com.

"I checked the weather, and we'll hit some rain on the way," Johnson said, changing the topic.

"I don't think it'll slow us down," Martinez added.

"Can you keep up with me?" Logan asked, changing lanes.

"We've got the police scanner. Plug in your radar detector and let's fly," Cho said.

Sam smiled. "Thanks, guys."

"What music do you like, Samantha?" Cho asked. "Mick likes—"

"Don't tell her what I like," Logan said. "I'd like to know what she prefers before you make fun of my song selections."

She laughed. "I like the old stuff of Frank Sinatra and Dean Martin."

"Mick, you told her to say that," Martinez said.

Logan laughed. "I did not." He looked at her. "My favorites, too. Barrett brainwashed me."

She covered her giggle. "That's all I heard at the cabin with my father and Bear."

"Jeez, I suppose you both like John Wayne movies," Cho said.

"*Big Jake* is my favorite," she replied. Logan nodded and laughed.

"Oh for God's sake," Cho said. "You have too much in common."

"Best friends usually do," Logan replied.

Sitting back, Sam closed her eyes and smiled. She liked having Logan as a best friend. She would prove to him that she'd have his back, too. He covered her with his jacket. The warmth lulled her to sleep.

CHAPTER 28

AS LOGAN DROVE, HE GLANCED at Sam sleeping beside him. He missed her smile and laugh. When she had grinned at the guys back at the motel, he knew they finally understood his feelings for her. He adored her sexy sweetness. She complimented his bitter disposition.

She loved him, but which him? The one from the recording or the one she just met? When she got to know the real him with all his baggage, would she be disappointed? She had pined for Major McCormick.

Logan couldn't live up to that. He needed to talk to her; he didn't want any secrets between them. He had learned about the detriment of secrets from Jillian. With a sigh, he realized he loved the idea of loving his ex.

He worried that Sam would only love the ideal, too. As she slept, the team remained unusually quiet. They weren't resting either. He heard snorts and chuckles. Sam piqued their curiosity.

"Are you guys passing notes?" he whispered, glancing again at his sleeping wildcat.

"Maybe," Cho replied.

"I'm not backing out of my promise. We'll discuss it later," Logan said. "It's just ... she's been through a lot and she's still processing it."

"Is she sleeping?" Martinez asked quietly.

"Yeah," he replied, listening to her deep breathing.

"Did that Ugly Penis Man, uh, hurt her?" O'Brien whispered.

"No, I stopped him before he could. Karl, the assistant at the embassy, did," he replied. "She let him, so she could get the wreckage information."

"He's the one you killed?" Cho asked.

Logan sighed. "Yeah."

"Good," Johnson replied.

While they thought about Sam's sacrifice, they spent the late afternoon closing in on the wall of dark clouds. Every car in the eastbound lanes had on their lights. As they neared the storm a few miles away, lightning flashed. They'd have rain for the rest of the trip.

As the water started to pound the van, Sam sat up and looked around. "Where are we?"

Logan turned on his headlights and windshield wipers. "Almost to Columbus."

She looked at his speedometer. "How fast are you going?"

"Only eighty-five, the van starts to shimmy and shake at anything higher."

She shifted in the seat and readjusted her arm in the sling.

"Do you need to stretch?" Logan asked.

"Yes, I really have to go," she replied.

"Thank God," Cho said.

"I'm starving," O'Brien added.

"We're low on gas," Johnson said.

"You could have stopped sooner," she said.

"Talk to Iron Man Mick about that," Martinez said.

"What?" Logan asked. "We're in a hurry. Do I have to remind you that this is a national priority?"

"Come on. The girl's gotta pee," Cho said.

"Fine. We'll fill up at the next truck plaza. I have a fondness for that one anyway."

"Do we get a reenactment?" Cho asked.

"Sure," Sam said. "Cho can play the Major and O'Brien can be me."

Turning the wipers up a notch, Logan laughed. "Does O'Brien know how to use a fire extinguisher and put out a bus fire?"

"I can act like Mick and his superior air," Cho said.

"I am not putting my foot in your crotch," O'Brien replied.

Sam giggled. "Cho will have to carry you around like a rag doll."

"I'd like to see that," Johnson said.

"Forget it," Cho replied.

"Oh, come on, please," O'Brien replied with a laugh.

"Samantha, was there kissing?" Martinez asked.

"No," Logan replied. "But I got a very nice neck and shoulder massage."

Sam looked at him and frowned. "Why did you jump from the truck as if I hurt you?"

"He probably liked it too much," Cho replied.

When Logan mouthed that it was her feminine wiles, she giggled and turned pink. God, she made him feel so light. Heaviness had weighed him down for so long. He needed to kiss her soon. Maybe he'd carry her into the truck stop convenience store. He could say he was protecting her shoulder from the rain. He smiled. She'd see right through it, but he thought she'd still let him.

"Hey, are you passing notes?" Cho asked.

Before Sam could answer, the lightning lit the area and the thunder cracked above them. She gripped the seat with her good hand while the rain pelted the van. Even with the wipers on high, Logan could barely see. Dusk came a few hours early.

Watching the road, the team quieted. A few miles later, he slowed toward the off ramp of the truck plaza. He and Johnson drove directly to the gas pumps under the port, but the horizontal sheets of rain gave them only partial shelter.

Logan stopped Sam from leaving the car. "Wait for me."

"I can't. I really have to go," she said.

"Then, I'll go with you."

They saw the line up behind them as the traffic stopped until the storm passed. "We're in a hurry, and I've got my ear com. I'll be fine," she said.

"We'll walk with her," Martinez replied.

Sam and the rest ran for the store and diner across the parking lot. His wildcat was going to melt. While filling the tank, he and Johnson scanned the area. Johnson paid cash for both vans while Logan drove to a spot not much closer to the door. Cars and trucks quickly entered the parking lot. The mass rushed for the diner.

"I'm turning this off for a few minutes," Sam said.

"No," Logan replied, turning off the engine.

"Logan, I don't want you and the guys to hear."

"No, Sam." He heard a click. "Damn it. Who's by the restrooms?"

"Calm down," O'Brien said. "I watched her go in, and I'm standing next to the door."

"There's an abnormally large crowd because of the storm. Are you watching for Spetsnaz?" Logan asked, jumping from the van. The rain soaked him before he took a second step.

"The diner's clear," Cho replied.

"The store is clear," O'Brien said.

"I can't see a damn thing out here," Johnson said from the van.

"Where's Martinez?" Logan asked, rushing toward the front entrance.

"He's taking a dump," O'Brien replied.

Sam came out of the restroom and touched her com, turning it on. Logan met her next to the fountain drink area. He kissed her lightly at first and then deepened it briefly before stepping back. She gaped at him and swayed. He steadied her as she licked her lips. Grinning behind her, Martinez filled his Styrofoam cup with ice.

Logan moaned at his arousal. "Don't ever turn off your com."

"What'd I miss?" she asked.

"Nothing, you just need to be careful."

She smiled and touched his wet face. "If you kiss me like that when I turn it back on, I think I will turn it off again."

They heard the team chuckle. He raised her chin and kissed her nose. "Please, leave it on," he said.

She nodded. "Do you have any money for a snack?"

"Martinez and his smirk are buying. Stay with him. I'll be right back." Logan groaned at the long line for the men's room.

CHAPTER 29

IN THE PACKED CONVENIENCE STORE, Sam settled on some powdered donuts and a bottle of ice tea. While Martinez waited in the long checkout line, she wandered throughout the store. She found a pack of condoms and added it to his purchases.

When his eyes widened, she smiled. "Safe sex is important," she said.

"What the hell is going on?" Logan demanded.

"Apparently, I'm buying you a pack of Trojans." The guys laughed while Logan growled.

"What? Did you already buy some?" she asked.

"When have I had time?" Logan replied.

"When we were together, you said—"

"Where are you, Sam?" he demanded.

"Jeez, I thought I was being responsible. I didn't think it was a big deal. I'm going to wait in the van," she replied, walking swiftly to the side entrance.

Outside, the storm roared and pummeled the pavement. She barely heard her own words much less Logan telling her to wait for him. When lightning flashed, she saw Johnson running toward her.

"Stay here," Johnson yelled as the thunder cracked.

She nodded, and he entered the store. Under the roof's edge, she watched the river of water flow into the grate a few feet away. Squished against the building to avoid getting wetter, she walked to the front corner. O'Brien and Cho ran for their white van.

Between the thunder and pounding rain, she couldn't hear the team. As she returned to the side door, someone grabbed her from behind. With a wet hand over her mouth, her body left the ground. The motion wrenched her arm in its sling. She didn't hear it, but she felt her shoulder joint slide from the socket. A nervy zap shot to her head. She disappeared into the darkness.

"If you bite my hand, I'll snap your neck," the angry voice said.

Dizziness and nausea radiated inside her body while the rain pelted the outside of it. She recognized his voice. Ugly Penis Man would finally have his revenge.

Praying Logan and his team heard him, she looked for other help. She couldn't see anyone in the heavy sheets of water. Ugly Penis Man mumbled as he rushed toward his patriotic truck. Logan will see it, right? Not in this weather.

Before he opened the back of the trailer, she struggled against him. He squeezed her shoulder. The pain dropped her into a heap on the wet ground.

On a smelly mattress, she opened her eyes and blinked in the pitch dark. The rain vibrated the steel roof. She breathed in the stagnant air mixed with urine and body odor, making it difficult to calm her anxiety from the enclosed space. Her soaked body shivered.

She sat up and heard muffled cries from the space farther into the trailer. As the truck lurched forward, she touched her ear. She lost her com. Logan would be so angry.

CHAPTER 30

IN THE CONVENIENCE STORE OF the truck stop, Martinez paid for their items at the counter. Logan flew out of the restroom and stopped next to Johnson in the candy bar aisle.

"Where is she?" Logan asked.

"Just outside the door. You can't hear anything out there," Johnson replied.

Martinez met them with a paper bag and his super-sized drink. "Where's Sam?" Martinez asked.

Logan growled and hurried for the side door. The roar of the rain and thunder muffled the other voices in his ear. Sloshing through the river along the sidewalk, he turned the corner toward the front of the building. He didn't see her or any other cars past the ones in the handicap parking spaces.

"Sam," he yelled. "Anyone have eyes on her?"

Dismissing the weather, the team converged to his place at the corner of the building. "She's not by the black van," Cho yelled over the rain.

"Who saw her last?" Logan asked.

"I told her to stay put. She agreed," Johnson said.

Before they started a search, they heard a man's voice over their coms. "If you bite my hand, I'll snap your neck."

"Who the hell is that? He doesn't sound Russian," Martinez said, dumping the sack and drink in the nearest trash bin.

"Shit," Logan replied, wiping the water from his face. "That is the Ugly Penis Man. I should have strangled him when I had the chance."

"What are the odds that he'd be here?" Cho asked.

"Start searching for a patriotic cab with a semi-trailer attached. It's red, white, and blue with an American eagle on the hood. Hopefully, Sam will give us some clues."

The team raced in different directions of the enormous back lot. The fact that they couldn't see more than twenty feet in front of them made it worse. Logan put a hand over his com to block out the rain. He heard a steel door slam shut and silence. Was she inside his trailer with him?

"Who's closest to the ramp for the highway?" Logan asked, running toward the front row of parked trucks.

"I'm working my way over there," O'Brien replied. "There's a steady stream of semis that have already left."

Before he could reply, he heard Sam's voice. "Hello? Is anyone here?" she asked.

"Sam," Logan yelled. "Can you hear me?"

"We're here," a young girl replied.

"Her com must have fallen out," Martinez said. "It sounds like she's inside a trailer."

"Yeah, you guys get back to the van. I'll drive the black one around the parking lot first and then follow you out," Logan said. "We only have a mile range with the coms. Don't lose her."

Logan begged her to keep talking. In the van, he started in the back row of the lot and worked toward the front with no luck.

"Who's *we*?" Sam continued.

"With you, there are six of us now," the girl replied.

"My name's Samantha. Can you tell me who you are?"

"I'm Kerrie," she whispered. "The rest of the girls don't talk. He'll hit you if you make a noise."

"How old are you, Kerrie?" Sam asked.

"Fourteen. I ran away from home, and he grabbed me. I want to go home now."

245

"Are Janet and Barbara here, too?" Sam asked.

Logan groaned. "These are the girls from the Amber Alerts. Their pictures had been on the news for the last five days."

"Son of a bitch," Cho replied. "We'll race ahead on the interstate and monitor the coms' range."

"They can only go west, but there are a number of turnoffs," Logan replied. "Stay quiet and listen."

"I'm Janet," the timid voice replied.

"I'm here, too," Barbara said. "How do you know us?"

"Everyone is looking for you," Sam replied. "Are Amy and Tiffany here, too?"

"Yes, they're here. Our parents are looking for us?" Kerrie asked.

"Oh yes, they're worried and want you all home," Sam said.

The knot in his gut continued to tighten. What were the odds of this guy grabbing Sam again? Did he cruise the interstate for runaways like a shark honing in on his prey? Why? Logan cringed at the possibilities.

"Can you come closer to me so we can whisper together? That's much better. You're safe now," Sam said.

"But you're trapped here, too," Kerrie said.

"I have friends who'll find me. They're very good at their jobs."

"Is she talking about us?" O'Brien asked.

"Yeah, shut it and keep listening for some kind of clue," Logan replied.

"How do you know they'll look for you?" Kerrie asked.

"My best friend, Logan, has my back. I trust him to come for us."

"Will he find us soon?" Barbara asked.

"Well, we have to be patient. He has another job to finish first, but he'll track us down afterward."

Logan had forgotten about the memory card. She was right. He already had an assignment to stop an assassination attempt on the President of the United States. He should put that first, but he wouldn't. The greater good could go to hell. If anything happened to Samantha, he would never forgive himself.

"Listen guys," Logan started.

"Mick, she's a team member," Cho said.

"Leave no man or woman behind," Martinez replied.

"We'll get her back and finish the mission," O'Brien added.

"Besides, didn't you say the memory card is locked in the safe room?" Johnson asked. "It'll still be there when we get there."

"Agreed," Logan said. "Can you still hear her? She's starting to break up."

"Loud and clear through Columbus. We're getting closer," Cho said.

"I'm on my way," Logan replied, passing cautious drivers. He slowed slightly before he hydroplaned into the ditch.

"Did that man hurt you?" Sam asked.

"He's smacks us around," Kerrie replied, trying really hard not to cry. Sam must have sensed it, too.

"I'm a little wet, but we can hold hands. The darkness won't seem so scary," Sam said.

"What if your friends don't get here before he stops again?" Kerrie asked.

"Does he stop often?" Sam asked.

"It's hard to tell. We don't know when it's day or night," Kerrie said.

"Who was the first?" Sam asked.

"I was," Kerrie said. "He only opens the back door when he adds a girl. Sometimes he'll throw in some water and food."

"Well, the next time he opens the door, we'll be ready and we'll fight him. There are six of us," Sam replied.

"He has a knife," Barbara whispered.

"I'll grab his hand with the knife and the rest of you can jump him. We'll punch him in his fat gut and scratch out his eyes."

Logan groaned again. Sam couldn't defend herself with one arm. She was taking on the bastard and his knife. The team needed to help her before that happened. Sam and the girls remained quiet. He begged his wildcat to talk—just talk.

"Mick, we're in Columbus with many exits," Martinez said. The team also understood the need for a conversation.

"Give her a minute," Logan replied.

"What's the matter, Amy? I'm right here," Sam said gently.

"I saw his ugly wiener," Amy whispered.

His relief at hearing Sam's voice was short-lived as they heard the topic. Cho swore. Martinez told him to shut it, so they could hear.

"It's okay," Sam continued. "They're not all ugly."

Logan didn't care if she talked about ugly wieners as long as she talked. He accelerated on the slick highway. Her com static finally disappeared. He still couldn't relax. His wipers flicked water off the windshield. The motion shoved water aside; more blocked his view. The loud and rapid swooshes increased his heart rate as if the wipers also knew the significance of finding her quickly. He scanned every truck he passed. He couldn't get to the next one fast enough.

"Samantha, will you talk to us? I like hearing your voice," Barbara asked.

"Is your friend Logan your boyfriend?" Kerrie asked.

"I'm not sure. I'd like to think so, but he hasn't decided yet," she said.

Logan had decided. He wanted to be her best friend and her boyfriend. Keep talking, Sam. Help me find you.

"What's he like?" Barbara asked.

Logan cringed. "Have you spotted the truck yet?" he asked.

"Shut it, Mick. It's getting to the best part," Cho replied. "We were promised details."

"Well, he's handsome and strong. He's serious, but he jokes when I need him to calm my anxiety. His kisses make me feel like a chocolate chip cookie hot out of the oven— soft, warm, and gooey. He thinks he's tough and mean. His job needs him to be, but he has a gentle touch, too. He waltzed me around the dance floor like Fred Astaire."

"He sounds perfect," Kerrie said.

Sam laughed. "He's close, but he has an injured heart."

"He's sick?" Barbara asked.

"Someone lied to him. She broke his trust and his heart. I want to mend it for him."

"God," Logan mumbled. "She already had."

Before she continued, the girls cried out.

Sam groaned in pain. "It's all right," she called out. "He's only turning. Is everybody okay?"

"That was a sharp turn," Kerrie replied.

"Oh no, he's slowing down," Barbara whispered.

"Exit 62," Cho said. "It has a steep right turn off the highway."

"Do you see the truck?" Logan yelled.

"No," Amy cried. "He's stopping. Please, Samantha, don't let him take me again."

"We see his cab with trailer at a stop light in front of a trailer truck distribution center," O'Brien replied.

"I'm almost to the exit," Logan said.

"Don't worry, Amy," Sam replied. "He'll take me this time."

"Shit," Martinez replied, "He just turned into a fenced compound with hundreds of semi-trailers lined up."

"Can you follow him?" Logan said, slowing behind another truck for the exit.

"It's an armed gate," Cho replied. "Maybe we can sneak in."

Logan pulled in behind Cho who parked along the street a block from the gate and its guards. The compound had a center warehouse, but most of the trailers lined the enormous lot. If that bastard dumped the girls into another trailer, they'd never find them, especially in this downpour.

251

The team listened as the young girls cried. Sam tried to calm them, but Logan heard the angst in her voice, too.

CHAPTER 31

THE TRAILER HAD STOPPED AND then lurched forward for the second time. The girls had a grip on both of Sam's arms. The pain in her shoulder kept her alert. They had a plan. She could do this. She took off her arm sling for better movement to overtake his knife.

"Okay, I heard the engine turn off," Sam whispered. "Are you with me?"

"Yes," they replied.

"When the door slides up, I'll jump him and his knife. While he's off guard, you follow and start punching."

"I'm ready," Kerrie said before taking a deep breath.

They helped each other stand. Sam took a step toward the door as he messed with the outside lock and latch. The door rose two feet. The rain became louder and halogen lights beamed across the mattresses scattered across the floor. Three men looked up at them.

"They look ready for a fight," the one said with a Mexican accent. Another laughed and spoke in Spanish.

Ugly Penis Man chuckled, too. "Yes, this bunch is feisty and put up a good fight. I should get double the price."

"Nah, they look scrawny. Not much good for selling over the border to my Mexican friends."

"Then, how about some food and water?" Sam demanded, trying to stall for an idea.

What could they do now? They couldn't take on three men. It was an iffy idea taking on Ugly Penis Man. She looked around for some kind of weapon.

Not far from Ugly Man, her com teetered on the edge of the truck bed. If she could get to it, maybe she could hear Logan when he came for them in a day or so. She needed something to give them hope.

The men laughed and tossed in two wet paper sacks. She knelt down to retrieve them. Pushing the bags behind her, she thrust out her foot and connected with Ugly Penis Man's jaw. He fell backward.

When the other men watched him fall, she palmed the earpiece. In the pouring rain, he swore and demanded retribution.

The other man smiled at her and handed the man a roll of twenties. "She's worth the extra," he said, slamming the door back down. The girls wailed while Sam laughed. She sounded hysterical.

"Samantha, what's so funny?" Kerrie asked. "Our plan failed."

"Maybe this one, but we have some water and food now," she said, putting the com in her ear.

She listened and heard silence. With a sigh, she sat down and opened the bags. The girls reached out to touch her for support.

"If he's going to sell us in Mexico, we'll have to travel south. That may take a while. It'll give Logan time to find us," she said, handing them each what felt and smelled like Hostess apple pies. Nauseated, she left hers in the bag.

"It sounded like three men," Cho said in her ear.

"They're on the move again," Logan replied.

She listened in shock. "Logan?"

"Sam. Baby. Can you hear me?"

She wiped the tears from her eyes. "Yes, I saw the com by the door and put it back in."

"Thank God. We've been following your voice," Logan replied.

"Hang on, Samantha. We've got eyes on the guy pulling out of the gate," Martinez replied.

"Logan, we're not moving," Sam said.

"Samantha, who are you talking to?" Barbara asked.

"My friends are nearby. This will be over soon."

"You're not moving?" Logan asked.

"No, I think he disconnected us from his cab. Can you still find us?" she asked.

"You bet, Baby. Stay strong," Logan replied.

His voice renewed her energy and spirit. She knew he would come. When the girls started to talk as they ate. Sam suggested they go to the corners of the truck and listen.

"Cho, O'Brien, follow that fat bastard while Johnson, Martinez, and I figure out how to get inside the compound," Logan commanded.

"Do you want us to cut him off?" O'Brien asked.

"Wait until he stops. Then jump him. Turn on your phone. As soon as we get the girls, I'll call you."

"Can we punch him in the fat gut and scratch out his eyes?" Cho asked.

"No, let us do it," Sam replied.

Johnson spoke, "Welcome back, Samantha."

"Thank you." She blew out a shaky breath as the semi lurched backward.

"I hear an engine running at the front of the trailer," Kerrie whispered.

256

"Logan, I think we're being reconnected to another cab," she said.

"Damn it, and there are a few lined up to leave," Logan replied. "Sam, can you give me a play by play of your movements?"

She nodded in the darkness. "We just lurched forward."

"Good, we're at the gate. What else do you feel?" Logan asked.

"Um, we're moving slowly. Okay, now he's stopped," she replied.

"Are you moving yet?" Logan asked.

"We just started and now we're turning left," Sam said.

"I got ya in my sights," Logan replied.

"Are you sure?" she asked.

"Just to be sure, have you stopped again?"

"Yes, and now we're turning right," she replied as the girls huddled around her. They waited for news while she quietly waited to hear Logan's plan.

"Have you stopped?" Logan asked.

"Yes, and I don't hear the engine," she said.

She and the girls jumped at the noise by the trailer door. The door flew up. On a deserted road under an overpass, Logan and Martinez smiled. She cried with relief and crawled toward them. She slid down and into Logan's arms.

Dismissing her arm pain, she hugged him around the neck. Her cheek rubbed against his stubble. She was in the best place in the world. Sheltered from the rain under the overpass, she warmed quickly against his soggy chest.

"I knew you'd come," she whispered.

"I was never more than a mile away," he replied, squeezing her tightly. "How about you introduce me to your new friends?"

From his arms, she motioned the girls to the edge. Logan set her next to them. After the introductions, Logan and Martinez assessed the girls for injuries. Cars and trucks raced across the highway above them while they hid in the isolated area a few blocks from the gated compound.

"What happened to those men?" Kerrie asked Martinez. He held out his arms and helped her down. He pointed at the men sprawled out on the pavement with zip ties around their wrists and ankles. Johnson stood guard between them.

"Are they the men you saw earlier?" Martinez asked.

Kerrie nodded. "Can I go home now?"

"Yes," Martinez replied, lifting her back to the edge with the others.

"Sam, we need to talk privately for a moment," Logan said.

She slid back into his arms, and he walked to the side of the semi. She ran her fingers over his wet hair. He kissed her so tenderly that she melded into him. He stared at her as if he wanted to say something. Instead, he sighed.

"We can't be here when the police come. We can't afford any more delays," he said.

Hugging his neck, she nodded. "I understand."

He set her back on the edge while the girls watched him. Uncomfortable with the stares, he handed her somebody's cell phone.

Sam held it out to Kerrie. "I have to leave with my friends. You're back in charge. Call nine-one-one and tell them who you are and the names of the girls with you."

"We're on Senate near Fourteenth Street," Logan added.

"We'll stay until you make the call and then we'll wait in our van until the police arrive," Martinez added.

When Amy started to cry, Sam held her hand. "How about you wait in the cab for the police? It's warmer. You can lock the doors and you'll all be together."

"What should we tell the police?" Barbara asked.

"Tell them the truth," Sam replied.

"What about the fat man?" Kerrie asked. "He's still out there somewhere."

"No, he's not," Logan replied, holding his cell in his hand. "You can tell the police that he's tied up in the Denny's parking lot three blocks from here."

With shaking hands, Kerrie dialed and talked to the dispatcher. Logan and Martinez helped the rest of the girls to the cab. Martinez carried Kerrie to the driver's seat while she stayed on the line. Sam leapt into Logan's arms again, and they rushed to the black van. In the heavy rain, Johnson drove a block away and they watched as four Columbus police cruisers screamed toward the semi.

With the girls finally safe, Johnson left the area and pulled into the parking lot of the Denny's restaurant. He stopped next to Cho and O'Brien in their white van. Logan handed her his ear com and slid the door open. He slammed it shut.

In the rain, Logan stood next to the driver's side of the white van. O'Brien lowered his window and the team heard Logan speak. "Where is he?"

"We locked him in the trailer of his truck," Cho said.

Logan mumbled and then stalked toward the patriotic truck. Cho chased after him.

"Let him, Cho," Martinez said.

"Let him what?" she asked.

"Let him have some payback," Johnson replied.

Rubbing his knuckles, Logan ran back to the minivan. She handed him the com and tried to gauge his emotional state. Drenched, he clenched his jaw.

"What now?" she whispered.

"Since I smell like a wet dog, we need a place to dry off and regroup," Logan replied, flicking the water out of his hair.

CHAPTER 32

WEDNESDAY

AT ONE O'CLOCK IN THE morning, Logan checked them into two rooms at the Fairfield Inn. Dry clothes, clean sheets, and Logan's warmth sounded heavenly. Their brief side trip drained her. Sam had a hard time finding a distraction from the throbbing pain in her shoulder.

"We'll leave at seven and reach the cabin at dusk," Logan said, sliding the passkey into the slot of their room.

Logan tossed his duffle bag and her backpack on the queen-size bed. She shut the bathroom door without a word. Soot and grime covered her face, hair, and arms. Her clothes stuck to her body and weighted her down. Her mother was right; she looked like a boy. She hoped Bear and Martha were safe. She'd ask Logan about them later.

After struggling out of her clothes, she spent a good ten minutes standing under the hot water and another twenty washing one-handed. She hoped those girls would be all right now. She thanked her father for helping her find them.

After the shower, her arm had no strength to lift even the towel. In the mirror, she saw how purple and swollen her shoulder had gotten.

With a big fluffy towel around her, she laid her wet clothes on the heater in the room. Hearing the men talking, she peeked through the center door to the adjoining room. They stopped and stared. Logan swore.

"Would you fix my shoulder again? It's really hurting," she said.

"God," Logan said, meeting her at the door. He ushered her back to their room. "Johnson's our medic. I want him to look at it." He gently sat her at the foot of the bed and knelt beside her.

Johnson set his medical bag next to her. "Is there numbness as well as pain?" he asked as he prodded her shoulder joint.

Wincing, she nodded. When the guys surrounded her, she held her towel tighter with her good arm.

"The joint's twice the size as the other," Cho said.

264

"We can see that," Logan replied, clenching his jaw. "Give her some room."

"Cho, ice," Johnson said as he tested her range of motion.

Martinez tossed Cho the ice bucket. Biting his thumbnail, O'Brien shifted his stance behind them. When Johnson lifted her arm slightly, she gasped in pain. The guys cringed and stepped back. She would have laughed, but the pain made her dizzy.

"What happened to your sling?" Johnson asked, digging around in his bag.

She pulled the corner of the towel up to wipe her eyes. "It's still in the back of that truck."

When Cho entered with the ice, Johnson told them to leave. Logan reluctantly shut the adjoining door behind him.

Johnson chuckled as he set out gauze and white tape. He looked at her and quickly frowned. "Sorry, I'm not laughing at you. It's the first time Mick has followed my instructions without comment. It's also the first time we've seen him openly upset about anything. He's worried about you."

"I would never intentionally hurt him."

He smiled. "We're glad you're in his life, and we're all hungry for hot chocolate chip cookies."

"I guess I've met his promise for details," she said with a sigh. "Is my arm going to be okay?"

"Yeah, once the swelling subsides. How'd this happen?"

"Logan grabbed my arm to keep me from falling into a ravine."

"Do you have a spare t-shirt? I want to secure your arm to your body over the shirt."

She retrieved a gray t-shirt from Logan's duffle, entered the bathroom, then returned to the bed. Johnson wrapped the gauze and white tape around her arm and torso. He laid her on her back between the sheets and propped the plastic bag of ice on her shoulder.

Logan growled from the doorway. "What the hell?"

Johnson rolled his eyes at her and picked up his medic bag. "Twenty on/twenty off for two hours," he replied, passing him for the other room.

"I'm sorry," Logan said, kneeling beside her.

When he touched her hair, she started to sob. "You were supposed to get the memory card first."

Logan wiped her cheek. "I seem to be the guy who has to save the team members first. Can you put in a good word for another medal? The whole team will want one, too."

"That information on the memory card is too important. You should have gotten it first. We've come too far not to finish this," she whispered.

266

"You are more important to me, and we will finish this."

"I love you," she whispered. He opened his mouth, but she stopped him. "When you're dry, would you cuddle with me? I'm cold."

He nodded and kissed her forehead. She would patiently wait to hear the words—only when he was ready to say them. Knowing he cared about her was good enough.

CHAPTER 33

LOGAN PLACED A NEW BAG of ice on her shoulder. Sam shivered until he slid in next to her. Still half asleep, she sighed at the comfort. She turned her head as he lay on his side.

"Why aren't you asleep yet? You should be just as tired," she mumbled.

"I will in another hour. I want that swelling to go down before we leave."

"Sleep," she muttered. "I'll ice it in the van."

She slowly pushed the ice bag to the floor. Logan laid his head on her pillow and kissed her good shoulder. She smiled as his breathing deepened. At some point while they slept, he had put his head on her chest.

Coming out of a deep sleep, she inhaled his Irish Spring Body Wash. She had tenderly rested her good hand on his neck.

With her eyes closed, she rubbed her fingers through his short hair. Hearing a snicker, she opened her eyes and saw the team at the foot of the bed.

Dressed and ready to go, they smiled with their arms crossed. She tugged on his ear.

"Logan, we have company," she whispered. He swore.

The guys chuckled. "She's got drool all over her shirt," Cho said.

"We gotta find some hot chocolate chip cookies," Martinez added.

"Very funny," Logan said. "Get out and give us a couple minutes." She smiled and watched him jump from the bed. "They're going to harass me for the rest of the trip."

"Was it worth it?" she asked.

He laughed. "Yes. You make a very nice pillow. Thank you."

She grinned until she sat up. She groaned at the stiffness. It didn't throb though; it just ached. Progress. She found her dry jeans and struggled to pull them on one-handed.

Logan chuckled as she hopped around.

"I need help with the zipper," she said.

Logan sat at the foot of the bed and pulled her hips closer. As he zipped and buttoned her jeans, his fingers lingered on her skin. "You're wearing my shirt."

"It's softer than mine and feels good against my breasts." She stared into his gorgeous green eyes and smiled.

"I'd rather be taking these off you," he said, tugging on the belt loops of her jeans.

"I liked it when you called me *Baby*," she said.

"What?"

"You said it in a deep sexy voice," she added.

"You liked it when I called you *Baby*?" he asked in that husky voice.

She nodded and stepped closer. His hands roamed under her shirt and caressed her bare back. While she kissed him, they heard the guys clear their throats.

"Come on," Cho said. "We're burning daylight."

She stepped back while Logan mumbled about the interruptions.

"We're hungry," O'Brien said. "They have a free breakfast in the first floor conference room."

"Ooh, yum," she replied, slipping on her damp shoes. "What happened to that box of condoms you bought from the truck plaza?"

271

"I ditched the whole sack when you disappeared," Martinez replied.

"Well, we'll have to get some more," she said to Logan.

The guys stifled their laughs as they walked out the door. Logan leaned down and whispered in her ear, "I'll buy them later, Baby."

She shivered and followed the guys to the lobby for breakfast. On the midweek morning, a few retired couples ate at the tables in the dining area. Manners flew out the window when the guys smelled the food. She stood last in the line as they piled the muffins, eggs, and bacon onto their plates. Then, pushing two tables together, they joked like brothers. Maneuvering toward them, she balanced an orange juice and a plate with a blueberry muffin. The plate slipped from the hand of her sore arm. Logan caught it before it hit the floor.

"Just a muffin?" he asked, carrying her plate and juice to the table. The guys waited for her to sit first.

"Not much of an appetite," she replied, sitting in the offered chair.

"For food, you mean," Cho said with a grin.

She agreed as Logan shifted in his chair. "You don't have a ring on your finger. You have a girlfriend, Cho?" she asked.

"He had one. She dumped him," Martinez replied.

272

"Oh, I'm sorry," she said. "She couldn't take the constant sarcasm?"

Logan chuckled as Cho stuffed half a muffin into his mouth.

She looked at O'Brien. "What's your story?" she asked.

"I play the field," O'Brien said with a grin.

"When was the last time you went on a date?" Logan asked.

O'Brien scowled. "I admit. I've run into a slight dry spell."

She nodded and glanced at Martinez.

"Hey, I have a girlfriend and do just fine," Martinez said.

"Long term girlfriend?" she asked.

Martinez nodded and leaned back. "Six years."

"But you're not engaged," she stated.

"No, he's not," Logan replied, taking pleasure in their squirming.

Johnson answered before she asked. "I've been married for three years," he said proudly.

"Planning a family?" she asked.

Johnson stared at her and then glanced at the guys. "Rachel's seven-months pregnant."

The noise level hit a ten out of ten as the team congratulated him on his successful sperm. The other two

273

couples smiled and sipped their coffee. Sam ate her muffin while they kidded him about fatherhood with dirty diapers and the depletion of sleep and sex.

With the guys in line for seconds, she sat alone with Logan. "I want that someday," Logan said, before taking a bite of his toast smeared with grape jelly.

She smiled and sipped her orange juice. She wanted that someday, too. He may not have said he loved her, but he shared his thoughts. The significance touched her.

"Have you heard from Bear? Do you know if my mother is safe?" she asked.

He pulled out his cell phone. "Let's find out," he said, dialing. He handed it to her.

"Where the hell are you?" Bear yelled into the phone. Logan heard him and mumbled that he was glad she was talking to him.

"Bear, it's Sam. Are you and mother safe?"

"Yeah, the question is are you? Have you seen the news?"

"No, what's happened?" she said, watching Logan sip his coffee.

"That's what I'd like to know. Where's Mick?" Bear demanded.

Sam handed Logan the phone. He took it and sighed. "What?" While he listened, he put his elbow on the table

274

and rubbed the bridge of his nose. The team sat in silence. "They only know our first names. That's it." He motioned for Cho to turn on the TV in the corner of the dining area. Logan suddenly stood tipping over his chair. He seethed and whispered into the phone, "I understand the big picture, Barrett. You must have forgotten the smaller parts." Clenching his jaw, he handed the phone back to her.

"What's going on?" she demanded.

"You need to remember why you left the embassy," Bear said.

"I know why," she replied as the team gathered around the TV.

"Stop distracting him and stay on point," Bear said.

"I'm sorry," she whispered. She couldn't wipe her face so the tears fell.

"Sammy, listen to me carefully. You know the layout of the compound. Help them."

She sniffed her nose. "I will."

"Stop crying."

"I can't help it. You're being unfair."

"It's not about fairness. This is a breach of our national security." Bear inhaled. "Samantha, we have only hit the tip of this gigantic iceberg. Men are on their way to the cabin. They want that black box Intel and they want you—

personally—dead for your interference. This is not a game. Do you understand what I'm saying?"

"Yes. Does Mother know what I did and why?" she asked, biting her bottom lip.

"She's upset that you didn't trust her or Dmitri," Bear replied.

"That's not it. I thought I was protecting them. I've made a mess of things," she said.

"No, but you need to finish this. Make your father proud."

She handed Logan his cell and joined the guys by the TV. Ugly Penis Man's picture took up the whole screen. He had the purple eye that she had given him with the hubcap. He also had a cut on the other eye, a swollen jaw, and a split puffy lip. She glanced at Logan as he absently massaged his knuckles.

Outside the Columbus Police Station, a reporter interviewed Kerrie about what had happened. Kerrie said Samantha, Logan, and their friends saved them. The reporter went on about the police searching for the good Samaritans in the black minivan who had interrupted an extensive prostitution ring that abducted young girls.

"It's time to go," Logan said. Silently, they cleaned their mess and separated the tables. An elderly couple close to the TV observed the report and eyed them suspiciously.

"Kim, don't worry about your dress getting wrinkled," Logan said to her. "We'll be in South Bend for Craig's wedding in a few hours."

O'Brien laughed. "I can't wait to harass him about his losing Fighting Irish."

"Knock it off. How do you think we met our frat brother?" Cho asked.

"We haven't seen our cousin in a year and that's what you're going to hit him with?" Logan replied.

The guys continued the fake banter as they left the room. She looked back at the couple who dismissed their loud antics and finished their meal.

In the morning sunshine, the team quickly piled all their equipment and duffle bags into the back of the white van. The black one had mysteriously disappeared thanks to O'Brien.

Logan wanted everyone together, and Johnson wanted to recharge the ear coms for their use at the cabin. Logan helped her into the back seat with him while the guys climbed in after them. O'Brien took the first shift driving and floored it toward the interstate.

"Bear said other men will be at the cabin. Are they of the same team?" she asked, opening her backpack. She pulled out the hotel's stationery and a pen.

"Yeah, and they're probably already there," Logan replied. "We'll have to take them out before we get into the safe room."

"Why?" she asked, setting her bag on the floor.

"They're Russian military on American soil," Logan stated.

With her left hand, she started to draw a rough diagram of the compound. "There are underground tunnels."

Logan looked closer at her drawing. "Really? Where?"

"One tunnel runs from the gazebo by the pond to the safe room. The other is an underground path from an abandoned barn in a nearby cow pasture to a hidden place in the woods inside the perimeter. Barns, cornfields, pastures, and a farmhouse surround the cabin's property and belonged to Bear," she said, gesturing to her map.

"You're saying Barrett owns a farm?" Logan asked.

"He owns the land, but a farmer works the fields, milks the cows, and raises the cattle."

"So we can go from the abandon barn right to the safe room," Logan said.

"No, each tunnel is separate for security reasons, but they're close enough to get to."

Cho angled his body to look at her drawing. "We were there before without a problem."

"Nobody was looking for us then," Johnson said.

278

"The rail fences surrounding the property are hooked up to the motion detectors that alert the cameras in the safe room and the security company, but the perimeter security is still turned off. I never reactivated it," she said. "From inside the safe room, I can check the monitors and let you know where they are, so no one gets hurt."

"We'll sneak Sam inside and then take out the five men. They should be along here and here," Logan said, pointing to areas on her diagram.

"How do you know?" she asked.

"Russians are predictable," Logan replied.

"Up close, they're quick and deadly, but they're not much on strategy," Cho said.

"Couldn't we get the flash drive and wait for the Army to take those men?" she asked.

"We could," Logan said with his arm around her, "but they could get away and keep tracking us and you. It's safer to stop them now. I know it sounds callous."

"I get it. Kill or be killed," she replied.

O'Brien looked at her in his rearview mirror while the rest turned back to stare.

"What?" she asked.

"It's surprising to hear that harsh comment come out of your mouth," Cho said.

"Why? Because I'm a woman?" she asked. "My father was a General and Bear is my godfather. I've been shooting guns since I was eight."

Logan raised an eyebrow and smiled. Cho and the rest laughed. "You hunt?" Cho asked.

"Only skeet. I went squirrel hunting with Bear once. I shot one and cried."

"Are you any good?" Cho asked.

She shrugged. "Do I get a gun?"

"Can you hold one with your sore arm?" Logan asked.

"I can try. I'll want this gauze and tape off before we get there."

Logan nodded. "When we get there."

"Don't worry, Cho. I won't embarrass and outshoot you," she said.

"Hey, I have a hundred percent kill rate," Cho replied, taking her sketch for a closer look. Logan frowned and Cho quickly turned toward the front.

"I'm not as fragile as you think," she said.

"I'm learning that," Logan replied.

CHAPTER 34

WHILE CHO AND JOHNSON DISCUSSED the layout from the sketch, Sam leaned against Logan in the back of the van. He slid her across his lap, and she pressed her ear against his chest. His chin rested on the top of her head.

He had learned that Sam wasn't some fragile porcelain doll. The vulnerability was there, but she held her own more than once already. It didn't stop him from worrying about her safety.

The guys joked and harassed each other, but there wasn't a better team out there. They had counted on one another enough times not to doubt it. That's one of the reasons the military kept them together.

The elite Soviet group, called Spetsnaz, has trained for kidnappings and assassinations although their military denies it. They carry silencers, assault rifles, combat knives, and different types of hand grenades. That's just their basic equipment. These guys don't mess around.

Logan wasn't surprised that Ambassador Demas was afraid of these men. Over the years while the Russian government changed, their military had, too. Most Spetsnaz units were rogue and for hire now. They were not a pretty part of Russian history.

Sam's earlier assessment was partially accurate. *Kill or be tortured and then killed.* Logan wanted to leave her somewhere, but they needed her knowledge of the property. His team would be evenly matched in hand-to-hand combat. Their advantage was the detailed layout of the compound as well as the tunnels. He prayed that Sam understood the seriousness. He hadn't told her that he killed the other Russians by the ravine although she knew about the other three at the embassy. Did she understand that this was his job? He wouldn't always be as cold and heartless.

"Promise me you'll follow orders," Logan said, running his hand through her wafts of curls.

"I won't endanger the team or compromise your mission, but it'll cost you," she said.

"Cost me what?"

"A kiss now and sex later," she whispered.

He laughed. "My kind of deal," he replied, before kissing her cheek.

"On the lips, Mister," she said. "Make me feel like a hot chocolate chip cookie."

Damn! When she said stuff like that, he lost his mind. He made sure the team wasn't watching. He tipped her back and gently kissed her. When she bit his bottom lip, he groaned and deepened their kiss. God, she could get him so worked up. He wanted to climb on top of her. Cho swore, and they separated to catch their breath. He almost didn't care about their public display.

"If I drive off the road, it's your fault, Mick," O'Brien yelled from the driver's seat.

"Damn," Cho repeated. "Turn on the A/C. The windows are fogging up."

Sam blushed and licked the wetness from her lips. She was so damn sexy.

"Do I have to separate you kids?" O'Brien continued.

To keep from having his way with her, Logan set her back on the seat beside him. "Nothing more to see back here," he said, rubbing his hand over the top of his head. He needed to calm down. He shifted and tried to make room in his jeans.

"Samantha, will you make us some homemade cookies?" Cho asked.

"No," Logan replied. "They're all mine."

She smiled and pulled her knees to her chin. She rested her cheek against them and looked at him. She kept her voice low. "I want to rip off your shirt right now and rub my breasts against your chest." He groaned. He needed a larger pair of pants.

"Damn, I heard that," Cho said from the seat in front of them. "Do we have to hose you two down?"

"She started it," Logan replied with a chuckle.

"Don't make me stop this car," O'Brien said, scowling in the rearview mirror.

Logan had snuck kisses from her all morning. In the early afternoon while she dozed, he and the guys discussed their tentative plan. They'd alter it as needed. With the layout memorized, they quieted. He knew they ran through a set of scenarios in their head to prepare. He did, too.

After the last rest area, Logan drove and Sam sat next to him. The closer they got, the more she squirmed. "Are you scared?" he asked.

"No, you're with me. I'm excited to see Yellow Springs. I miss it."

"You grew up there?" he asked.

She nodded. "I thought I'd move back and teach dance. Ms. Anderson, the local dance teacher, is close to retirement."

Logan winced. What about him? Would she make room for him in her life? Were they temporary? He wanted to ask her, but he held back, especially with the guys watching his every move. He glanced at Johnson sitting behind Sam. Johnson caught his reaction to Sam's statement and frowned at him.

Johnson motioned for him to say something. When Logan shook his head, Johnson rolled his eyes and turned away in disgust.

As Logan drove into Yellow Springs, Sam looked out her side window. Before he could probe her idea to move back, Cho interrupted.

"What kind of hippy town is this?" Cho asked. "Every tree along the main street is wearing a knitted sweater around their trunks."

Sam smiled. "A lot of retired writers, musicians, and artists live here. My dad used to say that the town had committees for everything. They never got anything done except talk about it to death. Even though it drove him crazy with their inaction, he loved this town."

Sam pointed out the elementary school with its finger paintings in the windows, the small movie theater that was showing an art film on whale dancing, and an antique shop with an overgrown lawn that was supposed to be more an earthy statement and less laziness in lawn care.

Martinez chuckled. "They have an organic grocery store? You people only eat healthy tofu?"

"Some tofu, but mostly it offers food without pesticides. Quinn's Diner, over there, has the best omelets for breakfast and the best liver and onions for dinner."

Logan made a face at her. "How about a thick juicy steak?"

"Dugan's Bar, over there, has the thickest steaks. It's Bear's favorite restaurant. His picture's on the wall for eating an enormous steak. He gave me the t-shirt."

With an hour until dusk, Logan drove around the town. He enjoyed her enthusiasm and observed the families walking along the sidewalk toward the elementary school playground. A dad pushed a stroller out of an ice cream shop. It put ideas in his head. The town seemed to be a perfect place to live and raise a family.

"Oh," Sam continued, "Kassiopeia's Shop on the corner has bath salts, candles, and incense. It smells so good inside. There's a holistic health center next door. They offer reflexology, acupuncture, and massage."

"Massages? Now, we're talking," Martinez said.

"Therapeutic massage not the other," she replied. "Oh, and they have a park by Rabbit Creek next to the high school. Every Friday during the summer, they have different musical bands ranging from folk to rock. Since the cabin is only a couple miles from town, my dad and I would ride his tandem bike to the festivals." She took a deep breath and whispered, "We could do it."

The statement took him by surprise. What was going on in her head? Before he could respond to her question, the banter started behind them.

"What did she say?" Martinez asked from the very back.

Cho turned back to him. His whisper wasn't quiet enough. "She wants him to hang out with her here."

"I will if Mick doesn't," O'Brien replied next to Martinez. "I'll play house."

Johnson scowled at them. "Shut it and let them talk. Jesus, you guys are a pain in the ass. Stop killing their moment."

Frowning, Sam sighed. "Logan, if you take the next street on the left, we can park in a wooded area across the street from the farmhouse and pasture."

Having missed their moment, he nodded. After a few miles, she pointed him to a muddy two-track that disappeared into a thick wooded lot. He hid them from the road and quickly turned off the headlights. With the interior light on, the team silently unloaded their bags and changed into their black fatigues. She yanked on the gauze and tape. With the large sticky ball on the passenger seat, she found a black t-shirt in her backpack. She stripped off her oversize shirt.

"Whoa," Cho said.

"Sam, in front of the guys?" Logan asked.

"I'm sure they've seen breasts before and mine aren't even very big."

Logan stalked over to her. "They don't need to ogle my girlfriend's breasts," he said, blocking her from them. He helped her with the black shirt.

"Am I your girlfriend?"

"Yes, and I want a private tour of Yellow Springs later. For now, I need you to be careful and to keep me focused."

She nodded. "Do you have a handgun for me?"

He handed her his smaller backup. He smiled as she quickly checked the clip and reset the safety. After giving her an extra clip, he added his knife and sheath to his thigh. Johnson handed out the coms while O'Brien distributed the night vision goggles. Without a spare pair of goggles for her, she stuck the com in her ear.

They silently jogged down the two-track back to the road. The sun from the day had dried most of the leftover rain except a few deeper puddles. He hoped their boot prints wouldn't draw attention.

Before putting on his goggles, he scanned the pasture across the road. Thirty cows crowded the newer well-lit shelter close to the farmhouse while half a dozen wandered around in the dark by the abandoned barn in the center of the field.

CHAPTER 35

WITH SAM RIGHT BEHIND THEM, they ran toward the electric wires that created a barrier for the cattle. Logan quickly crawled under the bottom wire. Sam slid under without a problem. She tucked her gun in her back waistband and wiped the dirt from her hands to her jeans.

As the last one through, Cho bumped his long sniper rifle on the wire. It sent a jolt through him. He flinched but, at least, didn't yell. The cows chewed their cud and seemed to shrug at them as if soldiers invaded their pasture all the time.

The team continued to the dilapidated barn where the cows moseyed and mooed. While Logan scanned the interior, Martinez tried to shoo them away. Three partial sides and a holey roof housed two rusted tractors and bales of moldy straw. In a rush, Sam used her foot to push loose straw away from the middle of the barn between the tractors. Logan helped until Cho swore.

"I lost my com and stepped in cow manure," Cho whispered, wiping his boot on the edge of the bale.

"Here," Sam whispered, holding out hers. "Take mine."

"Jesus, Cho, you're making us look bad in front of Samantha," Martinez said.

"You smell like shit," O'Brien added. "My hay and mold allergies are starting to act up."

Sam stopped sweeping the straw with her foot. "Why are you joking? This is serious."

Johnson stood guard at the missing wall and prevented the cows from entering. He looked over his shoulder. "They think they're easing your mind."

She frowned at them. "Well, it's not, so shut it and focus."

"We should start calling you *Baby Bear Barrett*," Cho mumbled as he quickly stuck the com in his ear.

Scowling, Sam knelt beside the cleared space. One-handed, she yanked up a worn three-foot plank. Logan took it from her and pulled back two more. Below the wood floor, they found a three-foot cement hole with a sewer lid in the center of the slab. She dropped into the square space.

"You'll have to help me pry this open. I haven't the strength," she whispered.

Logan slid down next to her. "There's no security?"

"Down below," she replied. "Do you have a flashlight?"

Logan handed her the light from his leg pocket and pried open the heavy steel sewer lid. Sam aimed the light at the ladder adhered to the deep cement hole. He climbed down first, then Sam, and the rest. They heard the cows clomp into the barn as Cho replaced the planks and sewer lid. The team waited at various points on the twenty-foot ladder.

At the bottom of the tight fitting hole, Sam flipped up a cover over a security access box for the submarine type door next to it. "You have to type in the main password before I can type in the number code." While she held the flashlight on the box, he typed in the one word password. "That's lame," she said, looking around his arm. "The whole world could have figured that out."

He snorted. "Not as wrong as your previous password," he replied, stepping back so she could finish.

She punched in some numbers. "You didn't guess mine, did you?"

They heard the door lock release. Logan quickly turned the large circular latch and pushed open the door. They winced at the loud grating of the rusted hinges.

After taking the flashlight back, Logan stepped over the ledge and into the dark cement tunnel—no hunching necessary. The men dropped and entered. Their movements were incredibly loud and echoed in the silence. From behind them, Sam locked the door.

Taking the lead, Logan crunched on some dead bugs and pushed some webs out of the way. The stale air smelled like dirt and mildew.

"Samantha, you're holding my hand," Martinez said.

"There are spiders down here, so I don't care whose hand I've got," she replied.

Logan sighed and shone the light back at them. "Let her through."

He smiled as she latched onto his belt loop. He set a fast pace through the tunnel and finally stopped at another submarine door. Sam typed in the code.

"What hides the door above?" he asked.

"A large stump," she whispered. "It has a hinge and opens in the center. Dad and Bear liked watching Hogan's Heroes."

The guys snickered as Logan hustled up the ladder. At the top, he pushed up the lid and found himself in the middle of the wooded area inside the compound. Using his night vision, he scanned the area.

With an all clear, they slowly moved toward the edge of the woods. From the shelter of the trees, the men scanned the area. Cho set up his sniper rifle with silencer and aimed it at the man pacing next to the gazebo.

After Cho shot him in the head, Logan and Sam ran for the gazebo. He would assist her in the safe room and communicate the location of the Spetsnaz to the rest of the team.

Sam crawled under the two-foot gap between the gazebo floor and the cement slab. With his assault rifle in front of him, Logan crawled after her to another sewer grate lid. He pulled it up and slid it across the cement. They cringed again at the noise of metal on cement.

"Hold," Cho said in his ear. "There's a guy at the path's edge."

"Don't move," Logan whispered to Samantha.

They waited for Cho to shoot him. Seeing the man drop to the ground, Logan motioned for Sam to go first. She shook her head and whispered about spiders. He lowered himself a couple of steps into the hole. Before he could grab his weapon, a spray of bullets shredded the gazebo. Slivers of wood exploded in the vicinity.

As he reached for Sam, he lost his footing. He fell halfway before grabbing a rung. His night vision goggles shattered at the bottom.

The team fired at the wounded man who continued to spray the gazebo. Sam grunted. The man hobbled toward them and used the gazebo to block the shots of the team.

"Sam, slide me the rifle," Logan yelled, scrambling back to the top.

Lying flat on her abdomen, she reached for his rifle. In a jagged section of the gazebo floor, she saw the shadow move closer.

She aimed the rifle through the open space and shot the man in the chest just before the roof collapsed onto the wood floor. The abrupt silence of the weapons and falling gazebo made his ears ring.

"Baby, are you hit?" he asked, pulling her by her good arm closer to the ladder.

"My leg," she whispered.

He felt along the back of her thigh and found a sliver of wood sticking out. Thankful that it wasn't a bullet, he reached for his flashlight, but it dropped into the tunnel entrance.

"I need to pull out the wood. It doesn't seem like it's in too deep," he said.

"Hurry before more men come." She gasped as he pulled out a two-inch long piece of wood. "Cho's kill shot percentage just went down," she whispered.

"We'll have words with him later," Logan said, helping her into the tunnel. "Hug me and we'll go down the ladder together."

Before he lowered them to the floor of the tunnel, Logan pulled the round sewer plate back across the hole. It didn't matter since the gazebo partially collapsed around them. They'd have to leave through the safe room door.

While the team scattered and stayed hidden, Logan held Sam tightly against his chest as he climbed down the ladder. She typed the new set of numbers into the access panel by another steel submarine-type door. He spun the wheel and opened it.

Leaving the shattered flashlight on the cement floor, he walked quickly down the corridor. "God, this is worse than carrying you through the woods in the dark."

She laid her cheek on his shoulder and weakly held on to him. "My gazebo's ruined."

"I'm sorry. I'll fix it," Logan whispered in her ear.

"I got eyes on a third man," O'Brien said in Logan's com. "He just saw the two dead men."

"Take him out," Logan replied. He heard shots through his com and a lot of swearing.

"He ducked back into the woods," Martinez said.

"Stay out of sight. We're almost to the safe room," he said as Sam typed in the code numbers. "Hang on, Baby."

"I'll try."

With her good arm around his neck, Logan hurried up the ladder and pushed up on the plywood floor. The three-foot square piece slammed into the bed above it. After shoving the board away, he pushed the bed aside one handed.

"We're in," he said. "Give us a moment."

Logan carried Sam to the monitors and carefully set her down. She winced. While she clicked a few buttons, he palmed the satellite's memory card and slid it into his zippered pants pocket at his thigh. He scanned the monitors of the different areas.

"All right, we got one guy at the west end of the property by the pond. Martinez, take him out," Logan said.

"On it," Martinez replied.

Logan leaned forward. "The other two are by the pole barn and the driveway on the east side. Johnson, O'Brien, take them out."

"Yes Sir," Johnson said.

"Cho, take the north side of the property by the house. I don't see anyone else. Once you take out those three, we'll meet in the cabin."

Logan and Sam watched Martinez creep around the pond to a place in the tree line. Sam groaned while Martinez used his night goggles to sneak up on the man. Twenty yards away, the man turned and took a shot but missed. Martinez didn't. Sam blew out a breath.

They switched their gaze to the east side cameras. At the northeast corner of the house, a man had a grenade in one hand and his sidearm in the other. Logan informed the team.

Just after the man pulled the pin to throw it, Cho shot him. His body exploded as it hit the ground. Flesh went flying. Sam mewed and covered her mouth. Grimacing, she pulled her sore arm across her body.

"I'll clean that up," Logan said.

"That doesn't matter. I don't want the guys to get hurt," she replied.

While the team carefully tracked down the fifth man, Logan checked the monitors of the rooms inside the house. He caught movement.

"Sam, are there blind spots on the cameras?" Logan asked.

"Yes, if you know where they're located. Most people who visit haven't a clue."

"Damn," Logan replied.

He and Sam watched the fifth man run for the tree line, but he wasn't quick enough. Logan stopped the team from approaching the house.

"I'm seeing shadows. We have one maybe two more hidden in the blind spots of the cameras. Proceed with caution," Logan said.

"Logan, what's that by the backdoor slider?" She pointed at the faint wire next to the handle.

"Hold," he yelled at the team, "The door's been booby trapped."

"All of them?" Johnson asked as the team backed into the woods. They crouched down to wait.

"We're checking," Logan replied.

Slowly, Sam stood next to him and leaned on the table for a clearer view of the monitors. He stared at the blood on the chair from her thigh. She was ignoring her pain? He clenched his jaw as she zoomed in the camera to see explosives attached to the slider and the front door.

"What about the windows?" she asked.

"They're wired, too, except for the General's bedroom," Logan replied.

"Setup?" she asked.

"Yeah, a blatant setup," he replied. "Do you see any shadows?"

Suddenly, someone turned the camera in the living room upward. The General's office camera followed a second later.

"We have at least two in the house," Sam said, easing back into the chair.

"Damn it, we lost visual in the house," Logan said to the team.

"Leave through the tunnel," Cho said.

"What's left of the gazebo is covering it," Martinez replied.

"I'll do it alone. They may not know we're in the safe room," Logan said.

"Of course, they know," Sam said. "They just dismantled the cameras."

"She's right, Mick," O'Brien replied.

"If you have a better idea, I'm listening," Logan said.

Sam hugged her sore arm to her chest. "I'll help you."

"It's too dangerous out there. Stay here and listen through the monitors. I'll free a door and let the team in," Logan said, handing her his com. "You can't be my eyes, but you can be their ears."

CHAPTER 36

LOGAN TURNED OFF THE LIGHTS in the safe room and left before she could change his mind. In the silent dark house, he scanned the living room. He crept toward the slider and glanced at the detonator and explosives. He needed more time to focus on it without the interruption of someone wanting him dead.

Hearing boots on the carpet in the hallway, Logan moved toward the corner behind the couch. With his assault rifle resting on the back of the couch, he waited. The voice he heard next surprised him. Sam recited the Pledge of Allegiance from her bedroom. Footsteps thumped down the hallway and bullets sprayed her room.

Her tired voice came over the speaker in the living room. "Don't worry. I'm safe," she whispered. "Sounds like only two."

Logan smiled and worked his way toward the hallway for a better angle. He doubted they'd fall for her voice again. He stepped carefully down the hall. Sam's bedroom door slammed shut. He heard an argument behind it. Man, he wished he understood Russian. He slipped into the General's bedroom across the hallway. With the door left open, he watched Sam's door.

"Logan, get out of there," Sam whispered over the speaker in the General's room. "I understood a little. One of them wants to blow up the house after they get the drive. The other wants to blow it up without it."

"Sam, go to the gazebo. I won't let them blow up your house," he whispered back.

"Come back to the safe room. I don't care about the house. I care about you," she said.

Hearing Sam's voice, the men shot holes through the bedroom door in hopes they'd hit someone. When they stopped to put in fresh clips, Logan ran for the living room. Before he could type in the code, someone told him to stop. With his rifle, Logan slowly turned.

General Stovall aimed his pistol at him. "Drop your weapon."

Logan slowly sidestepped toward the slider and set the gun on the coffee table. He held up his hands in defeat. Stovall turned on the table lamp and tossed his goggles aside. With his jagged scar down the right side of his face, his smile reminded him of the melted face of a zombie with a weird off center crease.

"Give me the memory card," Stovall demanded.

"What memory card?" Logan asked.

"Don't be stupid, Soldier. Give it to me and you will die quickly."

"I don't have it," he replied.

Over the speaker, Sam's voice broke the tension. "I have it, General. Drop your weapon or I'll transmit this information to every news outlet around the world."

Her bravado sounded weak. Was her pain worsening? Logan stayed close to his weapon and casually lowered his hands.

"Samantha Randall, that may take a while. You're soft like your father. Give it to me now or this man dies."

"Have you ever heard of YouTube? All I have to do is press *Upload*," she replied.

Calling her bluff, General Stovall shot the ceiling. "Now, Samantha."

"Don't do it, Sam," Logan yelled.

A moment later, the safe room doors opened. From the doorway, her bruised arm dangled while she held her other hand behind her back. Letting down his guard, the General angled his weapon away from them and walked closer. With lightning speed, she pulled the backup handgun from behind her back and shot Stovall in the chest. Logan grabbed his rifle. After checking the body, he rushed to her.

"My father never liked him," she whispered, steadying herself against him.

Before he could shove her back into the safe room, General Yzemikov shot at them from the hallway. "That was a warning. Drop your weapons and move away from that room."

Logan tried to block Sam, but she stayed planted next to him. They were going to have a serious talk about strategy and tactics. The General's daughter should know better. He set their weapons on the floor.

Grimacing, Sam took a deep breath. "What kind of sad ... military do you run, General? A girl killed ... your soldier and a high ... ranking General."

Logan looked down at her and her heavy breathing. Was it nerves?

"For that, you will pay," Yzemikov replied. "I will enjoy torturing Randall's daughter. However, I can make it quick if you give me the memory card."

Sam held out a fake one. When she stepped between them, Logan reached for his combat knife. He waited for her to move aside. She slowly limped toward the General. Instead of setting the drive in his open hand, she slumped to the floor. The knife flew from Logan's hand and landed in Yzemikov's neck. The team's bullets hit the General's torso.

"All clear," Cho replied from the basement door. "Nice work, Samantha. She helped us out and dropped when we told her to."

"How'd you get in here?" Logan asked, kneeling beside Sam.

O'Brien, Martinez, and Johnson joined Cho in the living room while Sam clutched her bruised arm and started to pant.

"We came in through the pole barn's basement," Martinez said. "You showed us the way when we loaded up the satellite. Your code was lame."

"SAMANTHA was all I could think of," Logan said, looking closer at her. She wasn't moving. "Sam, what's wrong?"

Her shallow breathing made it difficult for her to answer. "My shoulder's ... on fire," she whispered.

Johnson set his gun aside. He slid his hand behind her shoulder and pulled out his bloody hand.

"Help me turn her onto her side," Johnson said.

Logan put her arm across her chest and held her steady while Johnson tore the neck of her shirt. A jagged hole tore through her soft skin between her spine and her bruised shoulder. Blood oozed. She had caught a ricocheted bullet at the gazebo. All this time, she had it inside her. Logan wanted to vomit.

"It must have lodged deeper when she fell. Get some towels and hot water. Mick, help me get her to the dining room table," Johnson said.

"Hang in there, Baby," Logan whispered in her ear as he picked her up.

"Don't let ... Mrs. Kelley ... see the mess," she said on a raspy exhale.

Johnson tossed a couple couch pillows on the table and motioned for him to lay her on her side with the pillows propping her at an angle. Cho had four towels, Martinez had a big bowl of hot water, and O'Brien held Johnson's medical bag.

Logan avoided looking at what he had done to her and focused on her face. He tried to sound as if this was a common occurrence with the team. "Who's Mrs. Kelley?"

"We'll get ... someone else ... to clean ... the house," she whispered.

Logan held the hand of her bruised and dislocated shoulder to keep her from flinching while Johnson worked. Logan moved closer. His nose touched hers.

"I'll put the Army on it. We'll have the place looking as good as new," Logan said.

Tearing more of her shirt, Johnson frowned and looked closer at her wound. "The bullet's between your ribs. Samantha, I need you to hold still. It's going to hurt. Mick, are you all right? You look a little green."

He wasn't all right. His stomach clenched into a tight ball. Johnson mouthed for him to hold her down. Pressing her lips together, she whimpered while Johnson used his forceps. The team surrounded her and fidgeted. She gasped in pain, and the guys gasped from her pain.

Johnson told them to disarm the explosives from the doors and windows. Happy with something to do, they ran from the room.

Logan kept her from squirming. Her cries of agony would stay in his head forever. He couldn't get past his incompetence. He should have checked her better for other injuries. He had jostled her causing the bullet to move deeper. He failed her. She had looked to him for protection. Now, her blue and green eyes pooled with accusing tears. How could he have let this happen?

"Sam, look at me. Does Yellow Springs have old crooners at their Friday night concerts?" Logan asked.

"Some ... times."

"Well, I'm not riding in the front on the tandem bike because I don't think you'd pedal in the back. You'd make me do all the work."

"Samantha, take a deep breath. This is going to hurt," Johnson said. She screamed and passed out. "I can't pull it out. It's stuck in her rib. It's affecting her breathing. She needs a hospital."

With Sam unconscious, Logan rushed to the safe room. He picked up the red phone and made his demands.

CHAPTER 37

THURSDAY

THROUGH A PAINFUL HAZE, SAMANTHA looked around. Inside the cabin, Logan issued orders over the whirl of a helicopter just outside. The swaying chandelier over the dining room table blinded her while the plastic smell of the oxygen mask made her queasy. Someone had strapped her to a flat board. Where was she going?

Glancing at the clock, she saw the hands at midnight. Where had the time gone? She thought dusk was only an hour ago.

Her back throbbed. It hurt to inhale. Her body jostled slightly as O'Brien and Johnson picked up the board. When the slider opened, the helo roared.

"Mick, she's awake," O'Brien yelled.

"Hey, Sam, you're going for a ride on a Blackhawk," Johnson added.

"Why?" she whispered against the mask. They must not have heard her.

"Hey Baby, I'm right here," Logan said.

Logan walked with her as O'Brien and Johnson moved her toward the roaring noise. She turned her head slightly and saw a group of soldiers next to the enormous Blackhawk. In full combat gear, the soldiers jogged toward Logan.

"Get her inside. I'll be there in a second," Logan yelled to O'Brien and Johnson. He turned toward the other men who saluted him. "Lock down the cabin and property. Nobody gets in until our mission has been verified as complete. Captain, document the scene. You can compare your findings with our written accounts later."

Sam grimaced as they lifted her into the Blackhawk. Logan jumped in after them and shut the side door.

"Let's go," Logan yelled.

Lying in the middle of the floor, she looked up at Logan's team. They sat back but didn't relax. She struggled to speak.

"Sam, don't talk right now," Logan said. "We gotta get you to a hospital, and the President thinks this is the quickest and safest way."

Cho leaned forward, so she could see him without moving her head. "Mick blackmailed the President of our United States."

"I did not. I just said that me and the satellite's memory card weren't separating until Sam was out of danger," Logan replied.

"It sounds like blackmail to me," Martinez said.

Logan shook his head again. "He offered to help Sam any way he could." He leaned in closer. "He likes you."

"Give her some room," Johnson said. "I want to add some pain meds to her IV."

"The helo came fully stocked with medical supplies. Compliments of the President," Cho said.

"I wonder if we'll get to meet him," O'Brien asked.

"Probably," Logan replied, "and a bunch of senators in a private congressional committee hearing. They want a play-by-play of all our activities."

"We were covert. Can they do that?" Martinez asked.

Logan nodded. "They want this international issue with the Russians resolved now."

Johnson squeezed the IV bag and snorted. "Many of those on the committee were pushing for the Russian oil treaty. They'll make us look bad to repair U.S. and Russian relations. Mark my words."

"Well, whatever their motive, we have to write individual reports," Logan said.

"They'll scrutinize everything," Cho said.

Sam had many questions, but the drugs lulled her to remain quiet. She vaguely remembered landing at a hospital.

What seemed like minutes later, she woke in a hospital bed in a private room. Large fragrant and colorful flower arrangements filled the windowsill.

The smell of roses wafted toward her and reminded her of the rose bushes at the cabin. She wondered if Mrs. Kelley and her husband had tended to them over the years.

She caught a glimpse at the three-thirty p.m. on the clock and an armed soldier just outside the door. Logan slept in the chair beside her. His notepad and pen teetered on his knee. She watched him sleep. He had a few days growth on his face. She wondered what he'd look like in a full beard. She'd bet it'd tickle.

She sighed. Her breathing had improved. Her whole right side still ached in the new sling, but the IV with more pain meds helped.

She couldn't believe she was shot and didn't even know it. The pain had been sharp in her shoulder and back. She had thought she wrenched her arm again. At the time, her thigh hurt more.

She hoped she'd be able to dance again. She couldn't go through another disappointment in her life. Missing her Juilliard audition because of her broken leg was heart-wrenching.

Logan looked relaxed as he slept. She wanted to be his true girlfriend not the woman he was on a mission with. Because of his loneliness, he may like her company just to have the company. He'd be settling for her. Could she wait for him to love her? Would it matter to her if he didn't? When the pad and pen fell to the floor, he jumped and almost slid off the chair. She smiled at him.

"Hello," she said slowly. "How ... are you?"

"Me? I can't take you getting hurt anymore, so stop it," Logan replied.

"Sorry," she replied. "What's ... happened?"

"You've been in surgery for a while. We'll leave for D.C. when you're up to it," he replied, taking her good hand in his.

She hid the twinge of pain from her deep breath. "Where are we?"

"Irwin Hospital at Fort Riley. You've finally reached your destination."

"No, you were," she replied.

Logan stared at their entangled fingers. When he didn't say anything, she looked away to hide her anguish. Outside the door, a ruckus brought their attention to the guard and away from their non-discussion.

In a blink, Logan yanked open the door. With his palm on Logan's chest, Bear pushed him out of the way.

"You have some explaining to do, Mick," Bear thundered. "How could you get my goddaughter shot?"

Logan stepped back and dropped his head. Sam raised her bed to sit up farther as Bear strolled toward her.

"It's not that bad," she said, before pausing for a breath. "It hardly hurts now."

Bear growled. "Yeah, because you're doped up on drugs."

"I'm alert," she continued, swinging her bare legs over the side of the bed. She'd prove it to him.

"Samantha Renee Randall, do not get out of that bed," Martha said from the doorway. Walking to the bed, her mother shot daggers at Logan and then tucked Sam's bandaged thigh back under the blanket.

"Mother, I'll be fine."

Martha ignored her and faced Logan. "Your job was to protect her."

Logan ran a hand over his head. "Yes, ma'am."

"Instead, she had surgery to remove a bullet lodged in her rib. What do you have to say for yourself?" Martha demanded.

Logan opened his mouth. He glanced at Sam. The distraught look on his face made her arm throb.

"I'm sorry," Logan whispered, before leaving the room. Bear kissed her cheek and stalked after him.

"I can't believe he put you in danger," her mother said, fluffing her pillow.

Sam clenched her jaw and pushed aside the blanket. She needed to find him. When she sat up, she swallowed her gasp of pain in her shoulder. "He's saved me more ... times than I care to say."

"You were shot, Samantha. That's serious. I thought he would be different and watch out for you. He used the General's daughter to further his career," Martha said.

"He did not ... He helped me."

Martha harrumphed. "He helped you get shot. You are a civilian whom he dragged into this mess."

"Stop, Mother, I ... involved him," she said, sapping her energy. "I love him."

"It's the adrenaline of the danger. You will return home with me. Bear's discussing his actions with him right now."

"Why?" Sam asked, standing. She steadied herself with her IV stand.

"He's not right for you."

"Leave, Mother ... I'm tired ... I don't want to fight."

Martha pressed. "His job is dangerous. He could be hurt or killed. I worried about your father all the time. Now that I know more about the Major, you will stay away from him."

"Stop trying to control me."

"Samantha, get back into bed," Martha said, crossing her arms.

"No. Get out." Ignoring the sharp pain in her thigh and gasps for breath, she shuffled toward the door. "Where's Logan?"

"Samantha, please. You're hysterical from the pain," Martha said, blocking the door.

"Mother, I swear to God ... if you don't get out of the way ... I'll scream."

"You are not leaving the room. The guard outside the door won't let you," Martha replied with her hands on her hips.

Sam's anger overrode the pain of the deep breath. "Logan!" She yelled so loud it took her breath away. Before she took another step, Logan flew through the door whacking Martha in the rump. "Please ... escort ... her out."

The nurse behind him motioned for Martha to leave so not to upset her. Too damn late. Her body trembled at her own outburst. Before her legs gave out, Logan picked her up and carried her four steps to the bed, pulling the IV stand with him.

He set her down. "What's going on?" he demanded, straightening the tubing of her IV.

"Please don't ... leave me here ... by myself," she whispered.

"You're not alone. Your mother's here and she means well. Barrett's here, too," he said, sitting on the edge of the bed.

He wanted to leave? His assignment was over now. She couldn't think of a thing to say to make him stay. The ache in her heart masked all the other pain in her body.

"Sam, what's going on in your head? Talk to me," he said, grabbing a tissue from the table.

She took the tissue from him and squeezed her eyes shut. After wiping them, she looked out the window. Defeat and depression covered her like a wet wool blanket.

"You're done now ... just go," she whispered.

"Go?" he asked.

"Your assignment's ... over."

The muscles in his jaw tightened. "Well, it's not that easy, Ms. Randall. You're stuck with me until the senatorial investigative committee is finished with us."

"What?"

"The Army's outside the door, the floor, the building, and the base. They have the task of protecting us until I deliver the satellite's memory card and you to D.C."

"We'll go ... together?" Maybe she could convince him to stay with what time they had left.

"Sorry, Ms. Randall. But yeah. We go together," he said with a raised voice.

"Logan ... I meant—"

"Get some rest," he said half way out the door.

She stared at the door. What happened? Did she blow her chance to be with him? She sobbed as the nurse changed her IV bag. The drugs made her sleep—a temporary reprieve from the heartache.

The sun lowered and shadowed her room. She glanced at the empty chair. More tears burned her eyes. Skipping the dinner the nurse brought, she waited for hours for Logan to visit. Glad her mother stayed away, she had hoped Logan would have checked on her at least once.

She saw Cho and Martinez walk past the room. They didn't even peek inside. It shouldn't surprise her that they were loyal to Logan. Technically, the team's assignment was over, too. They wouldn't say goodbye though? They were mad, too?

Sam sighed and pushed back the blanket. She tested her bandaged thigh by stretching it as she sat up. Standing beside the bed, she put her weight on her leg. It held, and she blew out a shallow breath of relief.

Using the IV stand as a cane, she limped to her flowers by the window. One arrangement had a single red rose surrounded by a dozen white ones. The smell filled her with hope. She'd find him and tell him she loved him. She wasn't much on seduction, especially in her present state, but she could try.

"You should be in bed," Bear rumbled from the doorway.

She ignored him and carefully inhaled her roses. She read the card stuck between the thorns.

To my Wildcat

Bear approached her with a yellow legal notepad. He looked at the cards on the other flowers.

"Why are they calling you *Baby Bear*?" he asked.

She smiled sadly. "I bossed them around ... and told them to *shut it*."

"That's my girl," he replied with a baritone chuckle. "I sent Martha home to be with Dmitri. He's in a pickle and trying to salvage Russia's relationship to the U.S. before it returns to the Cold War."

"He's not part of this ... Is he?" she asked.

"No, but he needs to clear his president's name before this gets out of hand," Bear said.

"How can I help?" she asked, touching the silky petal of a white rose. She missed Logan's closeness. She didn't think she would recover from this sadness.

"I need a detailed report from you," Bear said.

She smelled her red rose once more before shuffling back to the bed. "You already know ... what happened."

"The senatorial hearing will want specific details. They want to know everything, Samantha." Bear covered her legs with the blanket.

"Are you taking notes ... since I can't write?"

He nodded and pushed the chair closer to her bed.

"Where do you want ... me to start?" she asked.

"When you first suspected something was amiss," he said.

They spent the next few hours discussing the details. Her labored breathing and the emotional toll exhausted her. The more she talked about Logan and his sacrifice to help her, the more upset she became. No wonder Logan was so anxious to get rid of this assignment. By the time she described the shooting of General Stovall; she was sobbing and gasping for breaths.

Bear sighed. "I know you've been through a lot, but this is necessary."

322

"I know," she said, reaching for the tissue he offered. "Why are you ... mad at him? ... This wasn't his fault ... and Mother blames him ... and he's angry at me ... and I don't know how to fix it."

Bear sat back in the chair. "There's much more going on here, Sam," he said. "For now, you need to rest. Martha was upset and lashed out. I did, too. I forget how stubborn you are—just like your father."

Her lungs tightened as she spoke. "He's finished this mission ... He'll move on to the next one ... I'll never see him again."

Standing, Bear growled out the door for a nurse. A frightened young blond slid past him. "We want to go for a walk," Bear said.

The nurse unhooked Sam's IV and whispered, "Did he really save the President?"

"What?" Bear demanded.

The young nurse jumped. "Never mind," she replied as she ran from the room.

Bear offered his giant paw to steady her. With her right arm in a sling, Sam gripped his burly forearm with the other and took baby steps out the door.

An Army soldier with an assault rifle followed them at a distant down the hallway. She shivered at the floor's security. She didn't understand the importance.

At the end of the hall, Bear stopped at a conference room. She looked inside the open door.

Sitting at a polished metal table, Logan and his team had the same yellow notepads in front of each of them. Johnson flung his pen at the far wall where Fox News on the flat screen had them riveted. Logan massaged the back of his neck while Cho and O'Brien leaned forward to hear the report. Martinez swiveled in his chair and scowled at the TV. She gaped. A caption scrolled along the lower part of the screen.

Has the President postponed his national tour because of an assassination plot by the Russians?

Shepard Smith reported that his source in the White House confirmed the plot. "It is unknown at this time if the Russian president sanctioned the action, but two Russian generals were implicated. They are now missing. Are they perhaps hiding at the Russian Embassy? Supermodel Jillian Williams and her father, Colonel Seth Williams, are suspected of selling information of the President's itinerary to the Russians. Her ex-husband, Major Logan McCormick, is wanted for questioning. He may have been the one who foiled the attempt. In doing so, he inadvertently saved five young girls, who were abducted for the Mexican sex trade. How these two events are connected has yet to be determined ...”

When they flashed to a picture of Logan and Jillian, she gasped and Bear swore. How had that news gotten out so quickly?

Logan and the team turned toward her and Bear in the doorway. She understood the ramifications. The news report outed Logan from any more covert operations. His career was in jeopardy.

“I’m sorry,” she whispered. “It’s my fault.”

Logan leaned back in his chair and crossed his arms. “Did you out the rest of the team, too?”

Shocked by the question, she squeezed Bear’s arm.

Bear growled, and the team quickly made excuses to leave the room. They reassured her that it wasn’t her fault as they skulked past them.

Bear nudged her into the room and slammed the door behind them. “What the hell is the matter with you?” Bear demanded.

Logan rubbed his temple. “I’m tired.”

“I don’t care. Cry me a river. You’ve bitched to me for the last three months that you wanted something else to do. Here’s your fricking chance,” Bear said.

While her body shuddered from the chill and pain, Logan shoved his chair back and paced in front of the second-story window overlooking the base grounds. She couldn't think of anything to say. She ruined his career.

"You think I want this attention?" Logan said to Bear. "Jillian knew I hated any kind of spotlight, and now she leaked the information and threw me under the damn truck. The vicious bitch."

Sam flinched and her injured leg buckled. Bear helped her sit in a chair then muted the TV. "Well, her plan to discredit you didn't work. The report just said you foiled the plot and helped those girls," Bear said.

"You're a hero," she whispered, wishing she had a blanket and not just a drafty hospital gown and flimsy slippers.

Logan snorted. "I don't care."

"You're my hero," she said.

"Yet, you can't get rid of me quick enough," Logan replied, staring out the window.

Leaving the room, Bear mumbled about being a fricking matchmaker to two clueless morons.

"That's not true," she replied. "I asked you not to leave me alone ... You're the one ... who said my mother and Bear were here ... Please, don't be angry ... I didn't mean for this to happen."

Logan dropped his head and sighed. "You're not sending me away now that this is over?"

She shook her head. "I love you ... I'm afraid of what will happen next."

He knelt beside her chair. "I am so sorry, Sam. I really am tired. I've worried about your injuries and about protecting you. I'm afraid of what'll happen next with us. I need you in my life. It killed me when you told me to go."

"I thought ... that's what you wanted."

"It's so far from the truth," he said, taking her good hand in his. He kissed her fingers. He frowned as he touched her bare calf. "You're freezing."

"I haven't anyone ... to cuddle with."

He smiled. "You have room in that bed of yours?"

"I'll make some."

With his hand at her back, Sam limped toward the door. She shivered from the cold floor, the throb that had returned, and the stares. Nurses ogled them. Everyone now knew who Logan was. He groaned from the attention.

With labored breathing, Sam tried to hurry down the hall to get away from them, but she staggered. Logan swept her up and hustled her into her room. He held her beside the bed for a moment.

"Do you like ... carrying me?" she asked, resting her ear against his chest.

He finally set her on the bed. "I do," he replied, covering her with the blanket.

Outside the door, the nurse watched them through the window slit. Logan waved her in, and she checked Sam's vitals. After giving Sam a couple pills for pain, the nurse made a notation in the chart. They remained quiet until the nurse left. Gossip had started to buzz.

Sam carefully scooted to the side of the bed. He lowered it to an almost flat position. With his boots still on, he joined her. On her back, she sighed at his warmth.

"I've missed this," she whispered.

He played with a lock of her hair. "It's almost midnight. Tomorrow, we fly back to D.C."

"When's the hearing?"

"Tomorrow afternoon. I'm hoping it'll be a private affair and not a public circus," he mumbled. "The sooner we get it over with, the sooner I get a tour of Yellow Springs."

As the medication dulled the pain, she smiled and relaxed next to a wonderful man.

CHAPTER 38

FRIDAY

AT TWO IN THE MORNING, someone opened their hospital room door a crack. The sliver of light from the hallway woke her. When a camera phone flashed twice, Logan jumped from the bed with his gun.

"Hold it," he said, racing toward the door. A few minutes later, he stormed back into the room. "Our guard just returned from the bathroom. The bastard left us unprotected," he said, pacing.

"What does it matter that someone ... took a picture? ... You're the hero ... who saved the President and those young girls ... You'll become a part of our American history," Sam said.

"Stop it, Sam," he said. "The picture is of us in bed. I know we're clothed, but it's a private moment."

"So the hero's upset that someone ... saw you drool on me again?"

Dismissing her joke, Logan returned to her side and kept his boot treads off the bed. She relaxed, but he remained rigid.

"I don't want this hearing to get personal," he said, laying his handgun on the bed between their knees.

"We won't let it," she replied.

He kissed her cheek. "I know you, Sam. You like blurting out information."

"What if I promise ... to only answer direct questions ... without going off on a tangent ... Would that ease your mind?"

"It would. Liking my privacy has nothing to do with my feelings for you. I don't like strangers knowing our business," he replied.

"I won't embarrass you," she said.

"That's not what I mean," he said with a sigh. "The paparazzi following Jillian were torturous. I hated it."

"Logan, move closer ... and go to sleep."

The rumbling of a plane landing woke her from holding Logan's hand as they walked around Yellow Springs. Next to the bed, Logan packed his duffle bag that set in the chair. He smiled while she stretched.

Her shoulder extended only so far, but she felt like it was mending properly. She barely winced at the pain in her back rib. She didn't struggle for a breath.

Sitting on the edge of the bed, she watched him. He hummed. She took it as a good sign for them. He had shared his thoughts and concerns with her again. She'd follow his need for affectionate baby steps.

"You hog the bed," he said.

Although she didn't have to gasp for breaths, she still spoke slowly. "I'm injured."

"You get to use that excuse for three more nights," he said, attaching his gun to his hip.

She grinned. "You'll be in my bed for three more nights?"

Before Logan could answer, the team in their street clothes burst through the door. They also had handguns secured to their sides. "We've got a sweet ride to D.C.," Cho said.

Confused, she looked back at Logan. "That roar is Air Force One," he said.

"The President must really want the satellite's memory card," she replied.

"And you home safely," Martinez said. "We're your protection detail."

"Aren't you afraid of being outed?" she asked.

"We don't care. We're riding in Air Force One," O'Brien replied.

Bear pushed open the door to join them. "Let's go. I'll carry you, Sammy," he said with a grin.

Logan tossed his duffle bag at him. "I got her."

"May I have a few minutes to change please?" she asked.

While Bear and the team impatiently waited outside her room, she slowly washed and replaced her hospital gown with her shirt and jeans. Logan buttoned her pants and tightened her sling. He kissed her forehead and picked her up. Her legs were going to atrophy, but—right now—she didn't care. Since she's known him, she's liked being the cat cradled in his arms. She didn't think that would ever change.

Nurses, orderlies, and even doctors stopped and watched them leave. Sam would have ogled them, too. They were a spectacle with her and Logan leading the way, the team and Bear parading behind them. When Sam mentioned knights in shiny armor, heroes, and great Americans, Logan snorted and picked up his pace for the runway. She giggled and nuzzled his chest.

"I think it would tickle," she said.

"What would?" Logan asked.

"Your beard."

Logan rubbed his chin on her cheek.

"God, get a room," Cho said next to them. "It's becoming less cute and more annoying."

"Jealous?" Logan asked.

Cho moved ahead of them while the rest of the team stifled their laughs. Already tired from struggling to get dressed, Sam skipped the tour. She found a cozy couch, and the attendant offered her a blanket. Logan joined her, lifting her onto his lap. As he played with her waves of reddish hair, she dozed.

"Sammy," Bear said. "Your mother's on the line." He held his cell's receiver against his t-shirt. "Ask her for an outfit to wear to this shindig."

"No, you do it," she said as she stiffly sat up from across Logan's lap. Bear dropped the phone on her blanket and left. "I hate him sometimes," she mumbled to Logan.

He chuckled. "Do you want some privacy?"

"Please, stay," she said.

"Then be nice and get it over with," he whispered before kissing her cheek.

She sighed. "I'm sorry, Mother."

"Oh, Samantha, are you still in the hospital?" Martha asked.

"We're on our way to D.C. ... Are you at the embassy?"

"We're afraid to leave. Dmitri has been on the phone with both presidents. U.S. soldiers are stationed outside for our protection," her mother replied.

"Yzemikov and Stovall are dead ... They were at the cabin. Mother...they wanted me dead."

Sam paused at the realization. Logan turned her on his lap so she could use him like a chair. His chest heated the ache in her wound. She sighed when his arms hugged her waist.

"Samantha, you are a strong woman. Your father taught you to persevere," Martha said.

"Yes," she whispered. "And you did, too."

"Is the Major with you?"

"Yes," she replied, hoping Logan wouldn't hear Martha start to rant again.

"Well, I believe I was wrong about him. Dmitri told me what he did for you. Karl and Jillian kept you in a dog cage? My God, Samantha, I had no idea."

Sam didn't want to rehash the incidents again. It was still raw and engrained in her psyche. The tight space of the cage and darkness of the trailer had been horrible. She had thought the tunnels would be worse, but Logan and his team calmed her anxiety. Even so, she needed to avoid enclosed spaces for a while.

"Mother, would you choose an outfit for me for the hearing this afternoon? I could use a cosmetic bag, too."

"Of course, Dear. I'll find a pair of short heels, so you don't trip."

Logan chuckled, and she elbowed him with her good arm. "Thank you, Mother," she said, putting the receiver back to her ear.

"Samantha, walk tall and confident even if you don't feel it. Your father would be proud. Now, let me talk to Bear."

Sam blew out a breath as Logan yelled for him.

"Stay there and I'll have someone pick up her stuff and mine," Bear said, collapsing into the oversized chair next to them.

"What if I say the wrong thing? I don't want to hurt you or the team," Sam said, tucking her good arm under the blanket.

"That spy satellite is considered top secret. If you need to refer to it, call it *cargo* and you'll be fine," Logan said as Bear nodded.

"What if they bring up certain things like Karl and the dog crate?" she asked.

"Tell them the truth. Bear and I will be next to you for support. I won't let them isolate you. They'll get the three of us or none of us."

She sighed. "Tell me something we could do after this is over."

"You got any fish in that pond?" Logan asked.

With a snort, Bear stretched out his legs and crossed his arms. He snored a few minutes later. The rest of the team explored the plane. Security kicked them out of a couple restricted places. As much as she tried to stay awake, she couldn't.

CHAPTER 39

THE PLANE LANDED, AND THE group scattered. Logan's team left in separate taxis to shower and change before the proceedings while a black SUV waited for her, Bear, and Logan. Secret Service drove them to a back entrance of the Capitol Building.

Seeing the massive domed building with its prestigious political history made her want to throw up. Although her shoulder and back didn't hurt because of the pain meds she had taken earlier, she was dizzy with the idea of the limelight. She'd much rather hide with Logan at the cabin.

The agents escorted them through a cement basement that looked like cars could drive right into the building like a parking garage. She imagined that's how the President entered. Secret Service ushered them down a narrow hallway and stopped outside a private lounge area with bathroom and shower. Their clothes hung on a rack in the corner. She saw her overnight bag beside an ivy-patterned couch.

Bear claimed the shower first, and Sam checked the items her mother had packed. She smiled at the clothes on hangers. Martha chose an Army green skirt and jacket with a cream camisole. Sam held up the matching shoes to show Logan.

He laughed. "I thought she was going for a low heel. That's what? Two inches?"

"I'd call it an inch and a half. Does that mean she's confident I won't trip?" she asked.

"She must know that I'll be carrying you most of the time," Logan replied.

"And I thought you were going for less personal."

Logan turned back to his duffle and uniform. "That media circus we saw coming in won't let it stay professional."

"I thought we've done something good here. You act as if we'll be on trial," she said.

"Something tells me those politicians have their own agendas," Logan said.

"You're scaring me," she replied.

"You're scaring me, too," Bear said clean-shaven in his Army pants and untucked dress shirt. "You're a real fun-sucker, Mick. I think that beard's making you more pessimistic than usual."

Without a response, Logan grabbed his bag and headed for the bathroom since Sam had washed up earlier. She couldn't get her bullet wound wet for a week although a bath sounded heavenly.

"Wait," she said, meeting him by the bathroom door. She scrubbed his jaw with her fingers. "Kiss me before you shave it off."

Logan smiled and complied while Bear grumbled about being a third wheel. She needed that. It really did settle her stomach. While Logan showered, Bear kept his back to her so she could dress. She struggled with her sling again.

On the first level of the building—the one that had more pomp and circumstance than the basement—two Secret Service agents ushered them through the rotunda with its statues of Presidents and massive paintings of American history.

They stopped before a plain oak door at the end of the wide hallway next to the senate conference room. The agent held the door for Bear and Logan. Another agent showed her to a marble bench across from the room.

"She is not to leave my side," Logan said to the agent.

"Sorry, Sir. Military rank only. You and Sergeant Major Barrett have a private meeting with the President first for *The Exchange*. Agent Todd will remain with Ms. Randall."

Sam nodded that she'd be okay and then eased onto the cold hard bench. Leaning back, she winced. She'd rather sit in her Logan chair.

Standing beside her, the agent wasn't much on talking. She sensed someone yakking in his ear. Farther down the corridor, senators in their expensive tailored suits entered the conference room.

Bear had called this the *Bull Shit Hearing of the Asshole Prying, Accusing, and Condemning Committee.* Logan had laughed and agreed.

A mass amount of reporters, cameramen, and security people started to mill around the thick wood doors. The ten senators reveled in the attention, knowing this would be a newsworthy event. The reality of it made her sick. She had thought she could give the information about the truck route and satellite to the driver and disappear. So, so wrong. Although not all of it had been bad.

More news crews expanded to within twenty feet from her. A beautiful reporter with long, fiery red, spiraled curls looked her way. Averting her eyes, Sam moved to the edge of the bench and slowly stood. When the reporter stepped toward her, Sam tried to hide behind Agent Todd.

340

"Hey, you're Samantha Randall, General Randall's daughter," the curvy newswoman said, pulling the shirtsleeve of her cameraman. "Why are you here? Wait a minute. You were part of the Amber Alert. You're the Samantha who helped those abducted young girls. They talked about a Samantha and a Logan who saved them. Major Logan McCormick, right?"

Stunned by the firing of questions, Sam froze as the other reporters moved closer. Video cameras zoomed in on her freaky eye colors. She wasn't sure which question to answer first. Agent Todd let them shove microphones in her face.

The flashes of cameras blinded her. They bombarded her with more questions. She was in that dog crate again. She couldn't catch her breath. Someone yanked her sore arm to draw her attention. She cried out and backed up. The bench blocked her from moving. The room spun. In a panic, she lost her voice and her nerve.

Logan's voice boomed, "Excuse me. Make way, people."

Logan pushed through the crowd. With his back to the reporters, he took her hand. His team blocked her from the press. Before moving to the conference room, Logan scowled at the man who was supposed to protect her.

"Nice job, Agent Todd." Logan turned back to her. "I'm sorry," he whispered, squeezing her hand.

She casually dropped Logan's hand, so the reporters wouldn't ask about the meaning. Reading her mind, Logan offered his forearm instead. Reporters watched the interaction then exploded with questions.

Logan ignored the press while the team created a force field around her. With Bear and his bulky body behind them, the group walked as one into the large conference room for the hearing.

Columns with exquisite detail and grand paintings of the Revolutionary War intimidated everyone who entered. The stale air permeated from either the stuffy senators or the lack of ventilation. Voices immediately lowered to murmurs.

On a double-layered dais, the ten senators conversed and read over their reports. In the back corner, the team formed a tight circle around her. She blew out a breath and looked up at the Army men in their dress greens. She patted each on the chest and thanked them.

"Mick's not the only one who has your back," Cho said with a grin.

"I love you guys," she whispered.

"Sweet," O'Brien said, glancing behind him at the blinding news camera lights.

"Where will we sit?" she asked.

Martinez and Johnson separated six inches, so she could see the three empty chairs at a table with three microphones in front of the dais. "We'll be directly behind you in the first row of seats," Martinez said.

"Although the press will be on the floor between you and the senators," Cho added. Martinez and Johnson closed ranks and glared at Cho.

"Just like the hearings on C-SPAN?" she asked.

Logan nodded. "Let's get this over with."

"You gave the President the memory card?" she asked.

"Yeah, he and his people are going through it now. He gave us a heads up and will be observing from the private room," Logan replied.

She groaned. "Great, no pressure," she mumbled.

While the team continued to block reporters and their cameras, Logan leaned down. His breath heated her ear. "You'll do just fine, Baby," he whispered in that deep husky tone.

Shivering, she smiled. Like Moses parting the Red Sea, Logan walked her down the aisle to their seats. Bear followed. They sat and waited for the senators. Cameras flashed as the firing squad of senators aimed their weapons. Each made notations on their packet of reports about the last week.

God, it had been a full week. Within that seven days, she had leapt across balconies, hitchhiked with a trucker, had knives and guns pointed at her. She was yanked out of a ravine, made love and danced with the man of her dreams, was shoved into a dog crate, abducted, and—oh yeah—shot by a Russian Spetsnaz and impaled by her gazebo. She had killed men. Not just any men—a Russian General and his soldier.

Her brain said it was necessary to kill or be killed. Her heart reflected taking the lives of any man, even the horrible ones. There was a certain sadness connected with Logan's and her father's jobs to protect their country. She remembered her father's pain at sending men to war knowing they may not return. He never took the responsibility lightly. Logan hadn't either.

CHAPTER 40

BLOATED AND OVERLY TAN, SENATOR Grayson banged his gavel officially starting the publicized committee hearing. "We have read over the full accounts of Major Logan McCormick, Sergeant Major James Barrett, Samantha Randall, and each member of McCormick's unit. Due to the sensitive nature of the information, the press will receive their packets later."

Sam heard grumblings from the press in the gallery behind and in front of her. They'd be confused without all the information. She thought it would be good for her—less hounding after the hearing.

The other senators let Grayson take the lead with the first question, but they were prepared with their own. On the edge of her chair, she sat with a straight back. Logan and Bear sat at attention with their hands on their laps.

"Ms. Randall, what's your stand on the Russian Oil Treaty?" Grayson asked.

"Oh boy," Bear grumbled.

"I'm sorry. I don't understand," she said. The question took her off guard. What happened to *yes* and *no* answers?

"Do you know intimate details of the proposed Russian Oil Treaty?" Grayson asked impatiently.

"No," she replied.

"Your mother is married to Russian Ambassador Dmitri Demas, and you live at the Russian Embassy," Grayson said.

"Is that a question or a statement?" Bear asked.

Grayson glared at Bear. "I'd like to know if Ms. Randall had overheard details."

"No details," she said. "I do know it would make Dmitri very happy. He loves America and thinks having this treaty would further bond Russia and America in a supportive way."

Bald with tuffs of white fringe like Friar Tuck, Senator Healy adjusted his thick reading glasses. "What is your reasoning?"

Confused, Sam glanced at Bear and then at Logan. "My reasoning? I wanted to warn and help the President. I had overheard Dmitri's assistant, Karl Petrov, discussing an assassination attempt. Karl had information on the classified military travels of a memory card that could link Russia to the assassination plot. I thought it was my patriotic and civic duty to warn the driver about the danger to him and his *cargo*."

Grayson straightened his black tie around his waddle neck. "How did you know Major McCormick was the one driving the truck with the information?"

"When I asked him for a ride, I didn't know. He gave no clue as to his *cargo*. Later, I overheard Sergei and Ivan—the men who worked for Karl—describe him and his Army Ranger tattoo," she replied, sliding backward on her chair. She winced and wished she had taken another pain pill.

Grayson sipped from his glass of water then continued, "Of all the people to approach for a ride after your bus caught fire, why him?"

"He looked military." Out of the corner of her eye, she thought she caught Logan crack a smile. "Having been around military personnel all of my life, I felt drawn to him." Logan tense at her comment.

"You mean attracted to him?" Grayson asked.

She swallowed her grin as Logan balled his hands into fists. "Attracted in the sense that military men and women are of the same mind, I thought I could trust him."

Friar Healy looked over the top of his reading glasses. "Major, do you pick up hitchhikers on every assignment?"

"No."

When Logan didn't elaborate, Bear spoke, "Samantha is my goddaughter. The major dismissed her, but later saw her in trouble. I opted to stay in the trailer until we switched places the next morning."

Senator Flynn, an elder statesman who wore a toupee one shade darker than his real hair, cleared the smoker's phlegm from his throat.

"Major, are you saying you had no idea who Samantha Randall was?" Flynn asked.

"I knew her father and of her but didn't know who she was at the time."

Grayson worked to retake control of the questions. "Sergeant Major, why didn't you inform the Major that she was General Randall's daughter?"

Bear leaned forward, so his mouth almost touched the microphone. "For the fun of it. Do you know how boring those cross-country trips are?"

The press caused a stir with their laughter. Too Tan Grayson banged a gavel, and Phlegmy Flynn moved to change the subject.

"Ms. Randall, how did you get your injuries?" Flynn asked.

"I dislocated my shoulder when Sergei and Ivan chased me at a truck stop. I was shot trying to retrieve the memory card."

Before Flynn continued, Grayson jumped in with the next question. "Major, did you kill Ivan and Sergei?"

Logan leaned toward the table and its microphone. "I did, to secure our *cargo*."

The press murmured as the questions continued to jump around in no particular order. If she was part of the press, she'd be pissed at the lack of chronological order. She started to get the idea that the senators did it on purpose.

"Major, you never suspected your wife of espionage?" Grayson asked.

"My ex-wife, and no," Logan replied. He hadn't budged a muscle. Sam felt she was squirming so much that she looked guilty of something sinister.

Grayson pointed his pen at Logan. "During your marriage, did you ever share information about your missions?"

"No. My failure to discuss my assignments led to my divorce."

While Fathead Grayson looked at his notes, Friar Healy asked, "Why did you escort your ex-wife off the embassy grounds before helping Ms. Randall?"

349

Logan gripped his thighs under the table as if staying in control. "Jillian was protected from prosecution there. I thought it was easier to trick her into leaving than to deal with weeks of red tape."

"Your unit also escorted Colonel Seth Williams off the grounds," Healy stated. "How do you feel about your father-in-law, who's also your superior, being arrested for treason?"

"Former father-in-law," Logan corrected. "He knew what she was doing and did nothing to stop it."

Flynn swallowed his phlegm before speaking. "Ms. Randall, why did Karl Petrov put you in a dog crate?"

As the press collectively gasped, she flinched and looked at Logan. He nodded his support.

She turned back to Senator Flynn. "I took a recording out of his safe. It had proof that Jillian provided the information and that Colonel Williams knew of the assassination plot organized by General Yzemikov, General Stovall, and Karl Petrov."

Grayson continued, "Who killed Karl Petrov?"

"I did," Logan replied. "He held a gun on Ambassador Demas. I shot him in the shoulder. When Petrov lowered his weapon to the General's daughter in the dog crate, I shot him in the head."

She wanted to reach out and touch his hand, but she remained stoic. When he turned his head slightly to see her reaction, she gave a brief nod, hoping it was reassuring.

"How did Jillian Williams get the Intel?" Grayson asked.

Bear smirked. "Through the seduction of many political and military men with access to the President."

"What are you saying, Sergeant Major?" Grayson demanded.

Again, Bear leaned forward, so his mouth was an inch from the microphone. "Don't be stupid. Men will do anything to wet their willies. Half you guys up there know that. To the extent of one's integrity is the real question. What's the harm in giving up a little Intel for a taste? It all added up, gentleman. Who's going to do the right thing and fess up first?"

Cameras flashed, and the press murmured again. Sam thought the reporters liked Bear's *No Holds Barred* attitude. Standing, Grayson banged his gavel to quiet the room. He threatened to kick everyone out if there was another disruption. Maybe they should stop now because Bear was just getting started.

"Why are you being insubordinate, Sergeant Major?" Grayson demanded.

"You're not my superior," Bear said with a growl. She smiled when Grayson twitched and returned to his seat. "I'm ready to retire, so I don't give a shit about your politics. I've done my duty for God and Country."

Grayson narrowed his eyes. "All right, let's elaborate on the Sergeant Major's responses," he said with a smile. "Major, the second part of your mission was to retrieve the memory card from the location you had previously stored it. Yet you went after Samantha Randall and her abductor first."

Leaning forward, Logan placed his hands on the table beside his microphone. "Is there a question in there?"

Annunciating each word, Grayson asked, "Did you ... let your feelings ... interfere ... with your assignment?"

"Samantha had knowledge of the security codes at the location the data was stored," Logan replied.

"Major, do you have feelings for Samantha Randall?" Grayson asked.

"She is the daughter of a General whom I have a great respect for. Her knowledge, strength, and perseverance have been exceptional as she has gotten the significant information to the right people."

Glancing at Logan, Sam tried to keep her smile in check. His groan proved her grin was too wide.

"Do you love her?" Grayson continued.

"Why would that be important to this investigation?" Logan demanded.

Grayson held up a picture of them in the hospital bed. Cameras focused on the picture, so the whole world could see. A low buzz filled the room again. This time, Grayson smiled as if he won some sort of battle against the three of them.

Bear swore and Sam turned her stiff body toward Logan. "I'm sorry. You were right," she whispered.

Grayson passed the picture to Senator Healy next to him. "You have a response, Ms. Randall?"

"As you can see, the Major is fully dressed on top of my blanket. I had just gotten out of surgery after being shot. I had killed two men to defend myself. I doubted the decisions I had made. The Major was reassuring me that I had made the right choices. I had done the right thing."

"Do you love her, Major?" Grayson asked again.

"Again, why would that be important to this hearing?" Logan asked.

"Your judgment is skewed, and we wonder about the reason," Grayson stated.

Logan paused. "I do, but, more to the point, we retrieved the female member of our team who had important Intel about the place where we knew a unit of Spetsnaz was waiting for an ambush."

Sam didn't hear the rest only the *I do*. The admission wasn't lost on her, the team, or the press. Cameras zeroed in on her unsuccessfully hidden grin and Logan's rigid posture.

"You need a young woman to help fight Spetsnaz? What's that say to our Army's training?" Grayson mocked while the other senators looked on in surprise of his tone.

"Jesus!" Bear said, silencing the room. "He just said she had knowledge of the security codes to gain access to the memory card. Sure, the unit can take out a group of Russians. But what's the point when you can't get into the safe? Are you even listening or are you worried about how an extra thirty pounds looks on camera? By the way, your makeup needs better blending at the jaw line."

That riled up everybody. Logan coughed to hide his laugh. She stared in shock. Senator Grayson turned bright red and absently wiped sweat from his brow, which streaked his foundation.

Bear held up his hand to stop the committee from their reprimand. "My point is that many times smaller tasks are completed first to accomplish the larger one. General Randall taught his men to adapt on an assignment, and his daughter understood that. She patiently waited in the back of that creep's semi-trailer with those girls. She knew the Major and his team would find them after their mission.

She just didn't understand that they needed her for her detailed knowledge of the place to give them an edge, which, by the way, paid off. Here's another realization for you: We had foreign soldiers on U.S. soil. Your military is defending our country abroad and on the home front."

Once the press settled down with their pictures of the wild grizzly bear, Senator Grayson narrowed his eyes on her. Sam cringed at the intimidating glare. Apparently, the others let him dominate. She was disappointed that none called him out with his personal agenda.

"Ms. Randall, you've come in contact with this kidnapping trucker, how many times?" Grayson asked.

"Three," she replied, shifting in her chair.

"Please, elaborate," Grayson demanded.

She took a deep aching breath. "At the first truck stop, I asked for a ride. He wanted to, uh, barter," she said with a shiver. "Logan rescued me." She hugged her good arm around her sore one in the sling. "At the second truck stop, he pulled a knife on Logan, so I whacked him in the head with a hubcap." She paused at the chuckle from the press. "Um, then he grabbed me in the downpour. That's when I met the young girls."

Grayson grinned at her unease. Logan and Bear watched her pinch her finger under the table. She shoved her tears back below the surface. She could cry later.

"Your report never called him by name only a nickname that you gave him," Grayson said.

Bear and Logan's jaws cracked in stereo as she whispered, "Yes."

Grayson crossed his arms and sat back. "The name?"

She lowered her head. "Ugly Penis Man," she whispered.

Grayson and a few of the senators laughed. Bear slammed his fist on the table knocking over the three microphones. Logan and the team jumped to their feet. Bear pressed his hands into the table as he rose to his massive height. The grizzly geared up for an attack.

"The fact that she refers to him as that is no laughing matter. What the hell does that have to do with us uncovering an assassination attempt?" Bear demanded.

Logan's roar was louder. "Her sacrifice for the greater good is not a joke. Your line of questioning is inappropriate and disrespectful. Samantha Randall has only tried to live up to her father's words that some here have obviously forgotten. Well, let me remind you of the quote: *Some men think there's a choice between right and wrong. Great men know there is none.* Samantha's actions over the course of the last few weeks reflected that. She had no choice but to do the right thing no matter the cost to her."

Reporters scrambled to take notes. Cameramen filmed them and the scolded senators. Logan helped her stand. The team led the way up the aisle. Logan held her hand, and Bear glared at anyone who tried to break through their wall.

"We are not finished yet!" Grayson yelled, pounding his gavel repeatedly.

"Re-read the reports," Bear said.

Martinez and O'Brien disappeared in front of them. Cho and Johnson pushed through the mob toward the front entrance. On the steps, news reporters surrounded them. The huge mass moved as one toward the waiting SUV with blacked out windows.

A reporter from the back yelled, "Major, why are you shielding her?"

Without stopping, Logan replied, "She was shot while preventing this assassination plot. She deserves better treatment than that political ambush they call a hearing."

Another reporter stopped in front of them to ask his question. Johnson picked him up and set him aside. The rest of the press gave them a wide berth.

"Samantha, how do you feel?" someone yelled.

They stopped beside the SUV. As she looked around, she wanted to say *vomit,* but she spotted something across the way that fired her up.

357

"Do you see that tattered and faded American flag over there?" she asked. "It symbolizes the sadness I feel right now. The flag is supposed to be a symbol of pride and respect for those who serve in all areas of our Armed Forces. I'm saddened and appalled by this political pettiness. I can take the bashing, but it has cost Logan his career for pursuing sensitive assignments."

Logan smiled and held the door open for her. Bear snarled when reporters stepped closer. They actually took a step backward.

With O'Brien and Martinez already in the car, the rest crammed into the back. As soon as the door shut, Bear roared with laughter. The team chuckled. Logan lifted her onto his lap to give them more room.

"What's so funny?" she asked. "That was a nightmare."

Logan kissed her cheek. "Barrett is laughing because your statement will create an uproar in Congress."

"How much trouble will we be in for leaving the hearing early?" she asked.

"None," Logan said. "The President warned us about their agenda to make the military look bad, so they can cut spending. He said to take it for as long as we could."

"Tomorrow, we'll have a private dinner with him," Bear said.

"Even us?" Cho asked.

"Oh yeah," Bear replied. "He will be issuing a citation to each member of the team."

"Awesome," O'Brien said.

"Does Sam get one, too?" Johnson asked.

"It's all of us or none of us," Logan replied. "Let's head for a bar. I need a stiff drink."

CHAPTER 41

FRIDAY

ONE WEEK LATER AT THE cabin, Samantha eased into the hot water and overflowing bubbles in her bathtub. She hated washing out of the sink for the last week. She couldn't stand the bandage on her back anymore and had already peeled it off. She had another two days before she could get her wound wet, so she'd be careful.

Her shoulder joint was a mixture of violet and dirty yellow. The stitches in her fiery red wound pointed out of her flesh, like hairs on the nose wart of the Wicked Witch of the West.

She had smooth skin on one side of her spine and a jagged puckered scar on the other—Jekyll and Hyde. Swimming was not an option anymore.

It had been one hell of a week in D.C. They attended a casual BBQ with the President who told them humorous tales of General Randall's squabbles with Congress. Then, they dodged the press while non-bias personnel debriefed them in private this time.

After the Bull Shit Hearing, the Asshole Prying, Accusing, and Condemning Committee made a formal apology, but complaints from their constituents and negative coverage from the media pretty much nixed their agenda and their plans for another term this November.

Having arrived at the cabin this morning, she opted for a bath first. Logan and Bear were touring the grounds to inspect the work of the construction crew. From what she saw on the way to her bathroom, they did a wonderful job. She didn't see any bullet holes, blood, or exploded flesh. Mrs. Kelley had replaced the damaged furniture and bedding. She had even stocked the pantry and refrigerator.

With Logan here, Sam looked forward to the possibilities and not the past incidences. She frowned at the thought of her cherished gazebo. The pond and meadow would be different without it there.

She reached for the washcloth on the sink counter next to a towel and condom packet. She hoped to entice him. They kissed and cuddled, but that was the extent. Within

362

the massive amount of rose-scented bubbles, she stretched out her legs as someone knocked on the door.

"Come in," she said.

Logan opened it. "I could have been Barrett."

"Bear doesn't knock," she replied, pulling the bubbles closer to cover more of her.

He folded his arms and leaned on the doorframe. "You can't get your back wet for two more days."

"Maybe you should join me, so I don't," she replied.

"Are you tempting me?" he asked, glancing at the condom.

"Yes. You're dirty. We'd be conserving water," she said with a smile.

"It would be good for the environment," he said, untying his boots.

She moved back to make room. "Do you always wear heavy boots?"

"Always," he replied with a sigh.

She ogled him as he stripped down. She couldn't wait to touch his nakedness. The water rose to an inch below the rim. He stretched out his legs, and she climbed on top of his thighs. While he caressed her hips, she soaped up her cloth.

"This isn't a good idea," he said.

She looked down at her soapy washcloth. "Is it because my back's ugly?"

"God, no. Is that what you think?"

"Sammy," Bear yelled from inside her bedroom. A second later, the door flew open.

While she hid behind the bubbles, Logan sloshed water as he sat up straighter. "You're interrupting!"

"I see that. You're going to smell like roses," Bear said with a grin. "Your team is driving through Yellow Springs and will be here in twenty minutes. Since it's a full house, I'll be at Mona's."

"Are you going to the concert tonight?" she asked, casually wiping the tear off her cheek.

"Yeah, I'll run point," Bear said. He left the bathroom door open on his way out.

"Thank you," she yelled. She turned back to Logan. "Please, don't look." In a bubble suit, she reached for the towel and backed out of the tub.

"Sam, I don't think that. I don't want to hurt you. Please, don't leave."

"They'll be here soon," she replied, shutting the door.

Sam left off her bra, bandage, and sling. In a buttoned down cotton shirt and jean capris with sandals, she set her pre-made batter on the kitchen counter next to the cookie sheets. By the time she pulled out the first batch from the oven, Cho, Martinez, and O'Brien burst through the front door.

"Are those what I'm hoping for?" Cho asked. "We smelled them from the driveway."

She smiled. "Just for you." While they shoved hot ones in their mouths, she greeted Johnson and his pregnant wife. "Rachel, I'm so glad to finally meet you."

"Hello, Samantha," Rachel replied shyly.

Sam looped her good arm into hers and led her to a stool next to the counter. "How was the trip? Can I get you anything?"

"How about a bathroom?" Rachel asked.

Sam laughed. "Of course," she replied, showing her the door down the hallway.

"Got any milk?" O'Brien asked, looking in the cupboard for a glass.

"They did some great work," Johnson said, looking at the newly plastered and painted walls.

"Is this really how you feel with him?" Martinez mumbled with a mouthful of cookie. "I want this."

"Where is he?" Johnson asked.

"I'm not sure," Sam said, pulling out the second batch. She couldn't get them off the cookie sheet fast enough. After sliding the last batch into the oven, she set the timer. "Can you watch those while I find him?"

O'Brien nodded. "No guarantees there'll be any left."

After searching the house, Sam headed down the path through the woods to the pond. She smiled. The construction crew added lighting along the path. She'd bet it was Logan's idea.

At the tree line, she braced herself for the empty space where her gazebo had been. She paused when she saw Logan under her repaired shelter. The crew had rebuilt her gazebo using many of the old pieces. With his blade in his hand, he was carving into one of the thick columns that held up the roof.

"They tried to save as much of your art as they could," Logan said as she approached him.

She wandered around. "What did you add?"

His hand blocked it. With his blade, he tapped her heart carving of *S.R. loves M.M.* above his hand. "I don't want you to love him. He was a figment of your imagination. I need you to love me."

"You're the same man."

"He's an ideal. I'm just a guy," he said. "Sam, I wear my boots all the time, so I'm ready for combat—even during the hot summer. How sad is that?"

Smiling, she leaned against the railing. "Did you ever wonder why I didn't recognize you at the truck stop? Wouldn't you think I'd check out your picture at least?"

"It crossed my mind."

"I didn't want to wreck the illusion," she replied, looking across the pond. She pointed to the woods. "From here I see plain nondescript trees, but the closer I get I can single them out. I see the details of the oak: the bark, the branches, the leaves."

"I want to be your oak," he whispered.

"You are. I loved Major McCormick for his bravery and selflessness, and then I met Logan McCormick, the real man who is so much more. You've saved me numerous times as I pictured the Major would. I've gotten to know your caring and loving side. I love all of you, Logan, and I look forward to learning more about you," she replied. "And don't forget I've got faults. You might not like them."

He grinned with his hand over his carving. "Like what?"

"I don't like socializing at fancy parties. I'm afraid of spiders." She lowered her voice. "And my back's repulsive."

"That will never be an issue. I have my own scars," he said, stabbing his knife in the railing. "I like Texas Rangers baseball. I've seen them play at every stadium in the league."

She frowned. "Ooh, a sports guy, that's a deal breaker," she said, stepping away from him. He followed her to the other side of the gazebo.

"Are you serious?" he asked.

"I adore the White Sox, so this'll never work," she replied.

Standing behind her, he gently caressed her upper arms. "It'll make things spicy when they play each other. Are you a betting kind of gal?"

"I am," she replied as he turned her around to face the pole with his carving. She gasped at the heart below her old one. He had carved *L.M. loves S.R.*

"I love you, Samantha Randall."

She turned around and hugged him. "I thought you could only show it and not say it—like a quirky thing."

"Not any more. Thank you."

CHAPTER 42

AFTER PROMISING TO RIDE THE tandem bike next time, Logan parked in the half-full high school lot next to the large grassy field beside Rabbit Creek.

Excited to be with her boyfriend and new friends, Sam grabbed the large blanket from the trunk. She didn't need a jacket; she had Logan to keep her warm. She couldn't stop smiling. He truly loved her.

In a green tee, jeans, and boots, Logan slid the camp chair strap over his shoulder. Also wearing green t-shirts and jeans, Cho, O'Brien, and Martinez each carried one. Johnson helped his pregnant wife from their car. Carrying two, he held Rachel's hand.

"Do you guys always color coordinate your outfits?" Sam asked as they gathered at the edge of the parking lot.

"Fridays have always been Green T-shirt Day," O'Brien answered.

"Old habits die hard," Logan said.

"I think we look bad ass," Martinez added.

"And our tight shirts will show off our muscles for the hot chicks," Cho said, looking around. "There will be single women here, right?"

"I'm sure they've already checked you guys out," Sam replied.

Cho and O'Brien scanned the area as if honing in on their prey. Sam thought it would be the other way around. She grew up with some of these women.

A few people milled around the blankets and chairs in the first three rows in front of the stage. The main crowd congregated by the vendors and the four port-a-jons by the road.

The aroma of a roasting pig and other greasy food made the guys drool. Sam smiled as the whole crowd stopped and stared at their group.

Logan groaned. "Are we going to get swarmed by the curious?"

Sam laughed. "No. They'll swarm Bear to indirectly get the scoop on us," she said, extending her good arm and waving at everyone. They waved back then dismissed them. "Yellow Springs is used to famous people living here. A couple well-known writers, a concert pianist, and a former soap opera star have property and homes in the area. And my father was fairly famous." She led them to the start of the fourth row by the trees next to the creek. "We'll set up first then you guys can race for the food line."

Logan chuckled as Cho eyed the line. "What do they have?" Cho asked.

"The usual picnic fare. The American Legion sponsors the food to help cover the expenses for tonight's music," she replied.

While the bluegrass band set up on stage, Logan propped open Sam's chair while Sam struggled to lay out the blanket for him. He rushed to help her and gave her a look that said she had better take it easy.

While Logan and the guys stalked toward the line, Sam stayed with Rachel, who eased into her chair. Sitting beside her, Sam watched a young mother in front of them, wrangling her two-year-old daughter from leaving the blanket.

A minute later, the father and their five-year-old son arrived and presented the mom with plates of food. The family formed a circle to share their meal.

"Rachel, are you comfortable?" Sam asked.

"I know where the bathrooms are located, so I'll be fine," she said with a smile. "You're good for him. He seems more relaxed now."

"He's good for me, too."

Sam silently thanked her father again for helping her find Logan. Her father's recorded voice played in her head. *I love you, too. Don't ever forget that.*

While she and Rachel watched the band test their equipment, an eight-year-old girl, in pigtails, a pink tutu, and flip-flops, pulled a red wagon toward them.

An assortment of homemade cookies in plastic containers filled it. The sign read: *For Summer Dance Camp $3.*

"Are you interested in some cookies?" the girl asked.

Sam smiled. "If you come back in twenty minutes, there'll be a group of men here who'll buy some."

Rachel laughed as the girl nodded and moved on to the next group of blankets. Returning with two full plates, Johnson set one on his wife's diminishing lap. Their eyes spoke volumes on their loving devotion to each other. They had a history and were creating a future. Sam hoped for that.

With mounds of food on their plates, Cho, O'Brien, and Martinez carefully sat in their chairs. With a grin, Logan handed Sam one of the two full plates then sat on the blanket. His back touched her knees. She liked that he wanted to be so close to her.

Sam sat forward and kissed his cheek. "I love you," she said in his ear.

"And I love you," he replied.

At Logan's declaration, the guys paused from inhaling their food. Martinez swallowed before he spoke. "I didn't think you'd ever say it again."

"I had to meet the right woman first," Logan replied.

Forgetting about her food, Sam reached out and caressed his neck. Rachel was right. Logan was opening up to her and the group more. "You smell like roses," she whispered.

He leaned back his head and gave her a peck on the lips. "We'll resume those activities later. I promise," he whispered.

"Whoa, who's that with Barrett?" Cho asked.

At the edge of the parking lot, Bear, in jeans and a clean green shirt, held the hand of a tall busty brunette in hip-hugging jeans and low-cut sleeveless blouse. Her makeup skillfully hid any fine lines. Her loose bun looked casual but a bit too perfect.

"That's Mona Wilson, Bear's longtime girlfriend. She owns the Yellow Springs Inn on the other side of town," Sam said.

"Barrett's got a girlfriend?" the guys said in unison.

"For as long as I've known him," she replied with a shrug.

The guys probably hadn't seen the domestic side of Bear before. Now that Bear was officially retiring, Sam thought he'd return to Yellow Springs permanently. Something Mona has been after him to do for a long time.

Bear and Mona stopped briefly with different groups as they moved toward them. As predicted, the crowd swarmed and grilled him. Clean shaven, Bear finally introduced Mona to their group. After the pleasantries were exchanged, the guys grinned at Barrett as if they now knew a huge secret about him.

Bear growled. "Shut it." Before he and Mona moved on, he kicked Logan's boot to get his attention. "Mick, when you're done eating, introduce yourself to John Byron. He's the guy wearing the Navy Vet baseball cap," he said, nodding at the man in the wheelchair a few rows back.

Before Logan could ask why, Bear quickly escorted Mona away. Frowning, the young girl and her still full wagon approached them.

Logan took out a twenty dollar bill and handed it to the girl. "I'd like twenty dollars' worth," he said. Her eyes sparkled. Logan turned to Sam. "I didn't get any of yours,

374

CHRISTINA THOMPSON

so don't let them eat any of mine," he said, standing. He took their empty plates and left.

While the girl piled Logan's cookie containers on the blanket, the guys scrambled for their wallets. Sam chuckled as the young tutu girl left with an empty wagon and a pocket full of cash. The guys quickly devoured their cookies.

When Mayor Rob Hillard announced that the music would start in twenty minutes, Sam and Rachel took the opportunity to use the bathrooms. As they waited in line, Sam heard someone call her name.

In a flowing orange dress with matching sandals, Ms. Anderson glided toward her. At sixty-eight, she still had a dancer's graceful body. Six of her youngest dancers followed her then stopped in a row behind her.

"Samantha, I heard you'll be moving back permanently," Ms. Anderson said.

"Yes ma'am, that's my plan," she replied. Bear had spread the news already.

"Well, I'm retiring in the fall, and I'm looking for a replacement. Bear mentioned you might be interested."

"Yes, ma'am, I am."

"Great. Come and see me Tuesday, and we'll talk specifics," Ms. Anderson said, before turning away. The young girls, like giggling ducklings, followed her through the crowd.

Excited with the possibilities, Sam strolled with Rachel back to their chairs. From behind, Logan grabbed her hand to stop her while Rachel continued to their place.

In the middle of the ogling crowd, Logan kissed her hand. "Mr. Byron offered me a job. I'm meeting with him tomorrow," he said.

Sam shared her news about taking over for Ms. Anderson.

"I'm thinking we need to make our relationship more formal," Logan said.

"I'd like that," she replied. The significance of the statement brought a tear to her eye.

They rejoined the group at their saved spot as Mayor Hillard asked everyone to stand and remove their hats for the National Anthem. A boy scout carried the American flag to the stage, and pageant winner, Juliet Cowley, with a *Miss Yellow Springs* sash, adjusted the microphone.

In front of them, the young parents with their son and daughter set their plates aside and stood on their blanket. The boy, with his cap still on, eyed Logan and the team who were opting to salute the flag while Juliet sang. The boy saluted them back.

Sam stepped forward, knelt down, and whispered to the boy as his sister watched. "Don't just honor these guys," she said. Taking off his hat, she turned him toward the flag. "When you take off your hat, you're honoring all American soldiers, past and present."

The boy stood up straighter and raised his hand to his brow. His little sister mimicked him. Afterward, as the only ones still standing, Logan kissed her in front of the grinning crowd.

Sam enjoyed the music and Logan's company. Earlier, he had chatted with Bear and Mona, who introduced him to a few folks. Logan became quiet afterward. She could tell he had something on his mind. She'd try to coax it out of him. Sitting on the blanket in front of her, Logan leaned back between her knees. She caressed his shoulders.

With his hand on Rachel's abdomen, Johnson talked to their unborn baby. On the other side of Sam, Martinez had his cell phone to his ear. He tried to speak, but his girlfriend was doing most of the talking. He finally hung up on her then took off toward Cho and O'Brien by the vendors. Laura and Kelsey Sinclair, in skimpy summer dresses, were flirting with them. O'Brien was flexing his bicep while Laura squeezed his muscles with both hands.

Logan watched them and chuckled. "Given the chance, Cho will show his scars."

Johnson looked over his shoulder. "Looks like Miss Yellow Springs has latched onto Martinez."

"Will he resist her?" Sam asked, with a frown.

"I hope not," Rachel said. "His girlfriend's toxic."

"They've been on-again/off-again for a while," Johnson added.

"Oh," Sam whispered, setting her hands on her lap, "I guess that can happen in relationships."

Her happiness high suddenly dipped. Breakups were a part of life. Take her parents for example; they were both good people. They had held no animosity toward each other; they just couldn't make it work. What if she and Logan couldn't make it work either?

Logan turned around. On his knees, he took her hands. "I swear, Sam, that won't be us."

He couldn't guarantee that. They were happy now but what about later?

"This has been a whirlwind just like it was with you and Jillian," Sam stated.

Agitated by the mention of his ex, Logan cringed. "Let's go for a walk."

"What about our chairs?" she asked.

"We'll pack up the chairs and blanket if you're not back in time," Johnson said, seeing their distress over the conversation.

378

In silence, Logan, holding her hand, walked her toward the parking lot. He seemed to be working out in his head what he wanted to say. Filled with dread, she remained quiet as they stopped by his Charger. He checked his watch and sighed.

"Logan, tell me what you're thinking," Sam said.

He helped her sit and slowly walked around to the driver's side. Gripping the steering wheel at ten and two, he sighed again. "You were right before. I had compared you to Jillian. You are so much more, Sam. I just can find the right words to explain how I feel. It's like night and day between you and her."

Sam set her hand on his bicep, squeezed it, and smiled. "Let's go home."

"Home?" he asked, glancing at his watch again.

"If you want it to be," she replied.

With a nervous laugh, he started the car. "I do want it to be."

At the cabin, he helped her stand. "How about that walk now?"

Logan held her hand, and they strolled around the cabin to the newly lit path in the woods. Crickets and other critters scurried in the darkness along the sides of the path.

"Logan, I love you, and I know you love me back. Why aren't you sharing your thoughts with me?"

He exhaled. "I had a private talk with your mother before we left D.C."

"What? When?" Sam stopped, dropped her hand from his, and stepped back. She didn't like that he was keeping secrets from her. "What did she say?"

"Well, I did most of the talking." Logan reached for her hand, but she stepped back farther. He scrubbed his hand over the back of his neck in frustration. "I told her that I love you, that I would never intentionally hurt you, and that I would protect you with my life."

"I don't understand. I know that, and so does she."

He stuck his hand into the front pocket of his jeans. "I also told her that, for me, this was the real deal. I asked for her blessing. Sam, we're best friends and lovers, but I want more." Her mouth went dry as he got down on one knee in the middle of the lit pathway. "Will you marry me?"

He held out a ring with small diamonds surrounding a larger one. She recognized the setting. Her father had given it to Martha when he proposed. Her mother had promised her the ring when the time was right.

"Your mother thought this would suffice until we could go shopping," he said.

With tears blurring her eyes, she nodded. Her father was giving them their blessing, too. "It's perfect."

He slipped it on her finger and pulled her closer. She hugged his neck. Standing, he carried her down the path.

"I wanted this to be special ... if you're up to it."

He pointed to the ground where a trail of rose petals led them to her gazebo. Around the railing, over twenty candles glowed. Netting hung from the roof keeping the bugs away. In the center on the flooring, more rose petals covered a futon mattress with thick bedding.

"Oh, Logan," she whispered. "It's lovely."

"I had a little help from Barrett and Mona. She invited the guys to stay at her inn for the night giving us the privacy."

Her life was just beginning. Logan carried her to the bed and gently laid her down. While she kicked off her sandals, he untied his boots. She slid under the blanket and quickly took off her clothes. She watched him undress and thought she'd never get tired of looking at her sexy Army Ranger. She held the blanket up for him then rubbed her hands over his muscular chest.

"Which position should we try first?" she asked.

His laughter echoed throughout the woods. "I can't imagine my life getting any better than this," he said.

She softened at his kiss. His hands on her skin warmed her, but she melted at his sweet words.

"I love you, Sam."

EPILOGUE

CHECKING HIS SIDE MIRROR, LOGAN backed the full semi to the warehouse door of the distribution center. He stopped, jumped out, and tucked his Army t-shirt back into his camo-pants.

Reaching behind his seat, he grabbed the clipboard with his logbook and slammed the door.

Before his two-week vacation with Sam, he had one more critical assignment after this one. He hoped to wrap them up in a hurry.

Standing on the platform, Jack Parker opened the trailer's back door. "Major, you've been at this for a year, and you've always managed to stop an inch from the building. What's the secret?"

Logan chuckled as he jumped onto the platform. "I'm just that good."

Jack nodded and stepped into the trailer to inspect the product. Shifting his stance, Logan waited for a signature on his clipboard.

He loved his job and took the task seriously. He had a responsibility to his wife now, and John Byron's offer allowed him to be home every night by six.

Today, he started early to get back before five, which was still pushing it. His assignment after this stressed him more than any other he's had in his Army career. Jack's laugh broke up his thoughts.

"Major, once again not a single one is broken. Not one egg," he repeated. "The last guy Byron had as a driver broke at least a fourth of them. This has got to be a record or something."

Logan handed him the clipboard. "Barrett's taking over for the next two weeks. Remind him of my record. I'll want to know how he does. Now, how fast can we get these unloaded?"

"Say, Major, when you get back, can I ask for some advice?" Jack asked nervously.

"When I get back, we'll grab a burger, too," Logan replied.

Jack nodded then started the hi-lo.

Logan moved the boxes of Byron's Fresh Farm Eggs to the pallet. After an hour, he shifted toward the highway.

Between this Memorial Weekend and the last one, Logan's life had changed drastically. He and Sam were married on July 4th last year in a huge wedding planned by her mother at the embassy. The former President even attended as a goodwill gesture to mend Russian ties. Logan wasn't thrilled to use their wedding as a political step although he couldn't remember talking to anyone at the reception other than his lovely wife.

They had quickly returned to the solitude of the cabin. That following Friday, they rode the tandem bike to the music festivities and paid for the evening's food extending their wedding bliss with the town. Sam enjoyed the evening while he tolerated the town's gushing. Sam had promised everything would eventually settle down by doing it that way. She was right, but he couldn't get a single person to call him *Logan*. They had become *Ms. Sam and the Major*.

Logan slowed his truck as he approached the Yellow Springs city limits sign. In the warm sun, many families walked along the sidewalk heading in the same direction. He cringed; he knew where they were going.

At the mid-town stoplight, he waited for a few to cross the walkway. The younger children, jumping up and down, waved at him. They recognized him and the truck. One little boy made a trucker's honking motion with his arm. Logan reached over. The deep sound of his horn blasted the area. Unalarmed, the families turned, smiled, and waved. This town was growing on him. Sam had said as much.

Logan continued through town. Byron's Farm was located on the other side of Rabbit Creek next to the high school and Festive Friday's field. Passing the high school, he winced at the full parking lot. More families had reached their destination from their walk. Sam would be waiting for him. And he was twenty minutes later than he wanted to be. Groaning, he parked the truck, grabbed his camo jacket, and then jogged back toward the high school.

Today was Sam's dance recital showcase marking the end of her first year of teaching. Dedicating the show to the Armed Forces, she planned it on the Friday of the Memorial Weekend. The whole town would be attending.

Sam had talked him into helping. He didn't want to, but he could never say *no* to her. His final assignment before their vacation was presiding over the showcase as the Master of Ceremonies. Even though he held his own when grilled by Congress and the media, he thought speaking in front of a packed auditorium would be ten times worse. After taking a deep breath, he put on his game face.

Slowing to a brisk walk, he passed the crowd standing in line and entered the auditorium's atrium where a mass of people laughed and talked excitedly about the show. He stopped at the ticket table. In uniform, Martinez helped Mona hand out tickets and take money. Mona pointed him toward the gymnasium at the end of the corridor where all the dancers waited.

As he strode past well-wishers, Logan glanced at the auditorium door where O'Brien and Cho, also in uniform, handed out programs. The Sinclair sisters took tickets beside them. His team had visited Yellow Springs often. Sam thought they'd move here soon. He agreed.

Logan yanked on the gymnasium door. The loud girly laughter, the clicking of numerous tap shoes, and the John Philip Sousa recordings of three different songs at once stopped him in his tracks as he took in the panoramic view. Six groups of young girls ranging from kindergarten to high school wore different patriotic dance costumes. Samantha's college assistants, dressed like Uncle Sam, corralled the younger ones. They looked chaotically organized.

As he looked for his wife, Logan paused on Barrett and laughed. Wishing he had a camera, he walked toward him. Logan wasn't the only one Sam had convinced to help in the showcase.

In his dress green uniform, Barrett sat on a tiny stool. The smallest group of girls dressed in red, white, and blue sparkles stood in a line in front of him. Each held their lipstick and giggled excitedly.

The first young girl handed Barrett her lipstick. He puckered his lips and the girl mimicked him while he reapplied her lipstick. Afterward, she kissed his cheek and went to the back of the line while the next one stepped forward.

Barrett turned to him and smiled. Different shades of red and pink lipstick kisses covered his face. Barrett was part of the routine for the girls to honor the Army. At rehearsal, Logan laughed so hard he cried. At center stage, the girls' burley Bear had mimicked their routine to help them remember their steps. It truly was adorable. All the little girls loved him, and Barrett basked in the glow of it.

"Where's Sam?" Logan asked.

Barrett thumbed toward the girl's locker room before returning to his lipstick duty.

Logan walked slowly toward the other side of the gym so not to knock over the tiny dancers jumping about. With her engagement ring from Martinez prominently displayed, Juliet Cowley, the former Miss Yellow Springs, adjusted the blue tutu on another little girl just outside the locker room.

Juliet called out to him. "Major, Ms. Sam's in the bathroom. She doesn't look well."

Alarmed, Logan gave notice that he was walking in. Without a reply, he rushed through the door, finding it empty, except for his wife. On her knees in the stall, Sam was throwing up. Had nerves gotten the best of her? He had teased her earlier that he would be the one hurling in the bathroom before he had to get on stage.

"Samantha, I know you're nervous, but everything's under control. You've had a great year. It's time to celebrate."

The toilet flushed, and she stepped out of the stall. She washed her hands and swished water in her mouth before spitting it out. As she straightened her Uncle Sam costume, she looked up at him.

"I'm not nervous, Logan. I'm pregnant."

Just when he thought his life couldn't have gotten any better, it had. Hugging her, he felt his heart overflow with pure joy.

XXX

DEDICATED TO MY FAMILY

Lieutenant Colonel John Bunyan Bennett, M.D.,
United States Army (WWI, WWII)

Parachute Rigger 1st Class LeRoy Stewart Thompson,
United States Navy (WWII)

Hospital Corpsman 2nd Class Hershall Floyd Bennett,
United States Navy/Marines (Korean War)

Senior Airman James Hershall Bennett,
United States Air Force

Corporal Caleb Weyrick-Greene,
United States Marines (Afghanistan)

Senior Airman David Stuart Thompson,
United States Air Force

ABOUT THE AUTHOR

As a former holistic practitioner with a science background, Christina enjoys writing about the physical science, the emotional workings of our mind and heart, and the spiritual energy that taps into our passions.

Her degree in biology from Nazareth College in Kalamazoo gave her a love of science and a background into the physical realm of the body. Her diploma in Traditional Chinese acupuncture from Midwest College of Oriental Medicine taught her that the mind and spirit affect the body in powerful ways.

The healing power of LOVE is incredibly profound. She currently resides with her husband, Kraig, in Michigan.

Learn more about the Eclectic World of Christina
at **ChristinaKThompson.com**

Thank you for taking the time to read

The Trucker' Cat.

~ Christina

Other Titles by Christina Thompson

Dearest Mother and Dad

The Garden Collection

Their Rigid Rules
(The Chemical Attraction Series Book 1)

The Kindred Code
(The Chemical Attraction Series Book 2)

Searching for Her: an anthology
(The Chemical Attraction Series Book 2.5)

Chemical Attraction
(The Chemical Attraction Series Book 3)

Chemical Reaction
(The Chemical Attraction Series Book 4)

The Garden Collection

A few words of encouragement can stay with you for a lifetime. Robert and Brianna's childhood friendship grew into respect for each other and their ideas.

Robert gave her the confidence to stand up for herself. Brianna helped him see his artistic potential and encouraged him to travel for his inspiration. He found it in the letters she wrote.

Now struggling to care for her six-year-old half-sister, Chloe, after their mother abandoned them, Brianna Carlson receives news that her abusive stepfather will be released from prison. Still limping from a once broken leg, she's terrified he'll come back to hurt Chloe this time. She decides to leave town.

While traveling for his family's jewelry business, Robert Donovan designed The Garden Collection, his newest line of necklaces, bracelets, and earrings. Returning home, he discovers Brianna had lied in every letter she sent. She never received any of his.

Before he can demand answers, she disappears without Chloe. As Robert learns about Brianna's life during his absence, he sets out to find her and convince her to trust him again

Their Rigid Rules

Taylor Valentine, a senior at Western Michigan University, has had her life planned out since kindergarten. After her parents died while she was still in high school, she had perfected it to make them proud.

Now with the help of her best friends, Joe and Eva, she focuses on graduation and a career with romance in the far distant future. However, when the visiting professor enters the lecture hall to a four-weekend Civil War seminar, her perfect plan hits a snag.

As a handsome history professor and former Marine, Dr. Stuart Morgan has his own set of strict rules especially with infatuated students. He enjoys his boring yet pleasant life until he starts receiving death threats.

With his unwanted bodyguard in tow, Stuart is unnerved by his reaction to Taylor. Their rigid rules discourage all but a flirtation.

As the death threats become evident, the FBI believes Taylor's the culprit, hindering their budding romance. When Taylor inadvertently becomes the target, Joe and Stuart whisk her away to protect her.

Meanwhile, Joe struggles with his feelings for Taylor. He's loved her since grade school. He won't let her go and stands in Stuart's way. The men push her to choose between the lifelong love of her best friend and the true love of her new boyfriend.

With the threats from family and foe pulling them apart, Stuart wonders if they can sustain the stress. Trusting their love, he must somehow convince Taylor to break her rules and embrace a new plan.

The Kindred Code

Taylor Valentine, Eva O'Sullivan, and Joe Roberts are siblings by choice. They believe in The Kindred Code: blood means nothing and love is everything. After all, they've been together every day since the third grade. As their lives take different paths after college, they wonder if their mantra will stay true.

When word gets out that Professor Stuart Morgan had dated Taylor while in his class, the publicity takes a toll on their relationship. While Taylor recovers from a gunshot wound, Stuart struggles with his PTSD. Instead of sharing their pain, they drift further apart.

With his son, David, at a sleepover, Officer Matt Connor invites Eva to his home. During their romantic weekend, volatile confrontations happen between Matt's mother and Eva and David's biological mother and Eva. The rural town enjoys the uproar. Even on her best behavior, Eva worries about the chaos she brings to Matt and David's lives.

Before Joe heads to the FBI Academy, Director Peter Bingaman asks for his help on an unofficial case. He needs an outsider, who's smart and quick on his feet. Joe jumps at the chance to test his skills. Before long, they uncover horrendous crimes. Suddenly, Joe's in over his head.

Will Joe's family put aside their problems and come to his aid before it's too late? And what will that mean for his career as an agent.

Chemical Attraction

FBI Agent Joe Roberts wants that instant chemistry like his sisters, Eva and Taylor, have with their husbands. After years of searching, he's ready to give up on that romantic notion. Then, he meets Madeline. The problem is she's his contact on this dangerous case.

Dr. Madeline Pierce works in nanotechnology research. When she discovers a criminal network within her medical facility, she's partnered with Joe.

Throughout the investigation into the production and distribution of illegal drugs, Joe and Madeline struggle to stay professional despite their intense attraction to each other. She wants to trust his sweet words but wonders if she's just a fling.

Police Chief Matt Connor adores his wife, Eva, and works hard to keep his family and rural town safe. When farm animals become violent and meth labs become abundant, his calm demeanor is tested.

Eva Connor, a petite spitfire, has an opinion on everything and you know it whether you want to or not. However, her confidence is shaken when she's used as leverage against Matt's inquiries.

With this case now personal for Matt and Joe, they will do whatever's necessary to protect the women they love. As the ensemble hunts for this new bio-weapon, the dangers intensify putting their lives at greater risk.

Love should trump evil, but will their love for each other survive these tests without severe repercussions.

Chemical Reaction

FBI Agent Joe Roberts and Dr. Madeline Pierce must track down a rage-producing nano-drug before it devastates the nation.

Staying in Detroit with the FBI, Madeline works to develop an antidote from the confiscated journals. She clashes with the women from Joe's past.

In West Michigan, Joe hunts for the bio-weapon. With a history as a player, he's worried his relationship with Madeline is at risk. Working apart, they attempt to focus on the threat.

Before Joe returns, agents are killed, Madeline is abducted, and the deadly nano-drug is put on the market. Without the journals, the mastermind needs Madeline to reproduce the drug.

While she plays a dangerous game of deceit, Joe struggles to put his fears of losing her aside to find the weapon first.

Her life, their future, and the nation's security are in jeopardy. Joe must now choose between his personal desire and his professional integrity. Can he live with the consequences?

Made in the USA
Monee, IL
25 January 2021